MURDER
IN THE
MUMMY'S
TOMB

A

G. K. Chesterton Mystery

KEL RICHARDS

RIVER
OAK
PUBLISHING

Murder in the Mummy's Tomb
A G. K. Chesterton Mystery
ISBN 1-58919-963-4
46-606-00000
Copyright © 2002 by Kel Richards

Published by RiverOak Publishing
P.O. Box 700143
Tulsa, Oklahoma 74170-0143

ACKNOWLEDGMENT

The author wishes to thank Dr. Karin Sowada for her kind assistance with matters archeological and Egyptological. Details regarding such matters that are correct in this book are due to her input. Details that are incorrect, or merely fanciful, are entirely the product of the author.

THE CHARACTERS

Philip Flinders—a young archeologist

Prof. Henry Fell—a famous Egyptologist and leader of the expedition

Elspeth Fell—Fell's young second wife

Amelia Fell—Fell's daughter by his first marriage

Sir Edward Narracourt—another Egyptologist and Fell's arch rival

Laurence Wilding—a young assistant archeologist

John Farnsleigh—an expedition artist

Nathaniel Burrows—an expedition photographer

Dr. Brian Lamb—an expedition doctor

Ambrose Hoffman—an expedition engineer

Madeleine Sutton—the secretary to Professor Fell

Rev. Dr. Billy Burton—an American clergyman, popular author and lecturer on archeology, and representative of the American foundation funding the dig

Farouk Bahri—the *reis* (or head man)

Rami Bahri—Farouk's wife and the expedition cook

Colonel Race—a British Army Intelligence officer

Mamur Zapt—an escaped convict and revolutionary leader

Neville Page—a journalist

Elliot Jones—a rival American journalist

Canon Harry Poole—a clergyman and archeologist

Rebecca Poole—Poole's wife

G. K. Chesterton—a famous author, lecturer, and writer of detective stories

Frances Chesterton—Chesterton's wife

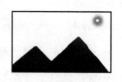

EGYPT, 1919

From the low hill where I stood, I could vaguely discern—in the dim, purple twilight—the gravel road from Luxor that ran through our camp from east to west. Lined up upon the northern edge of the road were the huts of the archeological team, mine among them, constructed of grey mud bricks and the roughest thatch. One or two of the huts were larger; these were to accommodate visitors. The largest of all was rather grandly called "the expedition house," but in fact it was merely a hut large enough to have three rooms.

At the western end of the row, on a level terrace, stood the oblong of the common room with narrow open slits for windows, bordered by wooden shutters that kept out the heat of the day and featuring double wooden doors, now standing wide open and spilling golden lamplight into the gathering darkness of the Egyptian night.

Clustered along the southern side of the gravel road were the tents of the *fellahin*, the Egyptian workmen employed at the dig. Their chattering voices drifted upward toward me on the night breeze accompanied by the aroma of roasting meat from their campfires.

Looking to the east of the camp I could see nothing but a purple, inky blackness that hid the broad expanse of the River Nile and, beyond, Karnak, the largest temple on earth. To the west was a clear sky sprinkled with a million stars that disappeared into the black, starless horizon that was the cliff face where we were digging.

I stood drinking in the coolness of the night air, a pleasant relief after the scorching heat of the day. It was only April, but already the Egyptian summer with its furnace-like temperatures had begun.

The cool air cleared my head and helped me summon up my courage. I had not climbed this hill above the camp just for the exercise:

I had come looking for Amelia. I had noticed her slip out of the common room after the evening meal, and from the doorway I had seen her clearly in the moonlight, climbing the hill's steep slope. *At last,* I thought, *an opportunity to talk to her alone.*

I had finished my coffee and hurriedly set off after her. But so far, although I had clambered more than a hundred feet above the camp buildings on the valley floor, I had not found her. I climbed higher, to the top of the ridge, and looked around. There she was. Her long white dress took on a bluish tinge from the brilliant moonlight, and her face, well, there never had been a more beautiful face since the creation of the world.

She was seated on a boulder and appeared to be deep in thought. She did not hear my approaching footsteps.

"Good evening, Miss Fell."

"Oh! You startled me."

"I'm sorry. In the future I'll try to make more noise as I approach."

"No. No. It's all right. My thoughts were a thousand miles away."

"And what were you thinking about?" I asked as I squatted on my haunches, facing her.

"Just . . . just thoughts, that's all."

"Let me guess. You were inspired by the view and were composing poetry."

"Poetry? Me?" As she spoke, her face, with its beautiful creamy complexion, seemed to blush faintly in the moonlight.

"I'm sure your soul is capable of the most beautiful poetry, Miss Fell," I persisted.

"Now you're making fun of me," she complained.

"Not at all. It seems to me that poetry must be of your very essence."

"I do assure you, Mr. Flinders, that I am a very practical, down-to-earth young woman. My father insists that I be, and I am."

"And yet I find you in the moonlight, dreaming dreams and seeing visions."

"We all dream," she said quietly.

"Ah, that is the poet speaking," I remarked.

She turned her face away from me.

"And what do you dream about when you are alone in the moonlight, Miss Fell?" I continued.

"I do wish, Mr. Flinders, that you would leave my dreams alone."

"But they are such beautiful dreams."

"Now you are being foolish. How can you possibly know whether my dreams are beautiful or not?"

"You have a beautiful soul, Miss Fell, and hence I conclude quite logically you must have beautiful dreams."

"You know as little about my soul as you do about my dreams."

"Your soul is written upon your face," I quietly remarked.

She turned toward me, and I discovered, to my alarm, that her pretty face was scowling with annoyance.

"Please don't mock me, Mr. Flinders," she said irritably. "And since you can see that I choose to be alone, perhaps you would be enough of a gentleman to honor my wishes."

"I apologize, Miss Fell," I said, rising to my feet, "for so insensitively forcing my company upon you when it is clearly unwelcome."

Before she could reply, I turned on my heel and began walking rapidly down the slope of the ridge, in the direction of the campsite. I heard her draw a sharp breath behind me, as if about to speak, but she said nothing.

Near the bottom of the hill, I stopped and sank down onto the sand in the inky black shadow of a towering boulder. I did not feel like rejoining the others in the common room. I wanted to be alone for awhile, to curse myself for my clumsy incompetence at every attempt I made to speak to Amelia.

I was still there several minutes later, still feeling my cheeks burning with embarrassment, when I saw a figure leave the bright yellow oblong that was the door of the common room and head in my direction. As the figure drew nearer, the moonlight revealed the darkly handsome features of Laurence Wilding. He was, like me, a recent graduate in archeology. We were both fortunate enough to be employed as assistants to the legendary Egyptologist, Prof. Henry Fell. While I was grateful for the chance to learn from Fell, Wilding, with his smarmy upper-class English manner, seemed to regard it as his birthright.

I sat very still in the shadows, and he walked within ten yards of me without noticing I was there. Then he began to climb the hill toward the ridge where Amelia dreamed in the moonlight. If I was ever to win Amelia's friendship, or, perhaps, something more than friendship, then Laurence Wilding must not be allowed to . . . well, he musn't, that's all. I stood up to follow him at a discreet distance.

I had to walk slowly and carefully so as not to reveal my presence by sending small cascades of gravel rattling down the hill. It was some minutes before I reached a point on the slope that was just below the ridge. And there I paused, for I could hear voices in conversation above me.

"On a night like this," I heard Amelia saying, "I sense something about the mystery of Ancient Egypt that I don't understand."

"Feel it, Miss Fell," replied Wilding. "Don't try to understand it."

"Ah, but understanding is what you are paid to do, is it not? Are you an archeologist or a poet, Mr. Wilding?" responded Amelia with a musical laugh.

"What can be understood I will understand, but there is always much more that one can only feel. To understand how an Ancient Egyptian felt about his world . . . well, that is like trying to understand what goes on in a woman's heart."

"Are we women truly such mysterious creatures, Mr. Wilding?"

"Utterly mysterious, Miss Fell, utterly."

"So, you abandon hope of ever understanding the gentle sex?" asked Amelia, the note of faint laughter still in her voice.

"Life is too short," Wilding replied in his amused, smug, self-assured, too-clever-by-half voice, "to fathom such mysteries. Life is far too short: 'The wind blows out, the bubble dies; the spring entombed in autumn lies; the dew dries up, the star is shot . . .'"

"'. . . the flight is past, and man forgot,'" completed Amelia.

"Well done. And can you name the author of those lines?" Wilding asked.

"One of the metaphysical poets, I think. But I can't recall which one."

"Henry King," answered Wilding, patronizingly, "but you did well to know it was one of the metaphysicals. And do you know how that famous stanza begins?"

"I'm afraid not."

"'Like to the falling of a star, or as the flights of eagles are, or like the fresh spring's gaudy hue, or silver drops of morning dew, or like a wind that chafes the flood, or bubbles which on water stood: even such is man, whose borrowed light is straight called in, and paid to night.'"

"You are a poet, Mr. Wilding," laughed Amelia, "wasted on archeology."

Shortly afterward, Wilding said goodnight and walked noisily away, kicking up gravel and chips of shale with his boots as he walked. Suddenly I felt foolish, and more than a little guilty, about my eavesdropping. And as quietly as I could, I crept back toward the camp.

As I did so, my embarrassment was slowly replaced by anger. Amelia would not speak to me. To her I was just an interruption. But she would speak to the odious Wilding!

As I pushed open the common room door, I was not in the best of moods.

"You like more coffee, Mr. Flinders?" asked Farouk Bahri, our *reis,* or head man.

"No!" I snapped and then corrected myself. "I'm sorry, Farouk. No more coffee for me, thank you."

Farouk walked, in his dignified way, back to the small kitchen that opened off the far end of the room, where his wife Rami worked. My little display of bad temper had gone unnoticed, largely because Professor Fell was fulminating loudly at the other end of the room.

"I'll dismiss them all!" he growled. "This is the last straw!"

"Who is he talking about?" I asked John Farnsleigh, the expedition artist. He was standing near the open door of the common room, as he always did, trying to catch any faint breeze that was passing. A pale, thin-faced man, he seemed to feel the heat more than the rest of us.

"The *fellahin*," replied Farnsleigh. "There's been another theft from the pantry."

"Another?"

"Making what . . . three all told?" murmured Farnsleigh in his usual, vague, artistic way. "At least three that we know about. There may have been other thefts of food that have gone unnoticed."

"But why? The men are fed well."

"Certainly as well as they would be fed back in their home villages. Perhaps better."

"It's not the *fellahin*," barked Burrows, the expedition photographer, joining our conversation. Burrows was a stocky, solidly built man. In the two months that the expedition had been working at the site I had come to respect his thorough professionalism and to be wary of his quick temper.

"Who else could it be?" I asked.

"Haven't a clue," snapped Burrows, in his blunt way, "but if the *fellahin* were going to steal food, they'd raid the storeroom near their tents, not our kitchen."

"Rubbish," snorted Hoffman, the engineer working with the expedition. "Of course it's the *fellahin*. Has to be. Stands to reason."

Without explaining what reasons he had in mind, Hoffman snatched up an old copy of the *Illustrated London News* and buried his head in its pages. The most unsociable member of the team, Hoffman lounged in a battered old cane chair, his feet thrust out in front of him. He rarely spoke, and when he did, he never bothered to explain himself. He always struck me as a man with a great deal on his mind, but his taciturn character made it impossible to guess what.

"Anyway," resumed Farnsleigh in his slightly whining voice, mopping his forehead with a large white handkerchief as he spoke, "it's not really the thefts that have Fell so upset."

"What is it then?" I asked.

"All these visitors who are due tomorrow."

"Chesterton and his wife?"

"Not them," Burrows snapped impatiently. "Fell enjoys showing off the dig to visiting pundits. No, it's the impending arrival of Narracourt that has his nerves on edge."

"That makes sense," I agreed. "I read Narracourt's attack in the *Times Literary Supplement*. Blistering stuff."

"I'd heard that he was threatening to sue," bleated Farnsleigh.

"Who?"

"Fell. Threatened to sue Narracourt. Claimed the article was defamatory."

"Just a rumor," I said, "and you shouldn't listen to rumors."

"Well, can we feed all these guests, or can't we?" Fell's raised voice came loudly from the other side of the room.

"I shall tell Farouk to send a couple of his most trusted men into Luxor, first thing in the morning, to purchase additional supplies," answered the calm, strong voice of Madeleine Sutton, Fell's secretary. "Until they return we have more than sufficient supplies to feed a dozen visitors."

"Well, what about coffee tonight?" snapped Fell, savagely biting the end off a cigar. "Is there any possibility of a man getting a decent cup of coffee tonight?" The professor's anger had flushed his round, jowly face a bright red, in the midst of which his blue eyes gleamed like chips of ice. Over the past two months I had discovered how prickly and difficult Fell could be, but I had also learned to respect him as an archeological genius: a singled-minded visionary, as great as Sir Flinders Petrie.

"You only have to ask, Professor Fell," said Madeleine as she left the room to find Rami.

"I think I shall go for a walk in the moonlight," said a female voice loudly and firmly. It was Elspeth Fell who spoke, the professor's young, and very pretty, second wife. There was a clear tone of disapproval in her voice directed at her husband's irritability. All eyes were upon her as she slowly tied a scarf around her head, pulled a light shawl around her shoulders, walked the length of the room, and stepped out into the night.

Conversations had become subdued during this incident, and it was Fell himself who broke the spell by growling loudly, "When are these blasted people arriving, anyway?"

"Sir Edward will arrive during the morning," said Madeleine Sutton calmly, re-entering the room as Fell spoke, "and the Chestertons are due at lunchtime."

"Pity," grumbled Fell as he puffed on his cigar and accepted the cup of coffee from Madeleine with ill grace.

"He's like a pocket tornado tonight," I remarked quietly.

"Just like a *khamsin*," muttered young Page. Neville Page was a journalist who, together with his colleague and rival Elliot Jones, had attached himself to our party for a few weeks in the hope of a good story. The journalists had been lounging in a corner of the room, drinking *arak*, the fruity Egyptian wine that was in such plentiful supply, and talking to each other quietly.

Page, the taller of the two, was the rather self-important *Times* correspondent. A self-importance entirely unjustified, in my opinion, since he was simply a contributor, not a member of the *Times* staff. Jones, shorter, with flaming red hair, was on the staff of one of the illustrated evening papers.

"What's a *khamsin?*" I asked.

"You've never experienced a *khamsin?*" asked Page in disbelief, strolling across the room in my direction.

"This is my first season in Egypt," I explained.

"Well, you have something in store for you, then. It's a wind."

"It's a little more than a wind," chirped a man as cheerfully as if he were talking about a cricket match. "I say, just a little more than what you would call 'a wind.'" The Rev. Dr. Billy Burton was an American representing a foundation that provided half the funds for the dig. Tall, broad-shouldered, and barrel-chested, Burton was the irrepressibly hearty, constantly happy member of the expedition.

"It is a lot more than a wind," agreed Page, irritated by the implication that he was ever less than precisely accurate. "I was coming to that. It's a hot windstorm that blows in off the desert. It often reaches eighty or ninety knots, and it carries tons of sand."

"I lost a lot of equipment in a *khamsin,* season before last," Burrows barked, his bulldog-like face scowling at the memory. "It blew down the photography hut. Smashed everything inside."

"And the sand gets into everything, I say, absolutely everything. Into your mouth and ears and nostrils," Billy Burton chortled with relish, enjoying my reaction, "into the food and all the equipment. Oh yes, you have a real experience, I say, a real unique experience ahead of you, young Flinders, if we get a *khamsin* this season."

Just then Burton's gleeful description was interrupted by a sound from outside, quiet at first but rapidly becoming louder. Hooves could be heard rattling on the rocky floor of the valley, approaching rapidly from the direction of the Luxor Road.

"Now who the devil is that," spluttered Fell, "at this time of night?"

Fell strode across the room and flung open the common room door. We gathered behind him in a semi-circle and saw a rider approaching in the silvery moonlight.

The desert is a dangerous place to cross alone in the daylight—even more so at night. Whoever this was must have a strong reason to take such a risk. Then a sobering thought struck me: could it be a raider from one of the rebel bands we heard were nearby? I admit I am not an overly brave man—and even less so this far from home.

The rider was lost for a moment as he strolled deliberately behind the storage tent, then came into view once again as he pulled his horse to a halt a few yards from us and dismounted.

"Evening!" he called.

"Evening," mumbled Fell ungraciously.

"Sorry to intrude. Official business, I'm afraid. I wonder if someone could take care of my horse?"

"Farouk!" bellowed Fell. "Get one of the men to look after the horse. And you'd better come inside, sir."

As we all moved back and the visitor stepped into the warm lamp-light of the common room, we saw a short, bald-headed man with a ruddy complexion and a bristling moustache. He was wearing a British Army uniform.

"Race's the name," he explained. "Army Intelligence."

"Come in and take a seat . . . ah . . . Colonel Race," said the professor, glancing at the pips on the man's shoulder. "I'm Henry Fell," he explained, extending his hand.

"Yes, I know who you are, sir," said the colonel as he shook the offered hand. "Perhaps you'd like to introduce the rest."

"Ah, yes, of course." Fell cast his eyes around the room and rattled off our names, "This is my secretary, Madeleine Sutton; my photographer, Nathaniel Burrows; John Farnsleigh, expedition artist; Ambrose Hoffman is our engineer; young Philip Flinders there is one of my assistant archeologists; those two, er, gentlemen, Neville Page and Elliot Jones, are journalists; the Rev. Dr. Billy Burton here is paying half the cost of this dig . . ."

". . . not personally," explained Burton. "Not, as it were, out of my own pocketbook, which, to tell the truth, is thin enough. No, the fact is, I represent a foundation."

"The small man who has fallen asleep in the corner," continued Fell, ignoring the interruption, "is Dr. Brian Lamb, our expedition doctor."

At the mention of his name Lamb woke up, looking startled and blinking rapidly.

"And this," concluded Fell as the door of the common room opened, "is my daughter Amelia. You haven't seen Elspeth anywhere, have you, my dear?"

"I haven't seen my stepmother since dinner," Amelia replied coldly.

"Evening all," said Colonel Race, glancing around the room. One could tell this was a man who was used to being in charge. He rested his weight against a corner of the trestle table that ran the length of the room and continued, "As I said when I arrived, this is official business."

"To do with the rebels?" asked Page.

"Exactly," the colonel said grimly. "Saad Zaghlul is still causing trouble. I don't know how long you folks have been here in Egypt, but this year we've had a lot of . . . well, not to put too fine a point on it, political turmoil. These people don't seem to understand that since the start of the Great War this primitive country has been a British protectorate. The Suez Canal is vital for world trade, and we intend keeping it under a stable government. But still Zaghlul and his followers go on stirring up trouble."

"Still demanding independence, you mean?" said Elliot Jones, raising one eyebrow, "an absurd desire for self-government?"

"I take it you sympathize with the rebels, sir?" snapped Colonel Race, glaring at Jones.

"I don't sympathize with them," the young red-headed journalist replied cheekily, "but I do like them. I like anyone who gives me a story I can write up. Do you have a story for me, Colonel?"

"We have a good lead on Zaghlul, and he'll be under lock and key before long, you can depend on that," Race said to Fell, ignoring Page as much as he could.

"And then what?"asked Page, like an aristocrat questioning a peasant. "He'll be hanged for treason?"

"Of course not! We're not barbarians. He'll be exiled. In the meantime, we have another problem. One of Zaghlul's henchmen has escaped from British custody in Cairo. He has been traced to this vicinity, and I've been sent to find him and bring him back."

"What's this fella's name?" I asked.

"Mamur Zapt."

"Never heard of him."

"Not many people have. He's not one of the front men of the rebellion; he's one of their undercover people. We caught him spying on the British government offices in Cairo. Ideally, I'd like to catch him before he has a chance to communicate with Zaghlul."

"What can we do to help?" asked Fell.

"I was rather hoping you could put me up for a few days," said Colonel Race, "while I search this district."

Fell rubbed his chin and looked doubtful. "We have a number of visitors arriving tomorrow," he explained.

"There won't be a problem," interrupted Madeleine Sutton briskly. "I'm sure Farouk can find a spare hut to accommodate the colonel."

"Well, if Madeleine says there won't be a problem, there won't be. She knows more about the organization of the camp than I do. Farouk!"

Fell turned around and was slightly startled to discover that our ever efficient *reis* was already at his elbow.

"A cup of coffee for the colonel here," commanded Fell. Farouk walked rapidly to the kitchen, where he threw open the door and barked an order in Arabic.

The rest of us gathered around Race and began firing questions at him.

"What's this Mamur Zapt character like?"

"Is he dangerous?"

"What can you tell us about him?"

Race chose only the last question to answer.

"Not much, I'm afraid. Average build, average height, no distinguishing features. He could easily hide himself among your workmen, and you'd probably never notice."

"That's a thought," Fell said, an anxious expression on his face.

"How many *fellahin* do you have working on this dig?" Race asked.

"Fewer than fifty," replied the professor. "We had over ninety until a month ago. But then most of the heavy work came to an end, and we let half of them go."

"Still, fifty is a large number. I'd like a chance to move among them tomorrow and ask some questions, just in case I spot something."

At this point Rami came in, carrying the colonel's coffee. I noticed her hands were trembling, and she almost spilled some as she handed the cup to her husband, who then carried it with the aloof dignity of a head waiter to the colonel.

"Farouk,"snapped Fell, "find a hut for the colonel to sleep in tonight."

The *reis* glided away to carry out his instructions.

"Very decent of you, Professor," said Race, "to put me up like this at such short notice."

"If we're able to help, we're more than happy to," Fell replied although, to be honest, he didn't look particularly happy.

The group gradually broke up into several smaller clusters, each engaged in its own conversation. I found myself talking to Burrows, our expedition photographer, and the two newspapermen, Page and Jones.

"Be jolly handy if this spy fella gets caught here," said Jones with the strange combination of cynicism and enthusiasm that marks the professional newspaperman. "First-class story in it. And perhaps a photograph as well?" he added, looking in Burrows' direction and raising one eyebrow.

"I work for Professor Fell," said Burrows in a guttural tone that was little more than an ill-tempered growl, "not you gentlemen of the press."

"Well, just a thought," said Jones with a shrug and a grin.

Over Burrows's shoulder I saw Elspeth Fell enter the room. She had obviously been for a long and vigorous walk—her face was flushed, and she appeared to be short of breath. I watched her walk across to her husband, who introduced her to Colonel Race.

"The British public isn't interested in Egyptian politics," Page was lecturing in his superior manner when my attention drifted back to the conversation around me. "The glamor, the mystery, the occult spirit of Ancient Egypt—that's what they want."

As we stood there talking, none of us, I'm sure, had any idea of what was about to burst upon us—the poisonous tensions and violent death that were about to invade our archeological expedition. For a long time afterward we debated the power of Ancient Egypt to send its curses down the centuries to haunt those who disturbed its graves. But that Monday night, as we stood there talking, and as the clock crept toward midnight, all of that still lay before us.

During our two months together, Fell had imposed a strict schedule of two work sessions per day. They were designed to make maximum use of the hours of daylight while giving everyone a rest during the oven-like heat of midday.

With the first session of digging due to begin at dawn, I excused myself and left the common room to walk back to my sleeping hut. Outside the well-lit room and the noisy conversation, I found myself surrounded by the darkness, and the silence, of the Valley of *Deir el-Bahri*. It was an old Coptic name meaning "The Monastery of the North."

Fifty yards away, I saw Wilding. He was standing very still, his back toward me, smoking a cigarette. I was about to call out a greeting, but I stopped myself. Remembering the way he seemed to be able to charm Amelia, I felt rather less than friendly toward him.

Walking toward my hut, I could hear nothing but the crunch of my boots on the gravel and the distant cry of a lonely night bird. My hut was one of a long, straggling line of more than a dozen, all identical, all built from grey mud bricks, roofed with rough planks, and thatched with stalks of Indian corn. The first hut in the row was less than ten yards from the common room, but, as a younger member of the team, I had been allocated one well over a hundred yards farther on.

Once inside, I lit a candle and proceeded to strip off my outer clothing. The hut was small, perhaps ten feet by ten feet. The floor was sand. On one side was a palm-stick bed, on the other two rough plank shelves. Against the wall was my shipping trunk, containing my clothing and personal possessions. Elsewhere the floor was chaos—a mixture of cans, tool, and antiquities. Pots of the eighteenth dynasty rubbed shoulders with a packet of ship's biscuits, a shaving brush, and a revolver.

Snugly tucked into bed, I enjoyed again the delicious pleasures of taking part in this expedition in such a remote and wild part of the world. I sniffed with delight the sunburned blankets, glimpsed the stars that peered furtively through gaps in the plank roof, and heard a wild dog lapping at the water in the canvas bath just a few feet away on the other side of the hut wall.

TUESDAY
5:OO A.M. TO 11:OO A.M.

The harsh and raucous jangling of my alarm clock jarred me to consciousness long before I was ready to wake. It was five o'clock in the morning, and the first shift on the dig was due to start in half an hour. I washed in the chilly water of the canvas bath beside my hut, shaved, dressed, and set off for the common room and breakfast.

As I stepped through the one opening that served as both door and window to my tiny cubicle, I was seized once again by the beauty of the valley in which we were working. It was a vast, open space, bounded at its farthest end by a semi-circular wall of cliffs. These cliffs of white limestone, which time and the sun had colored a rosy yellow, formed an absolutely vertical barrier—accessible only by a steep and difficult path leading to the summit of the ridge that separated *Deir el-Bahri* from the wild and desolate Valley of the Kings beyond.

Built against those cliffs, and dominating our valley, was the mortuary temple of Queen Hatshepsut. The sun was just starting to rise over the Nile behind me, and dim pink rays were striking the Egyptian temple. The low, ruddy glow was casting long shadows over the ascending terraces, the central ramps that connected the terraces, and the remains of the colonnaded halls that embellished the temple.

Surrounding the campsite were low hills and ridges—remnants of the ancient quarry from which the temple had been built.

Most of the working party were already gathered in the common room when I arrived. Professor Fell was in a much better mood than the night before and was chatting cheerfully to Billy Burton. Lawrence Wilding and Ambrose Hoffman were engaged in sleepy conversation while John Farnsleigh and Nat Burrows were eating in silence, both looking less than half awake.

I took a seat beside our expedition doctor, little Brian Lamb.

"Morning, Flinders," said Lamb. He had one of those odd voices that made it impossible for me to pick which part of England he came from—a mixture of home counties with a hint of cockney. Very unusual.

"Good morning," I responded cheerfully.

"We're in for another scorcher, I'm afraid," Lamb remarked.

The medic was the opposite of merry and managed to look—with cheerful enthusiasm—on the gloomy side of everything. He had a long, thin face, dominated by a large, hooked nose and topped by a bald head with a monkish fringe of dark hair. I would have guessed that he was in his mid-fifties. He was a mysterious man in some ways—he never talked about himself or his personal life away from the dig or his family. But get him started on the subject of Ancient Egypt, and he would talk for hours. It was an obsession with him.

Breakfast was the same as it was every morning: fresh bread—small, flat loaves still warm from the oven—served with a dish of broad beans called *ful,* goat cheese, and sweet tea with goat milk. There were also jars of jam that Fell had brought with him by the case from London.

For a moment I had visions of sizzling frying pans filled with ham and eggs, and then I settled down to the reality in front of me.

"Will the tomb shaft be emptied today?" asked Lamb eagerly.

"Hard to say," I replied. "It's impossible to know how deep it is."

"Still, it must be encouraging that the shaft is still filled with limestone chips. Surely that means that tomb robbers have never broken into this particular tomb."

"I only wish it did. But there are a few instances of grave robbers looting a tomb and then refilling the entrance shaft with the same limestone chips the original builders had used."

"But why?" asked the little doctor, tearing a piece of bread from a small round loaf. "That doesn't make any sense. Once the tomb has been looted, why reseal the tunnel?"

"We're not sure why. Perhaps the grave robbers were superstitious."

"If so—why rob the tomb at all?"

"Human nature is a funny thing," I mused. "Perhaps their greed overcame their fear and superstition enough to allow them to loot the burial chamber of all its precious metals and jewels, and then superstition reasserted itself, and they refilled the tomb shaft to prevent the dead from pursuing them."

"So, what you're telling me is that even though this tomb shaft you're digging in now is packed with limestone chips, you may only find a looted burial chamber at the end of it?"

"That could be so. We won't know till we get there."

"And if it has been looted, it will all have been a complete waste of time," said the medic, shaking his head gloomily.

"No—not at all, Dr. Lamb. The things that tomb robbers leave behind as being of no worth are of great value to archeologists. We are not just looking for treasures to fill museums. We are looking for pottery, for clay sealings and stone inscriptions, for feasts of hieroglyphs, for those everyday items that will tell us the story of the past."

"Come on, you lot. Let's get going," called Professor Fell from his place at the head of the long trestle table. I scooped up the last spoonful of broad beans, swallowed the last mouthful of tea, slapped my old broad-brimmed felt hat onto my head, and followed the straggling line of my fellow archeologists out into the early morning sunlight.

As we turned toward Hatshepsut's mortuary temple and the cliff face behind it, John Farnsleigh fell into step beside me, dabbing at his thumb with his handkerchief as he did so.

"I've cut my hand," he bleated. He was a man for whom even the smallest wound was a major medical event.

"How did you do that?"

"I carried a pile of breakfast dishes out to the kitchen to help poor, overworked Rami. And when I put them down, I cut my hand on a blasted piece of broken glass on the bench top."

I made suitably sympathetic noises. As we passed the end of the main camp building, I glanced in through the kitchen window and saw Rami, red-eyed and weeping. *Odd*, I thought, *that she should be so upset over Farnsleigh's little accident.*

"The devil of it is," Farnsleigh was moaning, "that if this cut keeps on bleeding I can't work. I'll end up getting smudges of blood all over my drawings."

"Let me look at that," said Lamb briskly. A look of annoyance spread over his pudgy face. "A piece of sticking plaster will fix that. Step into my hut. You can catch up with the others later. Anyway, it will take less than five minutes to clean and dress that little cut."

Lamb and Farnsleigh turned and headed back toward the row of huts just as Fell turned around.

"Hurry up, you . . .Where's that blasted Farnsleigh going now?"

"He's cut his hand," I explained. "Lamb is patching it up for him."

"He'd just better be back on the job before we reach the end of the shaft, that's all."

On our left we were passing a temporary village in the sand, every inch of which was packed with the tents of the *fellahin*. Farouk's voice could be heard rousing them up and hurrying them toward the site of the morning's dig.

Their low-pitched tents were woven from some dark brown-colored material, and as they emerged they were laughing and talking loudly. Bubbling on fires around the campsite were pots of the strong coffee these men liked to drink. Breakfast appeared to be bread, cheese, and coffee.

One man was crouching on the ground near one of the campfires. Beside him was a woven wicker cage containing several small birds. As I watched, he reached into the cage, pulled out one of the small birds, and, to my horror, snapped its neck. For a moment it twitched and then lay dead in his hand.

Fascinated by what I was seeing, I stopped and looked. The man proceeded to pull an evil-looking knife out of his belt and slit open the body of the small bird. Other men gathered around him as he did so. He disemboweled the bird using the sharp point of the knife, talking to the circle of watching men as he did so in a strange, sing-song voice.

At that moment Nat Burrows caught up with me, his heavy camera and tripod slung over one shoulder. He looked like a bulldog who had slept badly.

"What on earth's going on?" I asked, not really expecting an answer.

"Haven't you seen that before?" grunted Burrows. "That man does it every morning."

"But why? What's he doing?"

"Reading the entrails. Consulting the oracle of the bird."

"I don't understand."

"The *fellahin* want to find many treasures in these tombs and earn much *baksheesh*. He is like a fortune-teller. He is telling them whether it will be a good day or not."

"What superstitious nonsense!" I snorted.

"Don't be so arrogant about other people's beliefs. If it's true for him, then it's true for him," growled Burrows pugnaciously.

"Rubbish!" I snapped. "Things are either true or false. Full stop."

At that moment Farouk appeared, shouting instructions.

"Farouk!" called Burrows. "Ask the priest of the bird what oracles he has for us today."

Our *reis* gave Burrows a quizzical look, as if to say, "You've never been interested in this before." Nevertheless, he turned to the man crouched on his haunches over the tiny corpse and asked a series of questions in Arabic. The man gave long and incomprehensible replies.

"He says that today will be successful on the dig," Farouk interpreted.

"There you are, good news," said Burrows, slapping my shoulder, a wicked grin on his bulldog face.

"He says that today we shall reach the end of the shaft and find the burial chamber," continued Farouk.

"Now there's a real test, Flinders," Burrows added. "By the end of today we'll know whether the oracle of the bird is right or wrong."

"That's not an oracle; that's just a well-informed guess," I snorted. "We're already more than eighty yards into the shaft. So it's a fair guess that we'll get to the end before the day is out."

"Was there anything else, Farouk?" asked Burrows.

"Yes, sir. He also says that today we shall see death."

"Of course, we'll see death!" I responded. "Once we enter the burial chamber, we will see ancient death, hopefully well preserved."

"What a nasty, old sceptic you are, Flinders," laughed Burrows. "Tonight you and I shall compare notes, and if the oracle of the bird was right, I shall teach you to respect the beliefs of others. That's all, Farouk. Thank you for your help."

"My pleasure, *effendi*," said our head man, bowing in a polite *salaam* of respect and hurrying off.

"Stop dawdling, you two!" shouted Fell from the head of the line, and Burrows and I hurried to catch up.

To reach the mortuary temple, we first had to descend into a vast pit and then climb up the broad ramps that led from one terrace of the temple to the next. On either side of us rose a broken and incomplete row of slender stone columns.

Ambrose Hoffman, the expedition architect, split off from the main group accompanied by one of the *fellahin* who carried his surveying and charting equipment. He had his own task of drawing up a plan of the original building as it would have been some three and a half thousand years earlier. The problem was that Coptic monks had later reused blocks of stone from the temple to build themselves a small monastery. Hoffman's task was to find the original building lines under the Coptic rebuilding.

Hoffman had begun this task back in 1894 when the great Swiss archeologist, Edouard Naville, had first excavated here. But he had not completed his work and had leaped at the opportunity to return with Fell's expedition.

Fell, meanwhile, was focused on possible tomb shafts that Naville had missed. During Naville's time, four tombs had been found. However, the inscriptions on the site had convinced Fell there were at least two more to be discovered, one of Fell's great skills being paleography (no, don't look it up; it means he was an expert in "ancient writing").

Professor Naville had simply run out of time during the digging season of 1894 to fully explore the site. And during the following seasons the Egypt Exploration Society had directed his efforts elsewhere. Then the Great War had intervened, leaving Fell convinced there was more work to be done at *Deir el-Bahri*.

Despite what I had said to Dr. Lamb, finding an unlooted tomb was Fell's great dream. Not that I had misled the doctor; it was just that an unlooted tomb would be a complete snapshot of Ancient Egyptian society—not a jigsaw puzzle with some of the pieces missing.

And so far, the signs were good. Behind Queen Hatshepsut's temple, and some yards farther to the north than Naville's excavations had reached, we had uncovered the entrance to a tomb shaft. Part of the shaft was filled with limestone chips, and the entrance was partly hidden by a rock fall.

It was a common tomb design in Ancient Egypt: a shaft dug straight into the rock face of the cliff. About sixty yards in, it took a sharp turn to the right. The day before we had emptied limestone chips from twenty yards or so of this branch of the shaft. Today, hopes were high that we would reach the end and uncover the burial chamber.

I was excited about what the day held for us. For years I had sat in dark-paneled, high-ceilinged lecture rooms at Sydney University, trying to concentrate on passing exams, while in my imagination I was already wearing a pith helmet in the Egyptian sun and opening up sealed tombs that revealed the strange truth about the ancient past.

And now, in my imagination, I was ready to return to my old university and, over a glass of port in the senior common room, talk modestly about being with Fell when he opened a sealed, unlooted tomb.

As we reached the last, and highest, of the temple terraces, I caught up with a red-faced Billy Burton, who was mopping his brow with a large, red-spotted handkerchief.

"Not puffed already are you, Dr. Burton?" I asked cheerfully.

"I'm not as young as you, Mr. Flinders, not as young, I say, or as lithe, or, perhaps young sir, not as agile," wheezed Burton, "and even in the cool of the morning, the climb from the valley floor makes me hot as a hummingbird in a Mississippi heat wave."

"Tell me something, Dr. Burton."

"Anything, my young friend, anything, I say, anything at all."

"Why does this foundation you represent pour money into archeology?"

"Many reasons, Mr. Flinders, many reasons," replied Burton, stuffing his colorful handkerchief back into his pocket. "America is agog with the wonders of Ancient Egypt at this time, positively agog, young sir. That means that it is not difficult, in fact it's positively simple, to persuade a bunch of hardheaded Chicago financiers to support scientific investigation of the distant past. It makes them feel like explorers themselves and not what they really are, Mr. Flinders, which is, not to put too fine a point on it, dull-witted bankers. In addition to which, many of our most generous supporters are on the boards of America's leading museums. They know how to butter a slice of bread. They know their support will result in their institutions receiving a share of whatever displayable treasures are found. Pretty things, young sir, pretty things the public wants to see."

"But you're not an archeologist yourself, are you?"

"Good grief no! Far from it," laughed the Rev. Dr. Billy Burton. "I say, far from it, very far from it. I am a man of God, Mr. Flinders, a man of God."

"Then why are you interested?"

"I am a popularizer of archeology, an explainer to the public, to the masses of America, to those hungry for news of the work of the real scientists like Professor Fell."

"There's that much interest in America?"

"There is indeed. When I return I will undertake a public lecture tour, a nationwide tour I should add, entitled 'The Bible as History'—illustrated with colored lantern slides. And if it's anything like my last tour, it will be a rip-roaring, I say, a *great* success."

The group came to a halt before a square-cut opening in the cliff face. This was the entrance to the tomb shaft. Fell removed his pith helmet and mopped his brow.

"Farouk," he called, "who are you using as pick man today?"

"Hamoudi is the most reliable man I have. I shall use him."

"Fine. Get him to work then, with a good spade man behind him and three or four basket men. Flinders—you supervise."

Farouk proceeded to make these arrangements, and I followed him.

"Wilding," I could hear Fell saying behind me, "set up a checking station for the rubble."

Each time I entered the shaft, my blood tingled with excitement. Today was no different. It was like entering Mr. H. G. Wells's time machine and setting the dials for Ancient Egypt. The rock walls were not smoothed and finished as they would have been in a tomb built for royalty or wealthy nobles. Whoever was buried here was a senior servant of a king or queen but not himself a member of the royal family. Unless, of course, the tomb had been built in haste—which sometimes happened.

We were working on the assumption that all the shaft tombs in this valley had been dug for the most senior and loyal servants of Queen Hatshepsut herself. In the first excavations, twenty-five years earlier, Naville had uncovered the tombs of the queen's architect, a priest, a manager of the royal household, and someone who was roughly the equivalent to a "lady-in-waiting."

We had debated among ourselves why the tomb of a mere public servant—albeit a senior one—should be filled with limestone chips. Fell's latest idea was that the chips were simply dumped in the tomb shaft when another, more important, tomb was being dug nearby. In other words, that it had been used as a dump site. But, whatever the reason, we were all haunted by the question: what would we find at the end of the rubble-filled tunnel?

I had a hurricane lamp to light my way, but I still stumbled occasionally over the rough-cut floor of the shaft. The tunnel was not a large one, and I had to stoop to walk. Some sixty yards in from the entrance, the shaft took an abrupt ninety-degree turn to the right. Another twenty yards down this part of the shaft, I stopped at the workface.

The only light was from the hurricane lamp—a light that disappeared in the deep well of darkness behind me and flickered over the uneven barrier of limestone chips ahead. The shaft had its own particular smell—not the damp smell you might expect underground in wetter climates, but something more like dust. It was, I told myself, the dust of the centuries that I could smell.

Before the men arrived, I rechecked the side walls. I did this at every stage of the digging, looking for signs that we might be getting close to the burial chamber and looking for traces of inscriptions.

By the time I had finished my inspection, Hamoudi was behind me with a pick in his hand. He had been chosen, not just for his size and strength and his ability to swing a pick in a confined space, but also for his intelligence. Hamoudi knew when to stop digging and call for one of the archeologists.

"Salaam kefek?" ("How is your comfort?"), I asked Hamoudi.

"Kullish zen," ("It is well"), he replied.

This formal greeting exhausted my command of Arabic. I placed the hurricane lamp on the floor of the shaft to illuminate the workface and then stood back to let Hamoudi work.

Pushing back the sleeves of the body-length, shirt-like garment that all the Arab workers wore, Hamoudi swung the pick and struck the compacted limestone chips. The first blow produced no results. The second sent small fragments of limestone ricocheting off the rock walls. I ducked for cover as Hamoudi swung again. His third blow broke the surface and sent a cascade of rock chips rattling to the floor of the shaft.

A few minutes later there were enough lose chips to summon the shovel man and one of the basket men. The shovel man shoveled the chips into the large woven basket, which the basket man then half-dragged and half-carried back to the surface.

This procedure was completed time and time again.

Although compacted with time, the limestone chips were relatively easy to dig through, and as the morning advanced, we made rapid progress. After an hour we had cleared several more yards. It was time to spell Hamoudi, and he was replaced as pick man by Abdullah.

After Abdullah had struck no more than half a dozen blows, he turned to me and said something in Arabic. I called back down the shaft for Farouk. A few moments later our *reis* hurried to my side.

"Ask him what the problem is, Farouk," I said.

They conversed for a minute in Arabic, then Farouk said, "He has struck solid rock, *effendi*."

By gestures I indicated to Abdullah that I wanted the pick. I only had to swing once to discover that our pick man was right. Beyond the last layer of limestone chips was a solid rock wall. I tried to the left with the same result. I tried to the right, and here the pick bit deeper.

"Tell him the shaft changes direction, and he should dig this way," I said, waving my right hand toward the workface I wanted dug. Farouk conveyed this information. I stood back, and Abdullah resumed work. Before long, another yard of the shaft had been cleared. What we had exposed was another sharp right-hand bend in the tunnel. This sort of pattern was not uncommon in tomb shafts.

Soon, another yard had been cleared. While the spade and basket men cleared the rubble, I examined the workface closely, holding the hurricane lamp high.

Was it my imagination? Or was there a gleam of white that I could glimpse through the gaps between the limestone chips? I reached out my hand to Abdullah, indicating that I wanted the pick again. He handed it to me, looking puzzled.

Taking only short swings, I began to gently pick and chisel away at the surface. Yes, there was definitely something there. Standing on a pile of loose rubble, I lifted the hurricane lamp as high as I could and peered over the top of the compacted rock chips. It was a plaster wall! If I stretched out my arm, I could touch it.

Reaching out as far as I could, I ran my finger along the wall and withdrew it, to find it covered in the white powder of centuries-dried plaster.

"Farouk!" I yelled excitedly.

Picking up the urgency in my voice, Farouk ran to my side.

"Tell Abdullah to remove the rest of the rubbish very gently," I instructed. Farouk passed this on. "And now run and fetch Professor Fell; he'll want to see this at once," I added.

Abdullah used his pick in a chiseling, rather than a digging action. Progress was slower now, but gradually bits of the plaster wall were being exposed.

"What is it, Flinders?" Fell gasped, hurrying breathlessly to my side. Lawrence Wilding was with him. The two had been checking the limestone chips as they were removed, looking for fragments of old building materials or, indeed, anything that might be of interest.

"Perhaps this is the entrance to the burial chamber, Professor. Look!"

Fell, whose Arabic was excellent, told Abdullah to halt for a moment and, taking the lantern from my hand, made a close examination of the small area of plaster wall that had been exposed.

"This is wonderful, Flinders!" he exclaimed. "Wonderful! This is what we're looking for."

Stepping back several paces, he instructed Abdullah to resume.

As the clearing continued, Fell hurried backward and forward to the surface, passing on the news and making the necessary preparations. I stayed at the workface and supervised the clearing. Not that there was much for me to do: Abdullah was an intelligent and careful worker and knew how to clear the plaster wall with the minimum of damage.

At last it was done.

I turned around to discover half the members of our party packed into the narrow shaft behind me.

"Exquisite! I say, simply exquisite!" enthused Billy Burton over my shoulder. "What a wonderful, I say, *wonderful* story this will make for my next lecture tour."

"Let me have a look. I want to see," pleaded Dr. Lamb, pushing and edging his way through. At the sight of the plaster wall, he stopped and stared in wonder.

Around the edges of the plaster were hieroglyphic seals. In the middle was a painted panel filled with colored illustrations. In the flickering light of the hurricane lamp, the picture looked to be as clear as the day it was painted, three and a half thousand years ago. In my imagination I pictured the artist employed by the mortuary officials working with brushes and small jars of color.

"This is what I came to Egypt to see," whispered the doctor near my right elbow.

"Pretty impressive," admitted Wilding, coming as close to enthusiasm as his breeding would allow.

"Clear some room here, please," shouted Fell, pushing his way to the front of the group. "Dr. Lamb, I appreciate that you are an enthusiastic amateur," Fell laid much stress on the last word, "but it is now time for the professionals to do their work. Please return to the surface."

"But . . . but . . . ," the doctor spluttered.

"Out," repeated Fell firmly.

With clear resentment, Dr. Lamb turned and left, pressing himself flat against the wall to edge past the others.

"You too, Dr. Burton," Fell continued, "if you please."

"Yes, of course. Absolutely, of course," said the American and turned to leave without protest.

"Lend me your notebook, Wilding," said Fell when Lamb and Burton were gone. "These hieroglyphs here are the necropolis seal of the priests who supervised the burial, and these others just might give us the name of the occupant."

Time seemed to be suspended as Fell worked in silence. Finally, after perhaps fifteen minutes of sketching, he said, "This is the cartouche of Queen Hatshepsut, so the chap in here worked for her. And the hieroglyphs on this seal here might give us his name."

I could make out the symbols of two door bolts, and these, I knew, stood for the letter *s*. But this was what Fell was good at, and it wasn't long before he turned to me and said, "This fella's name appears to have been Menes. And I think he was probably Queen Hatshepsut's army commander. And, according to these other symbols, he was a priest of Thoth as well. Some of that's guesswork at this stage, but I'm pretty sure about the name."

We looked at each other. This could be a treasure trove of information for historians. Neither of us said anything, but we both recognized how significant it was that the plaster wall was not breached: this could be an undisturbed tomb!

"What about this illustrated panel?" I asked.

"I've been thinking about that. I've seen those sort of painted panels before—but on doors."

"Meaning . . . what, exactly?" asked Wilding.

"That this is not a wall, but a door; that is, a supposed door, a mud-brick 'door' with a plaster facing. The chamber beyond is where the spirit of the departed was meant to live for eternity. This plaster is painted like a door so that the spirit knows how to leave and re-enter the chamber."

"This panel shows the god Osiris, I take it?" I said.

"Clearly," sniffed Wilding, who objected to anyone but himself displaying knowledge. "Osiris attended by the goddess Isis. Correct, Professor?"

"Quite correct," Fell replied. "Osiris, wrapped as a mummy, holds the crook and the flail, the symbols of kingship. The green color of Osiris's face indicates his position as a god of fertility. This chap worshiping the god is almost certainly our friend Menes. The women behind him are probably his family—his wife and daughter. See how Menes is wearing a long, pleated, linen kilt, and the women have full-length, pleated, linen gowns. All three have incense cones on their heads, and Menes is carrying the spear and shield of the professional warrior."

"The problem is," I remarked, "how do we break into the burial chamber without destroying this beautiful art work? Or do we just record it, then pull down the plaster?"

"Exactly. We have no choice. Right," said Fell, gathering his thoughts, "let's get on with it. Wilding, fetch Burrows for me."

"I'm right here, Professor," came the photographer's gruff voice from the darkness in the tunnel beyond my flickering hurricane lantern.

"I want your equipment up here immediately. This wall must be photographed before we remove it."

"I'll get right onto it," Burrows said, and he turned and inched back down the shaft.

"Now, Farnsleigh," continued the professor, "the colored panel on the wall—I want you to copy it. The copy must be to scale, and the colors must be accurate. If you and Burrows can both squeeze in here and work together, that will speed up the process. If it gets too crowded . . . well . . . let Burrows finish his photography, then you do your work."

"Yes, Professor."

"Flinders, Wilding!"

"Yes?"

"We shall go to the surface and have a cup of tea while these gentlemen get on with their work. Farouk! Clear all your men out of the shaft except for those assisting Mr. Burrows and Mr. Farnsleigh."

Professor Fell was brimming with high good humor.

A few moments later, I stepped back out into the fresh air, blinking at the brilliance of the sunlight. Pulling my watch out of my fob pocket, I checked the time. It was only half past eight, but already the sun was blazing with heat. And in just three hours we had accomplished a great deal.

A small campfire had been started flush against the cliff face, and on this fire two of Farouk's men were boiling water for our tea. Glancing down the wide ramps that connected the terraces of Queen Hatshepsut's temple, I saw a group of people approaching from our base camp.

At the head of the group was a manservant carrying a tray of tea things. Walking just behind him were Elspeth Fell, Madeleine Sutton, and two men and a woman—whose faces were new to me.

I took off my hat, mopped my forehead, and glanced around the worksite. Two hundred yards away I spotted Amelia. She was seated on a fallen pillar with a notebook on her lap and a pencil in her hand. I took several steps in her direction and then paused. Natural curiosity took over. Before I spoke to Amelia I wanted to know who the visitors were.

They were quite close now, with Elspeth Fell now in the lead. Although there were only a few years' difference between the ages of stepmother and stepdaughter, Elspeth's face had a hard and knowing look that was a world away from the soft innocence of Amelia. Like her stepdaughter she was wearing a long, white frock. But while Amelia shaded her face under a wide-brimmed straw hat, Elspeth carried a delicate, fashionable parasol.

Glancing back toward Professor Fell, I saw a changed expression come over his face. It was immediately obvious that his good humor had disappeared and been replaced by ill-temper.

"Darling," said Elspeth to her husband as the group approached, "allow me to introduce our guests. This is Sir Edward Narra . . ."

"I know who this is," Fell snapped. "Morning, Narracourt. We've made a discovery this morning that is the first step toward proving you to be the abysmal fool that you are."

Narracourt, taller and more distinguished in appearance than Fell, sneered down a long, aristocratic nose at his academic rival. "Nice to see you again too, Fell," he replied.

"And this is," continued Elspeth as if nothing had happened, "Canon and Mrs. Poole."

"Delighted to meet you, I'm sure," growled Fell, extending the hand he had failed to offer Narracourt.

"Good morning, good morning," gushed the Pooles with wide, slightly embarrassed smiles.

"Poole? Poole?" Fell muttered, half to himself. "You're not the H. J. Poole who writes for the *Royal Archeological Quarterly?*"

"The very same," replied the red-faced, elderly gentleman. "Guilty as charged, I confess."

"Delighted to meet you, dear sir, delighted," and this time Fell's voice suggested that he was indeed as delighted as he claimed. "Your review of my last book was splendid, simply splendid."

"Well, I just wrote what I thought, you know. That was a very good piece of work of yours."

"Canon." Elspeth said. "I didn't realize you were a clergyman."

"Harry is a canon of Salisbury Cathedral," Mrs. Poole explained. "Although, what he does for the cathedral I can never quite work out. His enthusiasm seems to focus mainly on archeology, detective stories, and steam trains."

"It was Sir Edward who invited us to your dig," added Poole. "I hope we haven't done the wrong thing by accepting. If we're in the way, dear chap, just tell us, and we'll scoot."

"Not at all. Not at all. If Narracourt starts expressing some of his half-witted opinions, I shall be able to turn to you to back me up."

"Actually, dear chap, Sir Edward expressed rather the same thought."

"Did he indeed?" snarled Fell. "Well, more fool him. With two well-read and intelligent men to correct him, he'll have to eat his words."

"You seem uncommonly certain, Fell," intervened Narracourt, "that Poole will support you and not me."

"Of course I'm certain! Every archeologist worth his salt supports me! You don't imagine you're going to win this debate, do you?"

"I only enter academic debates I am certain of winning, Fell. As you will learn, sooner or later. And now, may I ask what has happened to the hospitality of this camp? Are we to be offered a cup of tea, or aren't we?"

"One lump or two, Sir Edward?" asked Elspeth, who, to my eye, seemed to be enjoying watching her husband squirm under Narracourt's haughty stare. Not very loyal behavior, I thought—Amelia would never be that way toward the man *she* married.

With thoughts of Amelia filling my head, I made two cups of tea, one for her and one for myself—I had taken care some weeks ago to learn how she liked her tea. With a tin mug in each hand—the camp didn't run to fine china—I set off to where she was seated, notebook in hand, two hundred yards away.

As I approached, my boots kicked some loose stones, and, startled by the noise, Amelia looked up. Seeing me, she hastily thrust her notebook into a small, canvas carrying bag by her side.

"Good morning, Miss Fell. You see, I have been careful to warn you of my approach this time."

"How very thoughtful of you, Mr. Flinders," she responded with a musical laugh.

"I must apologize for my boorish behavior last night," I said, handing her a mug of tea and taking a seat beside her on the fallen stone pillar.

"Not at all. I was the one being boorish. And for that I apologize most sincerely."

"Never, Miss Fell. I can never allow you to take the blame."

For a moment we both sipped our tea in silence, and then I broke the big news.

"We have reached the end of the shaft," I explained, "and found an unbroken plaster wall."

"How exciting!" Amelia said, her face lighting up with genuine pleasure. "After two months with such little progress, Papa must be thrilled. I've been watching Papa as the team have cleared and searched this top terrace. I've seen him become more anxious by the week, afraid that nothing of significance would be found. But now . . . an unbroken wall; that means an undisturbed burial chamber, I take it?"

"In all likelihood, yes. However, there is just a chance it may not be."

"But, what else could it be?"

"Some Ancient Egyptian tomb makers created false tomb shafts in order to lead would-be tomb robbers astray. Grave robbing is not a modern phenomenon. It began in antiquity, often almost as soon as the tombs were sealed. Mind you, the presence of the unbroken plastered 'door' suggests we are safe."

"Yes indeed, wouldn't the looters have broken down the plaster and mud brick before they realized it was a false trail?"

"Not if they had a plan of the tomb. Some mortuary architects in Ancient Egypt appear to have made a nice little profit on the side by selling their tomb plans to looters."

"I see." After sipping her tea in silence for a few moments, she resumed. "I take it the decorated plaster will have to be broken down?"

"Unavoidable, I'm afraid. It is the only way to discover whether or not there is an untouched tomb behind it. But Nat Burrows and John Farnsleigh are busy recording the inscriptions and decorations on the wall first."

"I would love to be there when the tomb is opened."

"Well . . . I'm sure your father would be pleased by your interest. The only problem is the confined space at the end of the tomb shaft."

"In that case, I shall leave it to the scientists and come and take a peek only when I'm invited. Does Papa know yet whose tomb it is?"

"From the inscriptions he thinks it belongs to a man named Menes— an army commander."

"Papa will be delighted. The tomb of a senior official is sure to contain scrolls and valuable historical records. I'm very pleased for him."

We finished our tea in companionable silence. I stood up and collected Amelia's cup from her soft, delicate little hand.

"I noticed you were writing this morning," I said as I was turning to walk back to the worksite.

"Writing?" Amelia's face colored slightly as she responded.

"Yes. You had a notebook on your lap. Are you keeping a diary of the expedition?"

"No, not a diary."

"Not articles for a newspaper then? You're not a secret journalist?"

"Of course not!"

"Is it a secret? Or will you tell me what you were writing?"

Amelia pursed her lips. "It's not a secret. But it is private."

"I'm sorry," I stumbled. "I didn't mean to intrude."

"You didn't intrude, Mr. Flinders," replied Amelia firmly. "I didn't allow you to."

I turned away quickly to hide the hot flush of embarrassment that colored my face and walked slowly back to the worksite.

Having returned the tea mugs to the tray, I went looking for the professor and was told that he had returned to the tomb shaft.

Knowing that light would be at a premium, I lit an extra hurricane lantern and carried it with me as I re-entered the narrow tunnel and made my way to the workface.

"Ah, more light," cried Farnsleigh as I approached. "Over here, Flinders," he said, twisting his shoulder in the uncomfortably confined space in which he was trying to paint. "If you hold your lamp over this page, I'll be able to get on much quicker."

"Where's Burrows?"

"All done. His man just finished carrying all his gear back to the surface."

Farnsleigh was sitting on a small canvas camp stool in the corner of the final sharp right-hand bend in the tomb shaft. From there he had an excellent view of the painted plaster wall just ahead of him. Or he would have if his view had not been constantly interrupted by Fell and others who kept edging past him to look at the seals that covered much of the plaster, making notes in notebooks, and edging away again, pressing themselves flat against the wall to avoid bumping Farnsleigh.

At that moment, Fell and Narracourt were standing between Farnsleigh and the wall.

"Hardly anyone very important, this Menes," Narracourt was saying.

"Once again, you are missing the point," growled Fell. "What is significant is not *who* he was, but *what* he was."

"Meaning?"

"Stop being deliberately bone-headed. A senior officer of the court, of course! There may be papyrus scrolls and other valuable historical records."

"Perhaps. But that's not certain, of course."

"Likely, though. Very likely. And if there are . . ."

"Ah, now you're saying 'if,'" said Narracourt smugly.

"If there are," persisted Fell, "as seems most likely, then I will be able to prove once and for all that you are wrong about the royal families of the eighteenth dynasty."

"But you won't. Because I'm not wrong. And whatever records you turn up must, of necessity, support my view."

"Excuse me, Professor, Sir Edward," I interrupted, "but Farnsleigh's finding it difficult to see the wall and get on with his work."

"Yes. Yes, of course," muttered Fell in a slightly embarrassed tone. My comment had made it appear that his passion for debate was obstructing his management of the dig. Which, of course, it was.

"Shift yourself, Narracourt," said Fell, shifting the blame as quickly as he could. "My people have work to do."

Ducking their heads and doing the awkward shuffle that was necessary in that tunnel, both men departed.

Some time later Farnsleigh had made good progress, and I returned to the surface to announce that at least a small part of the wall could now be safely removed. Lawrence Wilding, Nat Burrows, and Dr. Brian Lamb were hovering near the shaft entrance, waiting for an opportunity to return to the site of the tomb.

"May I go and see the wall first?" asked the little doctor in his distinctive, high-pitched voice.

"I can't see any reason why not," I replied. And without waiting for any further invitation, Dr. Lamb shot into the tunnel.

"Why don't you keep on eye on him?" I suggested to Wilding.

"Supervise him yourself, if you want to," sneered Wilding. But as I turned away, I noticed that he was heading for the shaft entrance.

Fell was standing in a group with Narracourt and Poole, under the shelter of a temporary canvas awning that had been erected against the towering rock wall of the cliff. Mrs. Poole and Mrs. Fell were nowhere to be seen. Presumably, they had returned to the greater shade and comfort of the camp buildings.

"Follow me, gentlemen," said Fell when I told him that the wall could now be breached. As he strode toward the shaft entrance, he called out in Arabic to Hamoudi, who reached for a pick and an army entrenching tool and followed us into the darkness inside the cliff.

We followed one another in single file, heads ducked, shoulders hunched. While two men could pass each other in the tunnel, it was a slight squeeze, so single file was the easiest way to proceed.

Around the last corner we found Wilding and Lamb discussing the painted panel in the middle of the wall.

"Now this seal here near the lower left-hand corner . . . ," Wilding was saying in his most professorial manner.

"Wilding, stand back, please," Fell interrupted. "And Dr. Lamb, I want you back outside."

"Can't I see the wall taken down?"

"Professionals first, amateurs second. Outside, please."

"Excuse me, Professor," said Farnsleigh as the doctor glumly departed.

"Yes?"

"Are you going to take down the whole wall now?"

"That depends on how advanced your work is."

"Since I am trying to reproduce a detailed picture, full size and with precision, I have at least several more hours' work ahead of me."

"All we need do for the moment is take a look inside."

So saying, Fell issued an instruction to Hamoudi in Arabic. We all moved back a pace. The Arab pick man swung back over his shoulder and hit the plaster high on the wall.

It was a cautious blow that did little more than scratch the surface. He struck again and this time dislodged some plaster chips. On the third blow, the point of the pick went right through the mud-brick wall behind the plaster. With a fourth, and harder, blow Hamoudi dislodged a piece of the wall the size of a man's hand. Beyond, we could see nothing but darkness. Another blow doubled the size of the hole.

Suddenly we were struck with a gust of stale and putrid air.

Fell shouted a command to Hamoudi, who shouldered his pick and moved back. Fell and Narracourt hurried to the broken wall, shoulder to shoulder in the confined space, with Poole close behind them. Wilding and I, as befits younger archeologists, waited our turn.

"Intact!" cried Fell, disbelief mingling with excitement in his voice. He thrust his arm through the opening, holding the hurricane lamp high so that its rays fell into the burial chamber.

"Astonishing!" whispered Narracourt, struggling to catch a glimpse over Fell's shoulder.

"Jolly fine! Wonderful, in fact," the canon added, standing on his toes to see.

"I can't believe . . . ," Fell was muttering.

"So many pieces," Narracourt whispered, "and some of them will be treasures. Absolute treasures."

"Can I have a proper look, please?" asked Poole. Somewhat reluctantly Narracourt moved back a step, and Poole took his place.

"Beautiful," gasped the canon. "Such beauty! Such wonderful beauty."

"Just look at the craftsmanship," added Fell.

"Yes! Yes! Wonderful!"

"Come here, you two," said Fell, turning to Wilding and me. "Come and see something you will probably never see again in your lifetimes—a three-and-a-half-thousand-year-old burial chamber, untouched by looters. Narracourt, Poole—move back; let the young men have a look."

I moved forward and put my face to the hole in the plaster wall. The stagnant air was overwhelming, but I held my breath and kept looking. Fell was still holding his lantern at arm's length, and the flickering, yellow light bounced around the walls and objects in the tomb.

In the flickering light I could make out canopic jars, bronze mirrors, bronze daggers, and spears. There were small statuettes of Isis, Osiris, and Amun. Tall, sealed jars along the wall were likely to contain scrolls. And in the center lay—the sarcophagus!

"I never dreamed . . . ," I murmured as I stepped back from the wall to let Wilding take a look.

"None of us did," Fell remarked, slapping me on the shoulder. "We all dream of finding an intact tomb, but none of us, in our heart of hearts, believes we shall."

"But you have, dear chap," said Canon Poole, "you have. Well done. Congratulations. A fine piece of work."

"How much more of the wall can we remove?" asked Fell, turning to Farnsleigh.

"If you leave the remainder of it until after lunch, I can get this copy of the painted panel finished while the rest of you are eating."

"Do you have a revolver?"

Farnsleigh swallowed hard, "A revolver?"

"There may be precious metals in the burial chamber—there are certainly objects that would fetch an excellent price at the bazaar—and if you are working here while the rest of us are at lunch, you should have protection. As well, I'll leave a man standing guard at the entrance to the shaft. Farouk, are you there?"

"Yes, *effendi*," came a voice from a long way farther back in the tunnel, where our faithful head man was awaiting orders.

"Who do you recommend, Farouk?" shouted Fell, "to guard the entrance, I mean?"

"Hassan would be best for that," came the shouted replied.

"Arrange it. Now that revolver . . ."

"I'm afraid I haven't . . . ," began Farnsleigh.

"I have a revolver back in my hut," I interposed.

"Would you fetch it, please, Flinders, there's a good man," said Fell.

I left the tomb and, at a steady jog, trotted through the now scorching heat down the long, sloping ramps of the old temple and across the floor of the valley. I was puffing and sweating by the time I reached my hut.

On a shelf was my father's old army revolver. I had been at the university all through the Great War and the long conscription debate that wracked Australia, determined to enlist as soon as I graduated. My parents were not happy about my plans, but since my father had served in the Boer War, he could hardly complain. But the same month that I sat for my final exams, the armistice was signed, and I lost the chance of testing my nerve against real danger.

When I won this job in Egypt, my father had insisted that I take his old army revolver with me. I agreed, wondering if here I would find the test of nerve and courage that I had missed in the war.

I put the revolver into one pocket and a box of ammunition into the other. Then I splashed water on my face from the canvas bath that stood outside the back wall of my hut and jogged back.

At the tomb, Fell was rounding up everyone and herding them out of the shaft.

"But I haven't seen it yet," Lamb was complaining.

"Later, Doctor. All in good time."

"Do you want photographs of the chamber?" Burrows asked.

"After lunch, when Farnsleigh's finished."

"May I take the ladies inside, sir? I'm sure they'd like to see the tomb," said Wilding in his typically oily fashion. I recognized this as another excuse to spend some time with Amelia. I was suddenly annoyed for not having thought of it myself.

"Leave it till after lunch!" snapped Fell. "All of these things can happen later. Ah, Flinders, you're back. Take that revolver in to Farnsleigh, please."

It was with great relief that I left the blazing sunlight and stepped back into the dark tomb shaft.

I found Farnsleigh hard at work—making precise measurements of each part of the painting as he reproduced it.

"Here's the hand gun," I said as I approached.

"I don't want it,"said the artist. "In the first place I've never fired a gun in my life. And in the second, if I pulled the trigger in this tomb, I'm sure I should be killed by ricocheting bullets."

"It's not loaded. Just stick it in your belt to keep Fell happy."

Reluctantly Farnsleigh accepted the revolver but refused my offer of the box of ammunition.

I left Farnsleigh to his work and returned to the surface to find that the entire party had started back to the campsite for lunch.

Tuesday
11:30 a.m. to 2:30 p.m.

The powerful sunlight had burned all the color out of the landscape. The rocks, the buildings, even the people, were the same faded, faint, dishwater-brown color. As I walked slowly back to camp, a lazy puff of wind carried the mingled smells of paraffin, garlic, smoke, and savory vegetables.

To my right, a donkey was being led toward our dump site by one of the *fellahin*, two baskets full of limestone chips slung across the animal's uncomplaining back. At the far end of the valley, where the River Nile lay beyond a strip of lush, green cultivation, I thought I could see a faint trail of dust rising off the road that led from Luxor.

Outside the common room I washed in a basin of cold water, placed on a rough wooden bench for this purpose. As I washed, I was joined by the normally taciturn Ambrose Hoffman.

"A good morning at the dig?" he asked. Apparently he was, for a change, in the mood to talk.

"You haven't heard?"

"I've been working on my own all morning, retracing the architecture of the original temple. I found this very interesting . . ."

"We reached the burial chamber," I interrupted, "and it looks as thought it's undisturbed!" My own sense of excitement returned as I reported the news.

"Never been looted?"

"That seems possible—even likely."

"Have you seen the contents yet?"

"Just a glimpse. It appears to be the tomb of an army commander. That tomb will have stories to tell."

"I'm very pleased for you. Fell must be excited."

"Over the moon."

"Good. Let me tell you what I came across this morning. I was tracing the eastern wall. And it looks as though the whole thing may have been several yards longer than I originally thought. You see . . ."

Still surprised by Hoffman's garrulous burst, I entered the common room with him to find most of the party already seated at the long trestle table. The odious Wilding had placed himself between Amelia and Elspeth and was busy being his usual smarmy self, chatting and smiling first to one of them and then the other. I noticed there were still a few spare places around the table and took an empty seat between Poole and Narracourt.

"Canon, perhaps you would give thanks for this meal?" asked Fell.

Canon Poole did so.

We were served by Farouk and Rami's two eldest sons. Farouk himself supervised the serving while Rami remained in the kitchen. Perhaps in honor of the morning's discovery or perhaps in honor of our guests, Farouk had dressed himself in a new, crimson fez with a blue tassel and had strapped a gaudy, striped sash about his waist.

Lunch was a meal of hot, freshly baked bread; plates of savory vegetable stew, into which we dipped our bread; boiled eggs; and goat cheese. In the center of the table was a basket of oranges.

We had not long started to eat when a commotion outside caused us all to lay down our knives and forks and listen. There was the clatter of a pony cart followed by raised voices.

"Archons of Athens! Take care, can't you? My wife is a delicate woman!"

Fell rose from the table, and several of us followed him outside. Clambering out of a pony cart that looked too small to hold him was an enormous man—not just fat, but tall and broad-shouldered as well. He was wearing a white linen suit made from enough cloth to provide sails for two or three of the *feluccas* that sail the Nile. On his head was a broad-brimmed panama hat. His face was round and florid. Clamped firmly on his nose was a pair of gold-rimmed pince-nez spectacles from which trailed a broad, black ribbon. Covering his upper lip and, indeed, a good deal of his face was a magnificent bandit's moustache.

"Which one of you is Fell?" he asked, squinting through his pince-nez at the group. Fell, speechless for once, advanced, extending his hand.

The visitor took it and shook it as if he was trying to pump water. "Chesterton," he said, by way of introduction, "and this delicate flower is my wife Frances."

"How do you . . . ," Fell began, but Chesterton hadn't finished.

"And these two warts on the face of humanity," he continued, "are, I believe, already known to you. They took it upon their own initiative to come and fetch us from the Winter Palace Hotel in Luxor."

It was then I noticed Neville Page and Elliot Jones, the two journalists. I had not realized until that moment that they had been missing from the camp all morning.

"Welcome to *Deir el-Bahri*," said Fell. "Come in out of the heat. One of the men will take care of your baggage. I'm afraid you'll find conditions here rather primitive."

"I'm a primitive man," boomed Chesterton, giving Fell a slap on the back strong enough to dislodge dentures. "My needs are simple. But we must take care of Frances, you know. She is a delicate little thing."

Indeed, Mrs.Chesterton was both short and slender. Tiny, in fact. Next to her husband she looked as though a strong breeze would snap her in two.

Inside, Fell made the introductions, ending with, "Now, please take your places at the head of the table." As he said this, he began to move people to make room.

Mrs. Chesterton raised her hand to stop him. "Please don't make a fuss. We will sit wherever there are empty places. Gilbert—take a seat here."

"Yes, m'dear," murmured the gentle giant beside her. I was to discover later that whatever instruction this tiny woman gave, Chesterton instantly obeyed.

Once we were all settled again at the table, meals were served to the Chestertons and to the two journalists. Chesterton and his wife bowed their heads while he said grace, aloud, and then they began to eat—she picking delicately at her food, he demolishing the meal like a blacksmith after a heavy day at the forge.

"I apologize for the rather limited range of food we can offer . . . ," Madeleine Sutton began to say.

"Nonsense, my good woman!"snorted Chesterton."Good, plain, hearty food—that's what keeps Englishmen healthy." So saying, he demonstrated his own health by biting into a slab of bread and goat cheese.

I was on the opposite side of the table from the Chestertons, and this position gave me a good opportunity to observe him. Beneath the wild mane of hair, the wide, open face was benign in the way a child's is, and the eyes behind the glasses frowned a little in the manner of short-sighted persons. The moustache, I now noticed, was rather like an ill-tended but luxuriant elderberry bush. His mouth was restless, even when it was not eating. And his body, I realized, was as broad as

it was long. In a map of Mr. Chesterton, the lines of latitude and lon-
gitude would be of equal length.

I felt rather overawed by the great literary figure facing me. I
remembered reading *The Innocence of Father Brown* and *The Ballad of
the White Horse* when I was in high school. Then, while I was an under-
graduate, I had discovered *The Man Who Was Thursday* and thought it
was the cleverest piece of writing I had ever come across. Of course, I
had known for several weeks that Chesterton was scheduled to visit our
dig, but the reality was far more overwhelming than the prospect. Fell
had received a letter from Chesterton announcing his presence in
Egypt and asking whether, on the grounds of his "voracious curiosity,"
he might be allowed to observe the dig.

In preparation for the great man's arrival, I had borrowed two of
his books of essays from Neville Page, *Alarms and Discursions* and
Tremendous Trifles. Page had looked down his nose as he handed over
the books remarking, "He writes quite well—for a Liberal."

And there he was, seated opposite, as real as life and twice as large.

"And to what do you attribute this enthusiasm for plain food, Mr.
Chesterton?" asked Mrs. Poole, in an attempt to overcome the
stunned silence in the presence of our celebrated guest and start
some conversation.

"To the fact," replied Chesterton, after swallowing a mouthful, "that
I had the good fortune to be born into a middle-class family—back in
the days when it really was a class and it really was in the middle."

"I love your Father Brown detective stories, Mr. Chesterton,"
chipped in Amelia. "I read them all in the *Strand* magazine."

"It's very kind of you to say so, m'dear," he replied, blinking at
her benignly.

"Now how can a man of your literary gifts, Mr. Chesterton," asked Narracourt, "justify squandering your energies on mere detective stories?"

"In the first place, dear old Father Brown pays our gas bills. And this is not an insignificant fact. It was Dr. Samuel Johnson who said that he who does not write for money is a fool. But in the second place, there is nothing 'mere' about detective stories."

"Of course not," agreed Amelia, "they are . . . delightful."

"Well put, m'dear. Detective stories are delightful in the same way that poetry is delightful. And for the same reasons."

This drew a quiet snort from Narracourt and the muttered remark that "the public like detective stories because they are bad literature."

"Utter nonsense, dear sir!" replied Chesterton, with a laugh that was like an explosion. "If lack of literary quality produced popularity, then the most popular book in England would be the railway timetable. That is a book totally lacking in subtle characterization and psychological comedy, and yet it is not read aloud uproariously on winter evenings."

Narracourt did not respond, so Chesterton continued. "In these stories the detective travels the streets of London rather like a prince in a tale of elfland. And in the course of those travels, the passing bus assumes the primary colors of a fairy ship. The lights of the city glow like innumerable goblin eyes, since they are the guardians of some secret which the writer knows and the reader does not. Detective stories, in short, are the poetry of the everyday—the poetry of the chimney pots."

"That's exactly how I see detective stories, Mr. Chesterton," said Amelia, her eyes glowing.

"Then you see clearly, m'dear. But that is not all. While it is the tendency of human nature to rebel against civilization, the romance of police activity reminds us that civilization is itself the most sensational and romantic of rebellions. The detective story reminds us that we live in an armed camp. The criminals are nothing but the traitors within our gates. The police force is only a successful knight-errantry. The law and order the detective imposes in these stories reminds us that morality is the most daring of conspiracies."

"Here! Here! Well said, sir," commented Colonel Race from the doorway. As he entered the room he introduced himself to the Chestertons, and, as he took his place in a spare seat, Farouk ordered that a meal be brought for the late arrival. Presumably, while we had been on the dig, Race had spent his morning hunting among our men for his missing convict.

"And how was the dig this morning?" asked Neville Page. "Did anything interesting happen while we were in Luxor?"

"You might say that," Poole said with a chuckle.

"We reached the sealed tomb door," Fell explained.

"You did?" exploded Elliot Jones, and suddenly the two journalists were listening intently.

Fell explained the morning's work and the great excitement of opening a small hole in the door that appeared to lead to a tomb with its contents intact.

"Mind you, it's only the tomb of an army officer," added Narracourt, "so it's hardly likely to yield valuable treasures for museums. The subscribers to Reverend Doctor Burton's foundation are likely to be quite disappointed."

"The real treasure is knowledge," said Billy Burton, wagging a finger playfully at Narracourt. "A treasure that does not perish, that moth does not eat nor rust destroy—as you, my good sir, know perfectly well."

"Pay no attention to Narracourt; he's just being a fathead as usual," snapped Fell, who went on to explain to the Chestertons, as well as Page and Jones, that the real value in the tomb was likely to be found in the inscriptions it contained.

"So," asked Mrs. Chesterton, "when do you enter the tomb itself? When do you start to explore and catalogue its contents?"

"After lunch," explained Fell, "as soon as work resumes on the second shift of the day."

"Now I certainly don't want to be a nuisance," rumbled Chesterton, "but I would dearly love to take a peek through this window into the ancient past. But only so long as I'm not under foot, you understand."

"That shall be arranged," Professor Fell responded, "but only after the position of every item has been noted. In archeology, where things are found can be even more important than what is found."

After luncheon was over and the group began to disperse from the table, I walked out into the fresh air to peel and eat an orange under the shade of the canvas awning that was attached to one side of the common room. I found Colonel Race already there, smoking his pipe.

"Have you been looking for your man this morning?" I asked, to make conversation. "I forget the fella's name."

"Mamur Zapt. Yes, I have. Without success so far, I'm afraid."

For a while Race smoked in silence while I began to demolish the orange.

"Tell me, Flinders," he said after a few moments, "have any thefts been noticed around the camp in recent days?"

"Thefts of what?"

"Of anything at all."

"Well, we've been a bit short of food the last day or two, and someone suggested that might have been due to theft. Mind you, I'm not so sure. It might just have been bad management and poor ordering."

"But the problem is a recent one?"

"Yes, only very recent."

"Interestin'. Most interestin'. Carry on. Anything else missing?"

"Well, on every dig there is always a degree of loss of some of the smaller antiquities. You allow for that. Fell calls it 'wastage.' Mind you, it still irritates him."

"I'm sure it does. What does he put it down to?"

"Same as always—some of the *fellahin* steal a few of the smaller objects to sell to the market dealers. We try to prevent this sort of thing from happening by rewarding every man who finds an object during the dig with *baksheesh*. That's to encourage the pick man and the shovel man to hand in any objects they find. Mind you, there will always be one bad apple."

"Meaning?"

"Meaning that there will always be one of the workers who will hand in objects, collect his *baksheesh,* and then steal the objects—or other antiquities—from the storeroom to sell to the market dealers. In any crowd there will always be some dishonest men—even among the *fellahin*."

"Yes, of course. I take it the storeroom is kept locked?"

"Of course."

"But there have still been thefts?"

"A few. Fortunately nothing important."

"Interestin'. Most interestin'."

For the next few minutes Colonel Race went on smoking his pipe in silence. I finished my orange and walked around the back of the common room to dispose of the orange peelings in the rubbish bin. As I rounded the corner, I saw a man trying to wrestle open the fly screen on the small high window in the back wall of the kitchen.

"Hey, you! What do you think you're up to?" I shouted.

The man turned and looked at me—not a look of fear, but a look of red-hot anger. For a moment his reaction startled me. Then I threw away the peel that was filling my hand and started to walk briskly toward him.

"Now look here, you . . . ," I began.

At that, he turned and took to his heels. I didn't know who this blighter was—our kitchen thief or the colonel's missing convict— but I had no intention of allowing him to get away. I began to sprint after him.

As I did so, I discovered I was not alone—Colonel Race had caught up and was at my side.

Our boots kicking away gravel as we ran, we followed the man up the slope behind the camp buildings. He managed to keep well ahead of us, his loose, shirt-like garment flapping behind him as he ran.

Sweat was running down my face, my legs were pumping like pistons, and my lungs were sucking in hot, dry air.

The flying figure ahead was slowly outdistancing us. We were chasing him up a slope of loose scree, and that made the ground treacherous under our feet and running difficult. He disappeared behind an outcropping of rocks on the brow of the low ridge.

By the time Race and I reached the rocks, the fugitive had disappeared. Ahead of us lay the northern side of the temple ruins with its piles of rubble. Farther away, on the right, was a line of palm trees, marking the start of the cultivation that occupied the banks of the Nile.

"The blighter could be anywhere," I puffed. Trying to talk was a mistake. For a moment I bent double, mouth open, gasping in air. As I straightened up, I discovered that the colonel looked remarkably unpuffed, and unruffled, by the run.

"Pity we lost him," he said, then clamped his pipe between his teeth and relit it. "Next time," Race muttered, more to himself than me, "next time I'll get him."

"Well . . . ," I gasped, still short of air, "if we've lost him, we might as well get back to the camp."

"You go. I'm going to mooch around here for a bit. See what I can turn up."

I wiped my sweating face on a handkerchief as I replied, "Stay out here in the sun if you want to. I'm heading back."

I walked back down the slope at a much more leisurely pace than I had run up it. Before me lay the long line of camp buildings: the store huts; Burrows' photographic hut; the long, low common room with its kitchen at one end and its canvas awning at the other; the rows of huts in which we slept—most of them tiny, but a few of them larger, to accommodate Fell and his special guests.

The sun beat down with a remorseless, scorching heat, and my boots felt like cast iron, threatening to slide from underneath me on the loose scree at every step. Coming a little closer to the buildings, I saw someone hanging around the back of one of the huts. *Curious behavior,* I thought, *why isn't that blighter inside, out of the sun?*

Squinting in the glare I recognized the figure as Wilding. And the hut he was moping around was Fell's. Why won't that blasted Wilding just leave Amelia alone? I thought savagely as I quickened my pace, determined to catch up to him so that he would not have another opportunity to speak to Amelia alone.

The path down the slope ended near the back wall of the kitchen. From there most of the huts were hidden by the bulk of the common room. When I came around the corner and the huts once more came into view, Wilding had vanished. Silently cursing the man, I poured water from a canvas water bag into the tin basin that still stood on its rough, wooden trestle under the awning. Then I stripped off my shirt and washed my face and head and upper body as thoroughly as I could.

Pulling my shirt back on, I stepped inside the common room, looking for a cool drink.

The long room was empty, except for our photographer, Nat Burrows, and the journalist Neville Page, who were in a far corner, heads together, huddled in quiet conversation. Whatever they were saying to one another, they stopped the instant I entered.

"I say, you chaps," I said. "Did either of you spot a man hanging around the back of the common room after lunch?"

"What sort of man?" asked Page.

"An ordinary sort of chap. One of the *fellahin*. He seemed to have a pretty ugly sort of face when he glared at me."

"I didn't notice anyone. Did you see anyone, Burrows?"

"Not a soul," said the photographer. "Sorry I can't help you, Flinders old chap."

I left the two of them to continue their conversation and stepped into the kitchen. In the corner was a small, wooden barrel that was filled with fresh water every day and kept draped in a damp hessian cloth. From this I filled an enamel mug and drank deeply.

Thus restored, I returned to my tiny cubicle of a hut. I glanced at the alarm clock that ticked loudly beside my palm-stick bed: twenty-five minutes past two. No time left for an after-lunch siesta. At that moment, Dr. Lamb stuck his head through the door of the hut and said, "I'm on my way back to the dig. Want to come with me?"

"It's almost time for the second shift—I might as well."

As I stepped back out into the sunlight, Dr. Lamb began burbling, "I am really most keen to see this burial chamber. And I wonder, Flinders old chap, if you would put in a good word for me with Fell. He seems determined only to allow archeologists into the tomb."

"You'll get your chance . . . ," I started to say, when a sound from behind caused me to stop and turn around. What I had heard was a thud, followed by a shout of pain.

Lamb and I spun around to discover, farther down the line of huts, two men fighting. Page and Jones, the two journalists, were squaring up to each other like boxers. As we turned, Jones, the shorter of the two, threw a punch. The tall, lean Page ducked his head back out of the way and then swung a punch himself. He caught the side of Jones's head.

I ran toward them shouting, "Hey! Break it up, you two!"

Reaching them, I grabbed Page's shoulders and tried to pull him back. He struggled violently beneath my grasp, his hautiness and poise completely lost. Dr. Lamb tried to push his way between the two men but was flung aside.

Jones, a red-haired picture of fury, had lifted his fist to swing a mighty punch at Page when he was frozen to the spot by a bellowed, "Stop that!"

It was the commanding voice of Fell.

"What in the blue blazes do you two think you're doing?" Fell's face was purple with anger.

"I will not allow fighting in my camp. I've had enough trouble with fighting among the *fellahin*. But I need them here to work. You two I don't need. If there's any repetition of this, you'll be banned from the camp. Both of you. Do you understand?"

There was no reply from either of the two amateur boxers, so Fell shouted his question even louder, "Do you understand?"

They both nodded their heads sheepishly and said they understood.

"Now that's settled—everyone back to the dig," growled Fell. "It's time for the afternoon shift."

The group that had gathered around the fight began to break up. I handed Page my handkerchief to wipe the blood off the side of his face.

"What was that all about?" I asked him quietly, letting the others go on ahead to the tomb site.

"That damned keeper of lunatics thinks he's a journalist," muttered Page between clenched teeth, but he refused to say any more. He returned my handkerchief, and I hurried to the tomb shaft. The burial chamber was about to be opened.

When I arrived at the shaft entrance, John Farnsleigh and his Arab assistant were spreading sheets of paper, still damp with watercolors, on some of the flatter rocks to dry in the sun.

"I've only just finished," he was explaining to Fell. "It's a good thing you didn't come back any sooner."

"I knew that you had a big job there," Fell commented.

"Careful with that!" shouted Farnsleigh to his servant. "Don't let it fold like that or you'll smudge the image!" He hurried over to the man's side and took over the task of laying the sheets over the flat, hot surfaces of the rocks. "Now, you stay here and keep an eye on them. As soon as they're all dry, pack them up and bring them down to me," Farnsleigh commanded.

"And you'd better go down to the kitchen and get Farouk to organize some lunch," suggested Fell. "Madeleine told Rami to save some for you."

"Thanks, I'm famished," said the artist as he started off back to the campsite.

"Now," said Fell, rubbing his hands with gleeful anticipation, "it's time to remove that wall and see exactly what we've got in the tomb. Flinders and Wilding, come with me—you two can remove the wall instead of one of the pick men. This is a delicate task; none of the contents of the chamber must be damaged by falling plaster or mud bricks."

I selected a pickax from a pile of tools near the entrance, and Wilding collected an army entrenching tool.

"Burrows, get your gear ready," continued Fell. "As soon as the wall is cleared, I want a complete photographic record before anything is touched."

"May Sir Edward, Dr. Burton, and I observe?" asked Canon Poole, somewhat hesitantly.

"Yes. All right," Fell agreed. "As long as you all keep well behind the work party."

"And may I?" asked Dr. Lamb, moving forward.

"No, you may not!" snapped Fell. "You will get to see the chamber later, when we open it up to everyone else."

I stepped inside the welcome darkness of the tomb shaft, with Fell in front of me and Wilding just behind.

"Where's Chesterton?" I asked, still feeling somewhat overawed by having such a celebrity visiting our expedition. In fact, I was probably as impressed by the presence of Chesterton as I was by the opening of the tomb.

"Resting," Fell replied as he shuffled down the narrow tunnel ahead of me. "I told him it would be awhile before we could let anyone else into the tomb, so he said they'd rest. Apparently his wife found the journey from Luxor tiring."

All three of us were carrying hurricane lanterns, and when we reached the plastered mud brick wall—or "door" as Fell called it—that divided the shaft from the tomb, we set our lamps down on the rock floor.

"Now, try to remove the painting intact—if you possibly can," instructed Fell as he squeezed back out of the way, leaving Wilding and me with some room to work—although there was very little room in that confined space.

I began by chiseling around the painted area in an attempt to separate the painted panel from the rest of the plaster-covered mud bricks. When it looked as though I had cut a fairly deep channel around it, Wilding and I tried to lever it out. I wedged my pick underneath one edge, and Wilding used his entrenching tool like a crowbar on the other.

"Careful! Careful!" urged Fell from somewhere behind us. Then with a shudder the central section of mud bricks came loose and fell forward into the shaft—shattering into fifty pieces as it did so.

"Sorry," I said ruefully.

"It was too brittle to save," explained Wilding.

"Saving the painting intact was only an outside chance at best. At least it fell forward into the shaft rather than backward onto the contents of the burial chamber," said Fell, trying to be positive. "I'll call in a shovel man to remove the debris."

Wilding and I continued pulling down the remaining sections of mud bricks. Wilding broke up the slabs I pulled down, and Fell arranged for a shovel man and two basket boys to remove the rubble—each of whom had to squeeze past the queue of archeologists waiting expectantly in the tunnel.

A little over an hour after we started, Fell, Wilding, and I picked up our hurricane lamps and stood, wide-eyed, at the cleared entrance to the burial chamber. Narracourt, Poole, and Burton were pressing in behind us, trying to catch a glimpse over our shoulders.

"Just look at that!" whispered Fell. "Magnificent!"

The chamber was perhaps twelve feet by twelve feet. In the center, and dominating the room, was a painted, wooden sarcophagus. There were other pieces of wooden furniture, a couple of chairs and a low table, and covering these and the floor of the chamber were dozens of small objects.

Suddenly I was no longer a citizen of the twentieth century. The centuries fell away, and I was looking at how the Egyptians lived, and died, three and a half thousand years ago. It was all so vivid, and, it seems an odd thing to say, but—*alive*. This was the furniture they sat on. These were the things that mattered to Menes in his daily life.

There were some beautiful pieces of the glazed earthenware called *faience;* a miniature box made of wood inlaid with ivory; the four canopic jars, which would contain the viscera of the mummified Menes; on the low table was a senet game board with playing pieces; and there were a number of *shawabti,* or funerary figures—of Horus, Thoth, Isis, and Osiris.

Against the walls were a number of tall, slender, sealed jars and wooden figurines—these, we hoped, would prove to contain historically valuable papyrus scrolls.

"Don't touch anything," Fell commanded as Billy Burton leaned past him and tried to lay a hand on the sarcophagus. "I want all of this photographed by Burrows. Then I want Hoffman to sketch a plan of the chamber, marking the position of each piece. Only then will we start to examine individual items."

I admired Fell's scholarly restraint: the desire to rush in and start handling all these beautiful pieces was almost overwhelming.

"Farouk!" Fell shouted over his shoulder, "I want two of your best men in here to clear away the remaining rubble from the entrance to the burial chamber. And I also want a couple of guards at the entrance to the shaft. There must be a guard on duty until we get an iron door installed at the shaft entrance. And send Burrows down here to me."

Somewhere behind me, way back in the tunnel, I could hear Farouk's footsteps hurrying away. A few moments later Burton, Narracourt, and Poole had to move back down the shaft to allow the shovel men through. Also squeezing through the congested shaft were Nat Burrows and his Arab assistant.

"All right! Move back everyone! Back around the corner," ordered Fell. "You men start on that rubble. Burrows, I want a photographic record of everything—and I do mean everything—in that chamber. But, mind you, don't touch anything. The rest of us will have to get out of the way."

As I backed away, around the bend in the shaft, Burrows's Arab assistant was setting up the tripod, and Burrows himself was unpacking his camera.

Some twenty feet down the shaft I found the others huddled in a kind of conference—if you can call a single file of archeologists jammed in a narrow tunnel a conference.

"You need to set up a very careful system for cataloguing," Narracourt was saying.

"I know! I know!" snapped Fell. "Don't try to teach grandmother how to suck eggs! Wilding, you go back outside and get a long trestle table set up right at the entrance to the shaft. Better still, two tables. We can do the preliminary sorting there. Canon Poole, you're good on pottery, aren't you?"

"Well, I have specialized a bit . . ."

"Good. Would you like to make a start on cataloguing the pots and earthenware?"

"Yes. I'd be delighted to help."

"Wilding will give you a hand. Dr. Burton," continued Fell, "why don't you assist young Flinders here with a catalogue of the *shawabti* figures."

"Professor Fell, you don't know, I say, you can't possibly know how happy this makes me," beamed the American.

"And Narracourt—if you can keep a polite tongue in that fat head of yours, you and I can work on the sarcophagus together."

By way of response Narracourt simply nodded. From time to time, as we talked, there was a brilliant flash of light from around the bend in the shaft, followed by the smoky smell of burned flash powder, telling us that Burrows was getting on with his task.

"You want me?" called Ambrose Hoffman, our architect, from the shaft entrance.

"Yes," shouted Fell. "Fetch your drawing equipment. As soon as Burrows is finished photographing, I want you to draw a scale plan of the chamber—with every item marked."

"I'll get my things" was the shouted reply.

"We can rope in the others to help us as well," I suggested.

"Good idea," nodded Fell. "Amelia and Elspeth will be happy to help clean and catalogue the smaller items. Mrs. Poole too, I'm sure, Canon."

Poole nodded his head and then said, "And your Dr. Lamb will be very keen to help."

"Yes, of course he will," Fell agreed with a chuckle. "He'll think it's Christmas if he's allowed to do some real archeology. Flinders, do you know where Lamb is?"

"Probably still hovering around the tunnel entrance, chafing at the bit to come and have a look at the burial chamber."

"Did you notice that one of the figurines in the burial chamber was . . . ," said Narracourt, and the conversation became very technical for a while. Around twenty minutes later the photographic flashes appeared to have stopped.

"Burrows!"shouted Fell, "How are you going?"

"Almost finished" was the yelled reply.

At that moment Wilding returned to tell us he had two tables in place, right beside the entrance to the tomb shaft. Fell continued making his plans for the next few minutes, stopping only when Nat Burrows returned, accompanied by his Arab servant, both loaded down with photographic equipment, which they were struggling to cope with in the narrow space.

"All finished," said Burrows as he squeezed past the line of waiting archeologists and continued toward the surface. "I've exposed over a dozen plates. I'll go and start processing them at once."

"Where is that blasted Hoffman?" grumbled Fell. "He should be here starting work now."

"Since he's not—shall we take another peek?" suggested Poole, a twinkle in his eye.

It took no more prompting than that. A few moments later we had shuffled in single file back to the tomb.

"Look, Fell," said Narracourt, breaking the silence. "I know this is your dig . . ."

"You bet your boots it is!" growled the professor.

". . . but, may I make a suggestion?"

Fell raised his eyebrows and waited for Narracourt to continue.

"Since Hoffman is not ready to start drawing the plan yet, why don't we—without touching anything else, mind—why don't we open the sarcophagus and take a look at the mummy?"

There was a murmured chorus of approval. Fell's scholarly restraint didn't take much pushing.

"I suppose it won't do any harm."

Taking great care where we put our feet, four of us stepped into the tomb—Fell and I on one side of the sarcophagus, Narracourt and

Wilding on the other. Since the tomb itself was wider than the narrow shaft, we were no longer jammed against each other, shoulder to shoulder, and could breathe comfortably.

The coffin before us was made of dark wood, brightly painted across the top and on both the long sides.

"Slip your fingers in there—where the join is," said Fell, unnecessarily, "and lift gently."

I reached out and touched the ancient sarcophagus softly. The wood was very dry to the touch, and I could feel the grain of the timber. It was an anthropomorphic coffin—roughly body shaped. Carefully I felt for the join between the lid and the base of the coffin. The join would be grooved, so we would have to lift it straight up. I eased the tips of my fingers into the join and felt the wooden lid shift. *Strange*, I thought, *that the lid seemed to 'give' so easily.*

"Everyone ready?" asked Fell in hushed tones. A murmur of assent ran around the small chamber.

The only hurricane lamp in the tomb was on the floor, sending its dim, flickering light toward the ceiling and casting dark shadows around us. All four of us took the weight of the sarcophagus lid simultaneously. We felt the lid easily come free from the grooved edge of the coffin base. It was much lighter than we thought.

"All right," said Fell. "Now slide it down toward the feet and lay it on the floor."

We lifted, slid it back, and rested it on the stone floor. Still the interior of the casket was invisible, hidden in black shadow. Billy Burton picked up the hurricane lamp from the floor and held it high—throwing its light into the interior of the sarcophagus. All of us leaned forward for our first glimpse of the mummy.

Fell swore, Burton gasped, and I felt as though my heart were going to explode: in the sarcophagus was no mummy but the body of Dr. Brian Lamb, a bronze Egyptian knife deep in his chest and his still warm blood filling the space around him.

Billy Burton was the first to recover from the shock.

"Quick—check to see   he's still alive," said the American urgently.

"He can't possibly be," responded Narracourt, his voice hollow.

Burton leaned forward, felt Lamb's neck, and then held a hand over his mouth.

"No pulse, and no breath," he reported. "He's as dead as a snowman in springtime."

"But . . . but . . . ," spluttered Fell, "that's impossible."

And he was right. We had left Dr. Lamb on the surface, and he could not have passed us in the narrow tomb shaft without being seen by every one of us.

"There must be another way in," Poole suggested.

"Most unlikely. Not," whispered Narracourt, "into a burial chamber."

"Narracourt's right," added Fell, their feud forgotten. "A tomb like this will only have one way in and out."

"But there must be another way!" insisted Wilding, a note of panic in his voice. "I mean to say, if there's not then . . . well . . . I mean to say . . . I don't know what . . ."

There was a long, heavy silence.

"Egyptian magic!" muttered Wilding. His eyes were wide and staring, and he was talking more to himself than anyone else. "The Ancient Egyptians had occult powers that we can't even dream about today."

"Nonsense, man! Pull yourself together," snapped Fell. "Flinders—make a careful examination of the walls. And the ceiling and floor as well. But be careful where you put your feet, and don't disturb any of the objects."

"What am I looking for?"

"A concealed entrance," Fell snapped.

I searched the whole chamber carefully but found no other way in or out.

"We must do something for this poor chap," I heard Poole's voice saying behind me as I searched. "We can't just leave him there."

"Certainly not," said Fell. "The question is . . ."

And for the first time since I had met him, I saw Professor Fell struggling to make a decision. "Wilding," he said at length, "get back to the surface. Send Farouk down here with two of his men and a stretcher. And send for Colonel Race—that's who we need here."

Wilding departed.

"Rotten business," said Billy Burton, "rotten, I say, simply hideously awful."

"No hidden doors or compartments," I announced, having completed my search. "But I've found something else."

"What?"

"The mummy. On the floor here, behind these chairs. This must be the mummy that was removed from the sarcophagus to make room for Lamb's corpse."

"Or for the living Lamb," said Narracourt thoughtfully. "We don't know if he was still alive when he was placed in the coffin and was killed in there."

"Why on earth would he do that?" Fell asked.

"I have no idea," replied Narracourt, in his most supercilious tone. "I am simply trying to canvas the options." And then he added, "Nothing like this has ever happened on a dig I've run. Or on any other dig, for that matter."

"Oh, shut up, Narracourt!" snapped Fell. "To have you crowing over archeology is bad enough, but crowing over a tragedy like this is beyond the pale."

"I wasn't crowing, Fell, please believe me. I think we're all suffering from shock."

"Yes, of course. I'm sorry."

There was a long and heavy silence as the stale air of the chamber, no bigger than twelve feet by twelve feet, seemed to close in on us. In the dim lamplight, surrounded by the artifacts of Ancient Egypt, it was possible to wonder if Wilding had been right. Was there some dark and ancient power in this tomb? What secret and dreadful knowledge did those ancient priests have that is now lost to us? Was there an evil presence moving in this chamber, a presence that could strike again at any moment? My breathing was shallow, and my nerves were on edge.

At last the silence was broken by Billy Burton, who asked, "Where did the knife come from?"

Fell leaned forward, holding one of the lamps high as he did so, and looked closely at the weapon.

"Bronze," he remarked, looking at Narracourt for support, "heavily embossed hilt. Eighteenth dynasty, I would estimate."

Narracourt nodded.

"Then it was probably part of the tomb furnishings," I proposed.

"The period is right," nodded Fell.

"What are you getting at, young man?" asked Poole.

"Well, it seems to me that the murderer . . ."

"Murderer?" yelled Billy Burton. "No one's mentioned, I say, no one's mentioned anything about murder yet!"

"What else can it be?" I said reasonably. "Look at him. It can hardly be suicide. And as for an accident . . . well . . . I can't imagine how. So, either it was some ancient curse—as Wilding suggested," I glanced around nervously as I spoke, "or else, well, a murderer, of flesh and blood just as solid as ours."

"Flinders is right," confirmed Fell. "We have to think in terms of murder. That's why I've sent for Colonel Race. He's an investigator; he'll know what to do. Flinders is absolutely right—suicide and accident are out of the question. As for that occult nonsense that Wilding was sprouting . . . well . . . that's just poppycock."

"The men won't understand that," commented Narracourt.

"Eh?"

"The *fellahin*. They'll start talking about ghosts and ancient curses. They may refuse to do any more work on the site."

"You could be right," Fell said thoughtfully. "I'll have to talk to Farouk and try to head off any trouble in that direction."

A clatter of footsteps could be heard in the tomb shaft, and Burton disappeared around the bend to tell Farouk and his men with the stretcher to wait for a moment.

"Why?" said Poole with a sad shake of his head. "Why would anyone want to do this to Dr. Lamb?"

"Why? How? I can't answer any of those things," Fell said with a helpless shrug.

More footsteps were heard, and a moment later Colonel Race appeared.

"You sent for me?"

"Take a look at this, Colonel."

Race leaned over the sarcophagus.

"Great Caesar's Ghost!" he muttered. Then he straightened up and said, "An ugly business. Who was the last of you gentlemen to see Dr. Lamb alive?"

We looked at each other for a moment, and then I said, "Perhaps I was. Or we all were."

"And when and where was that, Mr. Flinders?"

"At the entrance to the tomb shaft. He wanted to see the burial chamber, but he was told to wait."

"Who told him?"

"I did," volunteered Fell.

"And the rest of you came down the shaft, leaving him behind on the surface?"

We all nodded.

"So how did he come to be in the burial chamber, in the sarcophagus, with a knife in his chest?"

"We were hoping you could answer that question!"

"Have you gentlemen been in this burial chamber from the time it was opened until now?"

"Yes. Except for twenty minutes or so while Nat Burrows was taking photographs," said Fell, continuing to act as spokesman. "We all stood in the shaft, just around the corner from here."

"Where is Mr. Burrows now?"

"He'll be locked in his darkroom, processing the plates."

"I'll talk to him as soon as he emerges. Was Dr. Lamb a popular member of the expedition?"

"Not popular. Hardly that. He was too quiet, too unassuming to be described as popular."

"Unpopular then?"

"Not that either. Unless someone else noticed something I didn't. Flinders? Wilding?"

We both shook our heads.

"Did he ever speak of having any enemies?" asked Race.

"Not to me," Fell replied.

"How did you come to hire him?"

"I placed an advertisement for a medical officer for the expedition in *The Lancet*. Lamb wrote to say that he would be holidaying in Egypt at the time and applied for the job. Well, that meant I didn't have to pay his fare. It was an attractive offer. I wrote back confirming his appointment immediately."

"What do you know about his background?"

"Although he trained at Bart's in London, for the past twenty years or more he has practiced in Sydney, Australia."

"Interesting. You're Australian, aren't you, Mr. Flinders?" said Race, turning in my direction.

"Yes, I am. How did you know?"

"The accent rather gives you away, sir. We had quite a few Australian troops here in Egypt during the war. The accent is unmistakable—I recognized it at once."

"You don't imagine young Flinders had anything to do with this, do you?" protested Fell. "His professor at Sydney University—an old colleague of mine, I might add—wrote him a glowing reference. I refuse to believe that . . ."

"I'm not suggesting anything at the moment, sir," said the colonel in his calm, unflappable manner. "I'm merely exploring possible connections. Did you know Dr. Lamb before you joined the expedition, sir?"

"No, I did not," I responded. "Sydney is a big place. In fact, I didn't even realize that he was from Sydney. He never talked about it. In fact, he never talked about his background at all."

"That's quite right, I say, quite correct," volunteered Billy Burton. "The deceased was a quiet man all around, close mouthed even."

"Hmm . . . I'm sure he was," muttered Race thoughtfully. "I suggest we move the body back to one of the huts. Could it be held, temporarily, in one of the storerooms, Professor Fell?"

"If you wish. But with this heat . . ."

"Quite. I will inform the authorities in Luxor immediately. They will, undoubtedly, act quickly to remove the body to their premises and arrange for a proper medical report. In the meantime—I would like some photographs taken before the body is moved."

"Flinders," said Fell, "drag Burrows out of his darkroom, and get him back here with his equipment."

A few minutes later I was knocking on the door of the hut Nat Burrows had converted into a darkroom.

"Burrows! It's me, Flinders. Open up."

"Stop, please," said Burrows's Arab servant, who was squatting on the ground beside the door, as he grabbed my arm. "You cannot go in. The picture *effendi*, he has to stay in the dark. Go away, please."

I shook him off and pounded heavily on the door. "Open up, Burrows! It's an emergency!"

"What sort of emergency?" asked Burrows's voice, sounding very muffled through the door.

"There's been a murder."

"Murder?"

"They want you to take some photographs before the body is moved."

"You're drunk!"

"This is serious, Burrows. They want you now."

"Who wants me?"

"Colonel Race and Professor Fell."

"All right, all right! I can finish this process in . . . three minutes. I'll come then. Tell them that."

"I'll tell them."

I was about to leave when a muffled shout from inside the hut arrested my movements.

"Where? Where should I come?"

"To the tomb shaft."

"Tell them three minutes."

I turned around to head back to the shaft and found myself facing the towering figure of G. K. Chesterton. Under the shade of his broad-brimmed panama hat his face showed no beads of sweat. Clearly, he had only recently risen from his afternoon rest. The expression on his face was grim.

"I heard you employ the word 'murder,' young sir."

"Doctor Lamb has been murdered," I explained, "stabbed to death. We found his body in the tomb. It's tragic."

"Most assuredly. Murder is always tragic," agreed Chesterton as we began walking together toward the shaft entrance, Chesterton wheezing heavily as he walked with a heavy-footed tread.

"A sad death," I said, nodding my head in agreement.

"You mistake my meaning. It is a nonsense to think of a death as tragic, since we shall all die. Life is a fatal condition. No one gets out of here alive. None of us shall escape death. No, the real tragedy is that a living man has now become a murderer."

That remark brought me up short. In the strange, turbulent numbness that accompanied the finding of Lamb's body, I had not stopped to ask that one vital question: who killed him?

"Yes," I murmured quietly, "I suppose the murderer may be a member of our expedition. How extraordinary! To think that one of the people we have shared meals with, have talked to in a perfectly natural way, is a murderer."

"Not strange at all," remarked Chesterton with a fierce gleam in his eye, "entirely natural, in fact."

"Natural?"

"Murder is the oldest crime of all. The inclination to murder runs in our blood. We should not be surprised that a race who will kill their God will kill each other. The truly remarkable thing is that so many of us succeed in exercising restraint and venting our homicidal passions in more innocent ways, such as kicking a doorpost or writing a poem."

"I still feel sad about the passing of Dr. Lamb."

"Let's have none of the sumptuous humbug of the mortuary sentiment, young sir. It is given unto man once to die, and after that, to face judgment. That is the destiny of us all, as it has been of every human being since Adam. Why then should we, in hushed tones, pretend that every death is a surprise?"

"Would you not like hushed tones at your own funeral, Mr. Chesterton?"

"If there occurs to anyone a really good joke at the look of my coffin, I command him by all the thunders to make it. If he doesn't, I'll kick up the lid and make it myself."

We were approaching the shaft as Chesterton spoke, and as we reached the entrance, Colonel Race emerged. Seeing me, he asked, "Where's Burrows?"

"Not far behind us. He had to finish whatever chemical process he was engaged in. No more than three minutes, he said."

"That will have to do then. I'm glad you're here, Mr. Chesterton," continued the colonel. "This is a puzzling business. And if you have no objection, I would rather appreciate your assistance."

"My good sir, I am at your disposal. Although what I can contribute, I cannot imagine."

"A creative eye—that's what you can contribute, sir. I am just a plain soldier, and all I can supply is a methodical thoroughness. This case looks devilishly puzzling, but between us, Mr. Chesterton, we'll catch the swine who did this."

"Certainly we may catch him," said Chesterton, "but he will not turn out to be a swine. He will turn out to be something far worse—a man!"

The crunch of boots on gravel alerted us to the arrival of Burrows and his servant, carrying the heavy tripod and camera.

Race seized his arm and led him at once inside the shaft, to make a photographic record of the scene of the crime. I looked at my watch— just half past four.

Coming toward us, up the temple ramps from the floor of the valley, were Madeleine Sutton and the *fellah* whose special job it was to make the tea. He was carrying afternoon tea in his basket for the archeologists.

As they arrived I stepped forward to greet Miss Sutton, eager to share the horrible news. I gave a hasty account of what had happened. Miss Sutton looked concerned, and in response to urgent questions from the tea servant, she explained what I had said in her excellent Arabic. The tea *fallah* gave a little shriek of terror, put his basket on the ground, turned around, and ran back toward the camp buildings.

For a moment Madeleine Sutton was silent as she beckoned the men who had boiled water for the tea to bring their boiling kettle to the camp table where she proceeded to set up the tea pot. These men had been too far away to hear what Miss Sutton had said in Arabic, but if the tea servant's reaction was typical, we stood a real risk of losing all our *fellahin*.

"What will happen to the dig?" she asked quietly as she added tea leaves to the pot. "Will the expedition be canceled?"

"I don't know," I replied. "Perhaps not. What do you think, Mr. Chesterton?"

"I suspect that your patrons, and Dr. Burton's foundation, will be more insistent than ever that the dig continue."

"Good," said Miss Sutton firmly, averting her face from mine and, presumably, her attention from the subject. Then she began to pour the tea. I went into the shaft and rounded up most of the others. From their faces I guessed that they found it a relief to step out into the blazing sunshine and to something as normal as the ritual of afternoon tea.

Grasping an enamel mug of hot tea, I walked slowly away from the group. I was still feeling stunned.

Walking up the ramp toward me, from the lower levels of Queen Hatshepsut's mortuary temple, were Amelia Fell and Mrs. Poole, their heads together, deep in conversation. When they arrived, I broke the news to them.

"But that's horrible!" exclaimed Amelia, her face beneath her straw hat suddenly pale and her breath coming in short gasps. "Just horrible!"

"I'm a qualified nurse," Mrs. Poole said. "Is there anything I can do to help?"

"Not for Dr. Lamb, there isn't," I said, rather abruptly. Then added, "But you might be able to make some useful medical observations for Colonel Race." Mrs. Poole hurried off to find the colonel, leaving me with Amelia.

"I broke the news rather bluntly, I'm afraid," I said.

"There's no gentle way such news can be broken," Amelia responded. Despite her moments of dreaminess, she was a very sensible girl, Amelia—feet firmly planted on the ground. When what was needed was "practical," she forgot her dreaming and delivered "practical." You never got those silly, girlish displays of the "vapors" from Amelia—no dramatic fainting fits. I thought again, as I had thought so often before, that one day she would make some lucky man a wonderful wife.

"I feel a little guilty," she went on, "that I'm not more upset about poor Dr. Lamb. But he was so quiet that I hardly knew him. It's not wrong not to be upset over the death of someone you hardly knew, is it?"

I assured her that her reaction was perfectly normal and exactly the same as mine.

"I'm more worried about Papa. This whole expedition is his responsibility. I just don't know what this death—this murder—will mean for him."

"It may sound callous, but it will probably mean no more than an awkward, but momentary, interruption to the smooth running of the dig. Unless, of course . . ."

"Unless—what?"

"Unless the *fellahin* are a problem. I take it they can be very superstitious. Mind you, this is my first season in Egypt—you would know more about the workers than I do."

"Farouk can handle them," said Amelia with certainty. "He's the best *reis* we've ever had. They will come to him and talk darkly of evil spirits and ancient curses. Farouk will speak sternly to them. He will shame them out of running away. Then we will give them a slight increase in *baksheesh* payments, and they will stay quite happily."

"You sound very experienced at this sort of thing."

"I've been coming out here with Papa since I was a little girl. But murder is something we have never encountered before."

"Hello, you two!" chirped Neville Page brightly, the tall, thin journalist ambling toward us like a stick insect in a straw hat. "What's new? Any chance of a cup of tea?"

"Dr. Lamb's been murdered," I replied in a conversational tone. "I'm sure there'll still be tea available."

"Eh? What?"

I told the journalist what had happened. Before I was more than a sentence into my explanation he whipped a notebook out of his pocket and started writing furiously. When I completed my account, he fired questions at me, some of which I could not answer.

"Who could tell me more?" he asked. "Fell? Race?"

"At this stage, I don't think there's much more to tell."

"Right!" said Page as he flipped his notebook closed. Then he turned around and ran—ran in that scorching heat—back to the campsite on the valley floor.

As I watched his scurrying figure recede, I heard my name being called. It was Fell. I made my excuses to Amelia and hurried over to where Fell was standing, surrounded by most of the rest of our party.

"Flinders," said the professor, "I want you and Wilding to work with Ambrose Hoffman drawing up the plan of the tomb. As soon as the body is removed, I want you two to make a note of every item in that burial chamber and its position. You can do that while Hoffman is drawing his plan. If you've finished your tea, you can get started at once."

I put my enameled mug down on one of the trestle tables and was about to step into the shaft entrance when an emerging group made me take several steps backward. It was a group of workers, under the direction of Farouk. They were carrying on a stretcher the body of Dr. Lamb, covered by a sheet. I stepped away from the entrance to give them room to maneuver, and avoided looking at the sheet-covered corpse. I looked steadfastly down the valley while the mortuary party struggled past. I could see our row of huts in the blazing, white sunlight and an Arab horseman mounting up and riding hard toward Luxor.

Farouk and his men passed, moving in the direction of the store huts where the body would be housed overnight, and then Wilding and I entered the shaft.

Inside was a different world. The sudden darkness and the drop in temperature told me I was entering a kind of underworld—a realm of death. It was then that I remembered the oracle of the bird: "Today you shall see death." I shivered involuntarily, as though some invisible, ice-cold hand had clutched my heart.

"I'd much rather be outside. In the sunlight," said Wilding quietly.

Pulling myself together, I said, "Come along. Let's forget all this 'curse of the pharaohs' nonsense."

"Small minds like yours," sneered Wilding, "can't comprehend the dimensions of reality that surround us constantly."

"You sound like a second-rate Gypsy fortune-teller," I scoffed.

"Laugh if you want to, but Lamb is dead, and we don't know how. And, what is more important, we don't know who'll be next. When a dead hand can reach out of the ancient past to strike down the living, none of us is safe."

Wilding's voice was hushed and tremulous. He really believed all this stuff. Since he appeared to be impervious to common sense, I judged it best to keep my peace.

At the tomb we found Hoffman set up with his drawing board in the tunnel immediately before the chamber. He had already sketched the outline of the room and was working with a tape measure on the exact location of the sarcophagus when we arrived.

"Ah, Flinders, give me a hand, will you?" he said. "Write down these numbers as I call them out. And Wilding—will you measure and mark down the positions of those jars? That's a good chap." Wilding gave him a dark look but started to work.

The rest of that afternoon the three of us worked side by side producing a minute and accurate account of the burial chamber and its contents. When Ambrose Hoffman finally pronounced himself satisfied, he rolled up his drawings and instructed his Arab servant to pack up his drawing board and materials.

We stepped out of the tunnel, into the ruins of the old temple, to discover that the spectacular Egyptian sunset had begun. The sun itself had disappeared behind the cliff that towered over our heads, and deep, black shadows were creeping across the temple toward the huts of our camp. Beyond the shadow line, the valley was washed with the blood-red glow of the rapidly disappearing sunlight.

"Wonderful to behold, is it not?"

I turned to discover Chesterton at my side.

"Yes. I've seen it every night for the past two months, but I'm not tired of it yet. Every evening it takes my breath away," I agreed.

"There's an expression in one of Meredith's books," Chesterton remarked, "about 'the largeness of the evening earth.' The sensation that the Cosmos has all its windows open is very characteristic of evening."

Suddenly the moment was especially magic—before me was the spectacular sunset, and beside me was a great writer and poet interpreting the experience. I felt rather inadequate and remained silent for fear of spoiling the moment. For a long time we stood there, side by side, Chesterton breathing deeply and staring into the far distance. Then he sighed and turned away from the blazing spectacle.

"How is your investigation going?" I asked.

Chesterton blinked at me short-sightedly.

"The investigation into Lamb's murder that you and Colonel Race are conducting. Have you worked out a practical method of tackling that yet?"

"Practical? I leave all practical matters to the good colonel. My only contribution is to think, not to be practical. I can keep ten poems and twenty theories in my head at once. But I can only think of one practical thing at a time."

"And what practical thing are you thinking of at this moment, Mr. Chesterton?"

"That most practical thing of all—supper!"

Before joining the others in the common room, I returned to my hut to change. I had stripped off my sweat-stained shirt when I heard a low groaning sound. For a moment I paused, alert, listening—then I heard it again. It came from beyond the back wall of my hut. I went to investigate.

Making my way around the side of the hut, I heard it again—louder this time. Then I turned the corner and saw—a man, lying on the sand. On the ground, beside my canvas bath, was Elliot Jones, the red-headed journalist—bound and gagged.

"Thank God you've come along," groaned Jones as I undid the gag around his mouth.

"What happened?" I asked, working on the ropes that held his hands and feet.

"I don't know. I was struck from behind. Knocked unconscious. And when I came to, I was like this—trussed up like a chicken about to be baked."

"How are you feeling?"

"All right, I guess. Ow!" his face contorted with pain as he tried to sit up. He lifted a hand to his forehead and continued, "When I try to move, my head feels like it's splitting open. This must be the mother and father of all headaches."

The man was a mess. His shirt was torn, one side of his face was caked with sweat and dirt, and on the other side was a massive purple bruise and a cut running across his jaw.

"I'd better take you to Mrs. Poole—she's a qualified nurse."

"Why not little what's-his-name? Dr. Lamb?"

"He's dead."

"Dead!" Jones shut his eyes tightly, as if feeling another stab of pain. "Poor blighter," he continued. "What happened?"

"He was murdered. Stabbed to death with an Ancient Egyptian bronze knife. We found his body in the sarcophagus inside the tomb we're excavating."

"Wow! What a story!" gasped Jones, struggling to his feet, the pain momentarily forgotten. "The public will love this: 'Ancient Egyptian Curse Strikes Death Down the Centuries.' I've got to get this down on paper. I've got to get to the telegraph office in Luxor."

"You've got to get that head seen to, and then you've got to get to bed. That's what you've got to do."

"Listen, Flinders, I'm a newspaperman, and this is a story. Ow! Every time I move, my head hurts." As he spoke he tried to run his fingers through the tangled mess of his red hair.

"And pictures," he groaned. "I've got to get pictures. My editor will want photographs."

"Let me take you to Mrs. Poole before you do anything else."

"That's starting to feel like a good move," said Jones with another groan, clutching his head as he spoke.

I helped him back to the common room. As we entered, we were greeted by questions:

"What's happened here, then?"

"This wasn't another fight, was it?"

"Do you feel as bad as you look, Jones old chap?"

I ignored the questions and beckoned to the canon's wife.

"He's had a blow on the head, Mrs. Poole. Can you take a look at him?"

"Come back to my hut, young man. I have a first-aid kit there."

"But I have to . . . ," protested Jones.

"Don't argue! Come!" insisted Mrs. Poole, taking him firmly by the arm and marching him off. Once they were gone, the questions were fired at me again.

"What's wrong with him?"

"Was he attacked?"

"Who did that to him?"

"Quiet, all of you!" shouted Fell. "Now, Flinders—can you explain to us what's happened to Jones?"

I explained.

"Did this assault have anything to do with the murder of Lamb?" asked John Farnsleigh, looking pale and nervous.

"I don't know," I replied.

"This is the unluckiest dig I've ever been on," the usually silent Hoffman growled sourly.

"Did he have any idea who attacked him?" asked Neville Page.

"None, I'm afraid. Says he was struck from behind. Didn't see a thing."

"What a pity," Page said, sounding quite unmoved by his colleague's plight. "It spoils a good story—if you can't point the finger at a villain."

"Is that all you blasted journalists think about?" exploded Fell. "A man is attacked, and all you can think about is whether it's a good story or not."

During the silence that followed this outburst the professor's eyes swept the room, glaring angrily. Most did not seem to be greatly moved by the attack on Jones. Laurence Wilding was sitting at the dining table peeling an orange, Nat Burrows was cleaning out his pipe, Neville Page was lighting a cigarette, and Ambrose Hoffman had gone back to reading his magazine. Only Billy Burton and Canon Poole looked genuinely concerned.

Fell's anger simmered into silence as his wife, accompanied by Amelia and Mr. and Mrs. Chesterton, entered the room.

"Fell, old chap, what's happened?" asked Chesterton, picking up the atmosphere at once. Fell explained; then Colonel Race entered, and the story had to be told again.

Just then, Farouk threw open the door from the kitchen and announced that dinner was served.

In the general melee of movement to find places at the table, I ended up between Chesterton and Canon Poole and directly opposite Amelia. This was delightful since every time I looked up, I caught a glimpse of her heavenly face. Even more delightful was the fact that Wilding was down at the far end of the table, well away from Amelia.

That meal should have been a rather glum and depressed affair since Dr. Lamb, who had been among us at lunch time, was now lying dead, murdered, in one of the storage huts. But, for some reason, that night's meal was a particularly talkative one.

Perhaps a psychologist could explain what was happening to us as a group. It was certainly odd. Instead of being quiet and subdued, there was a babbling of words around that dinner table. Were we suppressing the horrible fact of murder? Were we overcompensating for leaden hearts with bright talk? Were we trying to ignore the dreadful reality by talking of other things? Was it because none of us was very close to Dr. Lamb? Were we relieved simply because we were still alive?

Whatever the reason, there was a strange lack of somber silence at the table.

"The journalistic profession," grumbled Fell from his place at the head of the table as he sliced another piece off Rami's excellent roast chicken, "is surely the lowest of the low." He looked pointedly at Neville Page as he spoke. "You're either fighting each other or trying to outdo each other or gloating over some awful tragedy as a 'good story.' Positively ghoulish."

"I say, sir, that's a bit harsh," protested Page.

"I consider myself," said Chesterton, "nothing more than a journalist. A chap, trying to be unpleasant, once said I was a mere entertainer— a 'jolly journalist' he called me. Well, it's a badge I wear with pride."

"Then how do you account for the difference in attitude between yourself on the one hand, and Page and Jones on the other?" I asked.

"Well," Chesterton replied, removing his pince-nez, blinking rapidly, and then balancing it back on the bridge of his nose again, "perhaps they are not jolly enough. Perhaps they take the trade of the journalist far too seriously."

"There's nothing wrong with being ambitious," said Neville Page defensively.

"My good sir, there is everything wrong with being ambitious. Let me ask you: what, exactly, is your ambition?"

"To make a name for myself."

"But you already have a name. You are Neville Page. You cannot make a greater name than the name your parents gave you."

"Mr. Chesterton," said Page earnestly, leaning forward in his chair so that his tall angular frame was almost halfway across the table, "I believe in myself."

Chesterton laughed explosively, "All the men who really believe in themselves are locked up in lunatic asylums. Believe in something bigger than yourself—very much bigger than yourself, young sir—or don't believe at all!"

Page looked extremely irritated by this remark, so I decided to change the subject. I turned to the Army Intelligence officer seated to the left of Canon Poole and asked, "Colonel Race, have you any idea yet as to who killed Dr. Lamb? Or how? Or why?" As I asked my question, Farouk entered from the kitchen, carrying a large plate of figs.

It was not a good choice of subject, for it brought all the murmured conversations around the table to a sudden halt.

"None at all. Not as yet, Mr. Flinders," admitted the wiry, sunburned little colonel.

"Baffling business," muttered Billy Burton.

"I know who did murder," announced Farouk in a trembling voice.

We all turned to look toward him, as Fell asked, "Who?"

"It was Menes!"

"Who is Menes?" asked Elspeth Fell casually, laying down her knife and fork and looking across the table through half-closed eyelids.

"That's the chap whose burial chamber we entered today," explained her husband. "It was in his sarcophagus that we found Lamb's body."

"Yes! Yes!" said Farouk, his face gleaming in the lamplight, "In Menes's coffin. Menes killed doctor."

"Menes has been dead for three and a half thousand years," sneered Sir Edward Narracourt.

"Body dead, but spirit wandering. Menes knew all the most powerful spells in *The Book of the Dead*. He protects his tomb."

"Farouk, tell your wife to make the coffee now," said Fell, as a way of bringing this surprising performance to an end. Farouk left the room.

"Well," said Madeleine Sutton, "that strange performance may mean that we need a new *reis*."

"I don't want to have to train someone else. He'll be all right in the morning," Fell said. "He'll pull himself together. He's a responsible chap at heart."

"I hope so," Amelia said, looking worried. "You'll need him, won't you, Papa, to keep the others in line?"

Fell nodded thoughtfully.

"Well, I think you're all fools," commented Wilding with quiet intensity, "narrow-minded fools. Farouk is quite right."

"What on earth do you mean, dear chap?" asked Canon Poole, looking startled.

"I mean, there are more things in heaven and earth than are dreamed of in your philosophy, Mr. Poole. And the Ancient Egyptians knew the secrets of those things the modern world has forgotten about."

"Do you really believe that?" asked Poole incredulously.

"Yes. And so do many thousands, many millions of others. As well as the world we can see around us, there is also the unseen world. And that is a powerful realm. We need to understand it and control it."

"Poppycock!" snorted Billy Burton, who was sitting beside Wilding and looking at him more in amusement than anything else.

"Look at all the millions," continued Wilding, waving his fork in wide sweeps, a note of real passion in his voice, "the millions who believe in astrology and tarot cards and palmistry and spiritualism and seances. I'm not Robinson Crusoe, you know."

"He's quite right," said Elspeth Fell, the passion in her voice almost matching that in Wilding's. "There are many millions around the world who believe these things."

"Of course there are," Chesterton offered. "When belief in God declines, belief in these other things increases."

"Surely," said Narracourt, "as belief in God decreases, scepticism increases."

"Huh!" snorted Chesterton. "Would that it did. The decline in Christianity, my dear Sir Edward, means the increase in gullibility. It is not the case that those who do not believe in God believe in nothing. Rather is it the case that those who do not believe in God will believe in anything! They have discarded their last protection against superstition—namely a belief in the God who is there."

"What I am talking about," Wilding resumed, ignoring Chesterton and speaking with a shrill intensity, "is powerful unseen forces. How did a living man pass by us unseen? Explain that to me. And how did he become a dead man in the coffin of the owner of that burial chamber? Explain that as well."

"Just at the moment . . . ," began Colonel Race.

"You have no explanation!" interrupted Wilding. "Yes, I know. And you never shall have, either. This will end up in your files as an unsolved murder. All because you close your eyes to the strange powers of Ancient Egyptian magic."

Canon Poole, and then Billy Burton, took up the argument against Wilding, but he refused to budge from his stubborn opinion. After a while we took our cups of coffee and drifted away from the table. The men of the party pulled some of the canvas-backed folding chairs into a circle in one corner of the room to continue the conversation. As we did so, Mrs. Poole and Elliot Jones, his head heavily bandaged, re-entered the common room. They found seats at the far end of the table and were served the meals that had been saved for them.

Fell, in honor of his guests, produced a bottle of port from his closely guarded supply and a box of fine Havana cigars. These were passed around among the gentlemen present.

I noticed that Jones was eating his food with one hand while scribbling rapidly on a sheet of paper with the other. Clearly *The Evening Trumpet*, or whatever paper he wrote for, was about to get a lurid account of Lamb's mysterious death. After a while he summoned Farouk and handed him the paper and some money.

After he had finished his meal, Jones joined us and explained, "I"ve written my cable story and arranged for it to be taken to Luxor and transmitted to Cairo. They'll send it on to London."

"Pity you've come in second," said Neville Page smugly. "Still, that's better than missing the story entirely." Jones did not respond but glared daggers at his professional rival.

"What did you make of Wilding's outburst?" Narracourt asked Chesterton as he passed the port to his left. "Personally, I believe in modern science and the Church of England," the archeologist continued, "and on both counts it seems to me that Wilding was talking sheerest twaddle."

"The problem," suggested Canon Poole before Chesterton could reply, "is not your range of beliefs, but their sequence. If you believed in the Church of England first and modern science second—better still, if you believed in the Bible first and modern science second—then you would understand that there is something in what Wilding said that is true. Ghastly, but true. What do you think, Mr. Chesterton?"

"I think," began Chesterton as he puffed out his cheeks, "I think that Wilding can see half the truth. Unfortunately, he can see the wrong half."

"You're a strange man, Mr. Chesterton, and you say some very strange things," said Billy Burton, as he pulled a large spotted bandanna out of his top pocket and wiped his forehead. "You'll have to explain that to me."

"With pleasure. You see all those things young Wilding mentioned . . ."

"Astrology, tarot cards, palmistry, seances, crystal ball gazing, or whatever?"

". . . yes, those things. They are either silly, but harmless, games or they are dangerous dabblings with powerful forces. Either way, they are not particularly nice."

"Which are they? Silly games? Or dangerous dabblings?"

"The latter, dear sir, the latter. You see, if you believe in God—seriously believe in God—then you must also believe in the devil. If God is ruler, then there is also, clearly, a dark rebellion against His rule. There are forces of light and forces of darkness. That's what God wants us to see. The devil wants us to see nothing of the sort. He is delighted when we regard him as a childish superstition."

"So then, I take it that you, Mr. Chesterton, believe in the devil?"

"I do. And I am not proud of believing in the devil. To put it more correctly, I am not proud of knowing the devil. I made his acquaintance by my own fault and followed it up along lines which, had they been followed further, might have led me to devil worship, or the devil knows what."

Chesterton took a sip of port and then continued. "As a young man I dabbled in spiritualism without ever having made the decision to be a spiritualist. My brother and I used to play with the planchette. What you Americans, Dr. Burton, call the Ouija board."

"This was when you were young?" asked Poole.

Chesterton nodded, "In my teens."

"Why did you stop?"

"Because our sessions with the planchette were always followed by splitting headaches. And after the headaches came a horrid feeling as if one were trying to get over a bad spree, with what I can best describe as a bad smell in the mind."

"But my question is this," persisted Narracourt. "Do you think there may be something in what young Wilding said?"

"There are certainly powerful unseen forces at work here," Chesterton began, holding up his hand to prevent Narracourt from interrupting after the first few words, "but whether those forces are human emotions or demonic influences—well, we shall know after Race and I have investigated."

"Have the authorities in Luxor been notified yet?" asked Hoffman.

"Yes," Race replied, stroking his short, bristling military moustache. "I sent a note in with a messenger before dinner. I expect they will be out in the morning to collect the body."

"And then what do you do?" inquired the pale, nervous John Farnsleigh. "I mean to say, how do you investigate? What sort of things do you actually do?"

"We talk to people." Colonel Race lit his pipe as he spoke. "We will have to interview each one of you, I'm afraid."

"More valuable time lost," grumbled Fell. "With that burial chamber open, we have a mountain of work on our hands."

"We'll try not to inconvenience anyone," said Race tactfully.

Fell grunted, sounding unconvinced, and then said, "I'm going out for a breath of fresh air."

"Mind if I join you?" asked Elliot Jones, trotting off at his heels.

"Gilbert—it's your bedtime," said a small voice from behind me. I looked around. It was Frances Chesterton.

"Yes, m'dear. 'Night all," murmured her obedient husband, and, so saying, the Chestertons left the common room.

I looked around the room and was alarmed to discover that Amelia was nowhere to be seen—and neither was Wilding.

"I think I'll . . . catch a breath . . . of fresh . . . ," I mumbled to my companions as I made my way hastily to the common room door.

Outside the moonlight flowed over the desert landscape like quicksilver. In the distance, near the ruddy glow of the campfires of the *fellahin* I could see Fell and Jones with their heads together in close conversation. But there was no one else in sight.

Just beyond the main building I climbed one of the low hills of gravel and looked around. I could see no one. If I looked directly west I could see the terraces and colonnades of Queen Hatshepsut's mortuary temple, white and ghostly in the moonlight.

To the east, far away across the Nile, was the massive Temple of Karnak—the largest temple complex on earth, covering hundreds of acres. The light of the moon washed all the color out of Karnak and made it a dramatic, although distant, image in stark black and white.

Standing there, on the straight line that ran between the two temples, it was almost possible to believe Wilding's strange theories about the power of Ancient Egyptian curses.

But Amelia was nowhere to be seen.

I climbed down from the hill and walked slowly along the broad, sandy avenue that ran through our campsite. I passed the common room, where warm, yellow lamplight still spilled out of its windows and door, accompanied by the murmur of quiet conversation. I passed the expedition house occupied by Fell and his family.

I walked down the long row of small huts occupied by Fell's European employees toward my own hut at the far end. I saw a figure emerge from between two of these huts. It was Amelia! Her long white dress gleamed bluish in the moonlight—and she was running toward me. I stopped in my tracks and waited for her. Then—disappointment! As she drew nearer, I saw it wasn't Amelia after all, but Elspeth Fell. As she drew level I remarked, "Good evening, Mrs. Fell."

She ignored me, ran past, and disappeared into the expedition house. Oddly, I noticed, she appeared to be sobbing as she ran. I hesitated, wondering if I should ask what was wrong, then decided this would be presumptuous.

For the next quarter of an hour I wandered about in the rich purple indigo of the Egyptian night, smoking a cigar. Then a figure appeared in the distance, on the dusty Luxor Road—a figure that shimmered in the moonlight. Having been mistaken once, I tried not to get my hopes up. But to no avail. My heart kept telling me this was Amelia. I walked toward the approaching figure.

Drawing closer I saw that it was, indeed, Professor Fell's beautiful daughter. We met on the outskirts of the camp. I fell into step beside her, and together we walked down the main path through the camp, toward the Hatshepsut Temple.

"Have you walked far tonight?" I asked.

"Not quite as far as the cultivation," she replied, "but a long way."

"You must enjoy walking in the moonlight."

"I love it," she said.

"So do I."

"Egypt is just . . . just . . . well, beautiful by moonlight," she continued.

"On a night like this," I said, "it is almost possible to imagine this timeless land is still ruled by the pharaohs, that Luxor is still known by its ancient name of Thebes, and that, at any moment, the captain of the pharaoh's guard may come clattering down the road in his chariot."

Amelia stopped in her tracks and stared at me. "Why, Mr. Flinders," she said, "I had no idea that you had such a vivid imagination."

"I'm sorry," I spluttered, "now I feel foolish."

"Please don't," said Amelia, laying her hand on my arm, "at least, not on my account."

"On your account, Miss Fell," I said in a rush of words, "I would be pleased to feel foolish—or to be foolish—or . . . or . . . anything in the world that would please you."

"You are being very gallant tonight, Mr. Flinders."

"I would quite like it if you would agree to call me Philip, Miss Fell."

"If you would like it, then I shall—Philip. And I insist, absolutely insist, that you stop addressing me like an old maid and call me Amelia."

"I shall. With pleasure."

We walked for a long time that night. We talked, but about what I cannot remember. We may have solved the riddle of the sphinx for all I can now recall. When at last she said goodnight and walked back to her quarters, I continued to wander for some time, feeling as though I had drunk several bottles of *arak*.

It was not until a gust of cool damp air blowing up from the Nile brought me to my senses that I realized how late it was. It was clearly time for me to retire for the night.

Walking in a leisurely fashion toward my hut, I noticed, some fifty yards ahead of me, the erect figure of Madeleine Sutton, clearly on her way back to her own hut. She was walking briskly, and I was ambling along rather slowly, so I didn't catch up with her. In fact, she had disappeared by the time I discovered, lying on the ground, a small, black book.

It was lying at about the spot where I had first seen Miss Sutton. Had she dropped it? If she had, I would return it to her first thing in the morning.

Back in my own hut I lit a candle, and saw, by the flickering candlelight, the word "diary" stamped on the cover of the book. That, of course, meant it was private, and I should not, under any circumstances, look inside. But, I told myself, I did need to check on the ownership of the diary. After all, someone other than Miss Sutton might have dropped it.

So I opened it up and, sure enough, there, on the top of the first page, was written "M. Sutton." I snapped the book closed. Well, that settled that. Mind you, it would be intriguing just to take one small glance at, say, the most recent entry. What does a spinster like Madeleine write about in her diary? Surely nothing very private, I told myself. Having temporarily anaesthetized my conscience, I opened up the small book to the most recent entry. On an otherwise blank page I read these three words: "Guilty! Guilty! Guilty!"

Suddenly I felt extremely guilty myself for having pried. I shut the book and put it on a shelf to be returned in the morning.

As I stripped off my outer clothing and prepared for bed I wondered what the words could mean. Of what was Miss Sutton guilty? Surely not of the murder of Dr. Lamb? She was not inside the tomb when he died. But then, of course, neither did he appear to be. Still puzzled, I climbed into bed and blew out the light.

In that kind of haze that overtakes the mind as we drift off to sleep, I heard, in the distance, two voices arguing. They were arguing violently; the desert breeze seemed to carry their voices in my direction. Did I recognize those voices? Yes, I did. It was Nat Burrows, our photographer, and Neville Page. Now, what did those two have to argue about?

With speculations and puzzles running around in my head, I fell asleep. As I slept, I dreamed of Amelia.

The alarm clock jangled loudly at the usual unearthly hour the next morning. Despite my late night, I managed to drag myself into something resembling a waking state, dress, shave, and stagger to the common room for breakfast.

Professor Fell, Sir Edward Narracourt, Canon Poole, Billy Burton, John Farnsleigh, Ambrose Hoffman, and Nat Burrows were gathered sleepily around the long trestle table.

Madeleine Sutton's small leather-bound diary was sitting in my top pocket, waiting for a chance to be returned surreptitiously.

"Ahem." Fell cleared his throat to attract our attention and then said, "I have decided to solve the problem of our battling journalists. To that end I have appointed Mr. Elliot Jones as official correspondent to the expedition. Mr. Neville Page will be given his marching orders this morning."

He looked around the table as if expecting this order to be challenged. Everyone, however, was either too sleepy, or too indifferent, to question the decision.

"Right, then," said Fell after a respectable silence, "let's get some work done. Murder or no murder, we have a burial chamber to sort and catalogue."

Suiting action to word, Fell rose and led the shambling, sleepy company out through the common room door. I hung behind, to finish my coffee and to find a way to tactfully dispose of Miss Sutton's diary. After looking around the room, I set the diary on a small table against the back wall. Hopefully, when Miss Sutton found it she would think she had left it there herself. It was a cowardly thing to do, I know, but it was also the easiest solution.

Hurrying out of the door, I caught up with the straggling tail-end of the party as they headed toward the temple and our dig site.

"Flinders!" bellowed Fell.

"Yes, Professor?"

"Go and rouse out Wilding. Find out what's keeping him."

I ran back to his hut and stuck my head in through the door. Lawrence Wilding was standing in front of a small mirror shaving, his hair still touseled with sleep.

"Better get a move on, old chap," I said. "Fell's yelling for you. And he's rather on the warpath this morning."

"I'm coming! I'm coming! I'll be there in two minutes."

Turning to leave, I noticed a scarf draped across the foot of Wilding's bed—a woman's scarf. It was of a design and pattern that were familiar to me. I was almost certain that it was Amelia's scarf. What on earth was a scarf of Amelia's doing in Wilding's hut? Had he stolen it as a keepsake? Or had she given it to him? Had she visited him in his hut and left it behind by mistake? Surely not! Not Amelia—I couldn't believe that, not for a moment.

Preoccupied and ill-tempered, I hurriedly caught up with the rest of the company and fell into step beside them.

"Shall we consult the oracle of the bird again this morning?" asked Nat Burrows as he shifted his heavy photographic equipment from one shoulder to the other.

"Of course not!" I replied, being in no mood to be ribbed.

"But the poor little bird's entrails got it exactly right yesterday— opening the burial chamber, facing death, and so on. How can you forgo such wisdom, dear Flinders?"

"Because, Burrows, old chap, unlike you photographers I don't see things in simple black and white . . ."

"Very good! For a man who's still half asleep, very good indeed!"

". . . .so I can see that the so-called 'priest of the bird' told us nothing yesterday that we didn't already know."

"He told us we would face death!"

"But by that he didn't mean that Dr. Lamb would be murdered," I protested.

"How do you know he didn't?"

"Because he didn't actually say that one of the expedition would be killed."

"Well, not exactly," Burrows grudgingly admitted, "but as good as."

"Not as good as, at all," I insisted. "To say that we would 'face death' was just his guess that we would open a sarcophagus in the burial chamber."

"That's one interpretation, yes."

"It's the most sensible interpretation. You're just reading things into his words after the event. Which is what the dedicated followers of all spurious fortune-tellers do."

"Don't get so heated, Flinders—I was just ribbing you a little, that's all."

By the time we caught up with the rest of the party, they were gathered around the mouth of the tomb shaft, and Professor Fell and Sir Edward Narracourt were arguing furiously.

". . . you have no answer to that, do you, Fell?" Narracourt was sneering as we arrived.

"What your thick-headed theory fails to take into account is the desecration of the images of Queen Hatshepsut after her death. What do you say to that!" Fell responded, somewhat savagely.

"Gentlemen! Gentlemen!" interposed Canon Poole. "Surely we can settle these matters in a calmer and more academic fashion—perhaps after a little more investigation."

"Quite right," said Fell. "I have more important things to do than stand around here having idiotic arguments."

Fell decreed that he and I would work in the burial chamber, removing each item from its place, allocating it a catalogue number, and noting where in the chamber it came from, along with a short description of the item. Narracourt, Poole, and Wilding, he said, could work on the long trestle tables cleaning, and thoroughly cataloguing and describing, the items as they were brought to the surface. At the same time, John Farnsleigh and Nat Burrows could sketch and photograph each piece.

The Rev. Dr. Billy Burton offered to act as go-between, carrying the precious items from the burial chamber to the surface in a straw-filled box.

Roles having been designated, we set to work, and for the next three hours I had my head down concentrating hard.

The first item we dealt with was the mummy itself. Although the public thinks that mummies are what Egyptology is all about, to the professional Egyptologist a mummy is a relatively uninteresting artifact. Other items—pottery, jewelery, carved figures, scrolls, and so on—actually provide far more historical information. However, mummies can tell us about the people themselves—their diet, illnesses, and environmental conditions. And sometimes they can help with the chronologies of the Ancient Egyptians.

Menes's mummy was still lying on the floor of the burial chamber—we had not returned it to the sarcophagus, which still, appallingly, contained the dried blood of Dr. Lamb. As Fell and I carefully lifted the mummy out into the open, I was struck by how small and light it was.

This was due in part to the fact that the Ancient Egyptians were, on the average, smaller than us. But it was mainly due to the mummification process, which emptied out much of the body's contents and caused some overall shrinkage.

When Menes died, his body would have been taken to the necropolis where his brain and viscera would have been removed, the viscera being placed in the four canopic jars. His body cavities would then have been sterilized, his body dried, anointed, and covered with molten resin. After a process that took some forty days, his body cavities would have been packed with resin-soaked linen, and the surface anointed with unguents. Sometimes a jeweled scarab was inserted in place of the heart; sometimes the heart was left in place. And finally the whole body was bound and bandaged.

The burial chamber in which he was laid was intended to be the room in which he would live for all eternity, with the furniture and items around the sarcophagus being the things that he would need in the afterlife. It didn't strike me as a particularly attractive form of eternal life.

The sarcophagus was next. It was made from some sort of dark wood. If Menes had belonged to the royal family, he would probably have had a stone sarcophagus, but wood was deemed to be good enough for an army captain (and was probably all his family could afford). The wood was painted and varnished, with the lid depicting Menes in the manner so familiar from Ancient Egyptian art. The goddess Nephthys was represented above his head and the goddess

Isis at his feet, both being protectors of the dead. (I wondered what, if anything, those two goddesses were doing at the moment for poor Dr. Lamb.)

The sarcophagus was anthropoid, or "mummiform," in shape, and painted with white bands suggesting mummy bandages. In between these bands were decorative paintings of small scenes with various deities and texts. On the lid was inscribed Chapter 72 of *The Book of the Dead,* the "spell for going forth by day and penetrating the netherworld."

Next came the four canopic jars. These were made from alabaster and had lids carved in the form of human faces, representing the four sons of Horus. As far as Fell and I could make out, the texts on the jars seemed to place each one under the protection of a goddess.

In a special box there were a number of small statuettes, or funerary figures, called *shawabti.* These represented people, or gods, who would assist the departed in his afterlife. A number of the figures represented servants and workmen, and such gods as Anubis, Amun, Isis, and Osiris.

There were dozens of other objects as well: wooden headrests, a bronze razor, a flat wooden comb, a small chalice, an alabaster bowl, a miniature box made of wood and inlaid with ivory, and, finally, Menes's military gear.

At this point Fell called a halt for morning tea, and I was astonished to discover that three hours had passed. My back was sore from bending over small objects, and it was a delight to return to fresh air and sunshine and to stretch the muscles.

Madeleine Sutton, accompanied by one of Farouk and Rami's sons, had arrived with the tea things. Amelia and Mrs. Poole were also there, on the top terrace of the temple, about fifty yards away from the shaft entrance. They broke off their conversation when they saw me approaching.

"I hope I'm not interrupting," I said.

"Of course not," said Amelia quickly.

"Just ladies' talk," Mrs. Poole added.

"How is the work going?" Amelia asked, as if to change the subject.

"Very well," I replied, "very well indeed."

"After morning tea we were intending to volunteer to help," Mrs. Poole remarked.

"We thought it would be helpful if we packed the cleaned and catalogued items," added Amelia.

"Indeed it would," I said. "The items have to be packed very carefully, but I expect you two are experienced at that."

"Papa has had me helping on digs since I was in pigtails."

"I'm sure you were very pretty in pigtails."

"Mr. Flinders! Don't be presumptuous!" responded Amelia, but she didn't look displeased. "The point is, that I know perfectly well how to pack precious objects so they can be safely stored or transported. And I also know the boxes cannot be sealed until the Inspector of Antiquities from Luxor has indicated which pieces he wants for the Cairo Museum."

"Amelia shall show me how to go about it," Mrs. Poole said. "My husband's archeology, until now, has been entirely theoretical."

The three of us wandered together in the general direction of the table where tea was being served. It was while I was nursing a hot cup of tea in an enameled mug that John Farnsleigh approached me.

"Flinders, old chap," he said, "would you mind very much taking this thing back. Just having it in my pocket makes me nervous."

So saying, he thrust my old army revolver at me. In all the excitement, I had entirely forgotten that I had lent it to Farnsleigh.

"Yes, I'll look after it," I said, pocketing the weapon.

Pulling my watch from my fob pocket, I saw that I had enough time to return the revolver to my hut before Fell would want me back at work in the burial chamber. With this mission in mind, I set off for the campsite.

On the way I passed the open doorway of Neville Page's hut. The tall, thin journalist was inside, packing his belongings into a rucksack. I stuck my head in through the door.

"Just thought I'd say cheerio, sorry you're leaving, and that sort of thing."

"Ah, it's you, Flinders. Yes, well, it's nice of you to say that. I'm sorry I'm leaving too, and my editor in London will be dashed angry about it."

"It's a pity really that you and Jones couldn't have got on better."

"No one could get on well with that keeper of lunatics."

"Still, given how things are, I guess it made sense for Fell to pick one of you. And, unfortunately for you, the coin came down heads instead of tails."

"There was rather more than a toss of the coin involved in this, Flinders, old chap. If I had any idea what strings Jones had pulled, I would have pulled them myself."

"I have no idea what you're talking about, Page."

"Yes, I know," said Page with a patronizing smile. "That's what's so endearing about you, Flinders, old man; you're such a naïve colonial."

I admit that I was smarting a bit as I returned to my hut, put the revolver on a shelf next to the box of ammunition, and turned back toward the dig site. Naïve colonial indeed! For a start, Australia ceased to be a colony eighteen years ago with the formation of the Federation. And in the second place, I was a university graduate—naïve indeed!

As I hurried back toward the temple at the western end of the valley, with the perpendicular cliffs rising behind it, I could feel the strength of the Egyptian sun on my back. The day was already hot, and the valley was flooded with that brilliant glare that strains the eyes and causes one to squint.

Passing one of the store huts, I heard shouting and sounds of a scuffle from inside. I pushed the door open and found Ambrose Hoffman holding Farouk firmly by both arms.

"What's going on?"

"I caught this beggar stealing," gasped Hoffman as Farouk struggled in his grasp.

The hut was one in which the smaller antiquities were stored. On the floor between the two men was a small, rather handsome statue of Anubis, carved out of a dark wood. Hoffman nudged it with his toe.

"I caught him stealing this," he said.

"Is not true," protested Farouk. "I not steal. I find statue. I return him to storeroom. I am not thief, Mr. Flinders."

"Why don't you let him go, Hoffman," I suggested. "He's not about to run off anywhere."

Hoffman released his grasp, and Farouk stepped back a pace and rubbed his arms.

"What did you actually see, Hoffman?" I asked.

"I was walking down this way, looking for a level spot to set up my theodolite," explained the expedition architect, "when I spotted the door of this hut standing open. Well, you know that we always keep it locked, so I investigated. Farouk here was inside, with this statue in his hand. And I happen to know that this is one of the antiquities that went missing almost a week ago."

"And what's your story, Farouk?"

"I found it," our head man replied, a resentful tone in his voice. "I found it lying on sand. Professor Fell, he trust me with key to this hut, so I return it."

"It rather looks to me as though Farouk is telling the truth," I said.

"If you're going to take his side . . . ," spat out the sullen Hoffman.

"I'm not taking any sides. But if the piece has been missing for a week, then he obviously didn't steal it this morning. That being so, why would he bring it back?"

"He came back to steal other items. He dug it up from its hiding place and had it in his hand when he came back to steal some other pieces to send—along with this statue—to the market dealers," said Hoffman, improvising.

"All three of us had better see Fell," I proposed. "He can sort this out."

Making sure the store hut was properly locked, I walked with the other two to the shaft entrance where Fell was waiting to resume work.

In as few words as possible I told him the story.

Fell gave it a moment's thought, then he said, "Farouk—you have my complete trust. I'm sorry about the misunderstanding."

"Thank you *effendi*," said Farouk, as he *salaam*-ed gracefully and left to take charge of his men.

Once he was gone, Fell said, "Even if you are right, Hoffman, I have no intention of giving up such a useful headman. Farouk is too good at his work to lose. We've had no trouble from the superstitious *fellahin* because they trust him. He has stayed, so they have stayed. We'll change the locks on the hut and leave it at that."

Sulking silently, the taciturn Hoffman left.

"Let's forget about this unpleasantness," Fell said, turning to me, "and get back to work in the burial chamber."

We resumed where we had left off.

We began with those items that related to Menes's military profession. There was a small, carved, wooden figure, perhaps representing Menes himself, firing arrows from a standing position in the back of a small, carved chariot. Not far away was a full-sized bow and a leather quiver full of arrows. Leaning against the wall was a bronze spear with a wooden shaft, a short bronze sword, and a bronze helmet. There was also a second dagger with a curved blade and a decorated hilt—the brother to the one that had, in some mysterious way, been used to murder Dr. Lamb.

Again the time passed quickly as Fell and I recovered the pieces, allocated them catalogue numbers, and recorded their exact location and general description.

When we emerged from the shaft tomb several hours later, it was to find many of the pieces already cleaned and set out on the trestle tables on either side of the tunnel entrance. Seeing them there gave a real sense of achievement and delight—many of the small things were exquisitely beautiful.

"I think we have all earned our lunch today," said Amelia, carefully laying down on the table the small pot she had been cleaning.

"Is there much left to do?" asked Poole.

"There are still some small items," Fell replied, "and then the larger pieces of furniture—the chairs and tables."

"I must say, Fell," commented Narracourt, "there are some very fine pieces among this collection."

"Of course there are . . . ," began Fell.

"Father!" interrupted Amelia.

"I mean . . . hhmmff . . . nice of you to say so, old chap. We have every reason to be pleased. All of us. Now, let's get down to lunch."

The long whitewashed common room was filled with men in khaki shorts and heavy boots and women in long light-colored dresses. The little table near the door was piled high with pith helmets, broad-brimmed felt hats, ladies' straw hats with ribbons, and Chesterton's panama. The air was very still, very hot, and very dry.

I had no sooner found a place at the table than Billy Burton said grace, and the meal was served.

It was Frances Chesterton who broached the subject that was on everyone's mind.

"Tell me, Colonel Race," she said, "how are your investigations progressing?"

"I am at square one," replied the colonel. "Which is a good place to begin—I have no suspects, no motive, and no idea how this seemingly impossible crime was committed. But I also have no presuppositions and no assumptions—which means I am open to any possibilities the clues may suggest."

"What about the disposal of Lamb's body?" asked Fell.

"That is a matter that I intended to raise with you after lunch," Race replied.

"Raise it now," grunted Fell.

"While you people were working this morning, a police sergeant arrived from Luxor. I gave him Dr. Lamb's passport and a couple of other personal documents. The sergeant will pass this information on to Cairo, and they will attempt to contact Lamb's relatives. He brought a doctor with him, who examined the body and issued a death certificate. The sergeant also brought a letter from Inspector Fahd of the Luxor police station, asking me to take official charge of the murder investigation."

"Fine," snapped Fell. "But what about the disposal of the body? Did they take it away with them?"

"No."

"What's supposed to happen to it then?"

"They've told us to arrange for burial here."

"Here? Where, for heaven's sake?"

"The sergeant suggested the old Coptic cemetery, near the ruins of the Coptic monastery."

"I suppose that's possible," muttered Fell doubtfully.

"Would it be practical to transport his body back to Australia? Or London? Or wherever the man's home is?" asked Chesterton.

"No. Of course not," Fell admitted.

"Or rather," Chesterton continued, "where his home was. His residence for the moment might be described as the Supreme Court of the Cosmos: 'As it is appointed unto men once to die, but after this the judgment.' His body is merely an empty tenement, no longer occupied."

"Besides which," said Canon Poole, "you have not one clergyman, but two at your disposal: the Rev. Dr. Billy Burton and myself. We would be prepared to conduct the funeral service, wouldn't we, Dr. Burton?"

"Indeed, I say, indeed we would. In fact, we would take it as our responsibility, in fact as our bounden duty," added Burton, "to give the man a Christian burial."

"Very well," agreed the professor. "The funeral shall be immediately after lunch. Farouk will organize two of the workmen to dig a grave. Any expedition members who wish to attend may do so, but attendance is not compulsory."

"Do you find yourself," asked Mrs. Poole, addressing the company generally, "infected by what one might call the Eastern attitude toward death?"

"And what do you mean by that, my good woman?" inquired Sir Edward Narracourt haughtily.

"Well, death does seem to be regarded rather casually, here in the East, does it not?"

"It is their way," Narracourt said with a shrug, "as it has been for thousands of years."

"It struck me only this morning," commented Chesterton, "that the stories of the Bible take on a particular reality and interest out here. By way of example, the Good Samaritan story has a reality here that it cannot have in an atmosphere of crowded streets, police, ambulances, hospitals, and public assistance. If a man fell by the wayside on the Luxor Road, or on the longer and more lonely desert road to the Valley of the Kings, the story could easily happen today, and it illustrates the enormous virtue compassion has in the eyes of all desert folk."

"How many of us," asked Canon Poole suddenly, "would really stop to care for another human being in conditions where there were no witnesses, no force of public opinion, no knowledge or censure of a failure to extend aid?"

"Everyone, of course," said Colonel Race firmly.

"Would they?" challenged Fell gruffly. "A man is lying, dying. Death, remember, is not very important here. Mrs. Poole is quite right about that. You are in a hurry. You have business to do. You do not want delay or bother. The man is nothing whatever to you. And nobody will ever know if you just hurry on, saying that, after all, it isn't your business and somebody else will come along presently and so on."

We all sat back and thought, and we were all, I think, a little shattered. Are we so sure, after all, of our essential humanity?

After a long pause Amelia said slowly, "I think I would. . . . Yes, I think I would. I would go on, and then feel ashamed and come back."

Lawrence Wilding had once again managed to seat himself between Amelia and her stepmother. He sat with his arms folded, head back, and eyes closed, as if this whole discussion was somehow beneath him. No one else seemed to notice Wilding's disdainful lack of interest. But I found it irritating.

Professor Fell said he thought he, too, would stop, but he wasn't nearly so sure about himself as he would like to be. "What about you, Mr. Chesterton?" he asked. "What would you do?"

Before he could reply, his wife spoke up. "Gilbert will tell you very modestly that he would have his head in the clouds and would be so dreamy that he wouldn't even notice the man lying there in distress. But the truth is that my husband's vast exterior hides a heart of pure marshmallow. He couldn't stop himself from helping. More than that, he would regard himself as a knight errant coming to the man's rescue. He would probably not only save the man, he would set up a Travelers' Aid Station on the spot to save future wayfarers."

Chesterton first blushed and then laughed to hide his embarrassment at his wife's praise.

"What would you do?" I said to Nat Burrows, who was seated opposite me.

"Me? Oh, I would go on. I wouldn't stop."

"You would? Definitely?"

The whole company looked at Burrows with interest.

"People die so much out here. One feels that a little sooner or later doesn't matter. I really wouldn't expect anyone to stop for me."

There was a murmur of protest around the table, but Burrows continued. "It is much better, I think, to go straight on with what one is doing, without being continually deflected by outside people and happenings."

"May I humbly suggest to you, Mr. Burrows," said Chesterton gently, "that what matters most in this life are the deflections. My friend Hilaire Belloc calls such things 'divine appointments.' God has not only made us, He has made us alive! To use the gift of life otherwise than as intended is like using a Rembrandt canvas to start a fire on a cold winter's night. It can be done, but it was not the maker's intention. And it would be a waste. If you were to pass by, Mr. Burrows, the life you would waste would not be the wayfarer's, but your own."

A lively debate continued for the rest of the meal.

While coffee was being served, Fell summoned Farouk and ordered that a plain, wooden coffin be knocked together by a couple of the craftsmen among the *fellahin*. The professor then announced that Dr. Lamb's funeral service would be held in one hour.

I was about to leave the common room when I felt a hand on my arm. It was Colonel Race. "It's time for us to begin interviewing the witnesses," he said, "and we'd like to start with you, Mr. Flinders, if you have no objections."

"Only too happy to help," I mumbled.

"Professor Fell has kindly lent us the living room of his house for the interviews," said Race, leading the way out of the common room and across the compound. "Come along, Mr. Chesterton," he said over his shoulder. "You promised your assistance, and I would appreciate your presence at all these interviews."

The expedition house, like all the other buildings, was made from whitewashed mud bricks. However, unlike the other buildings, it also had several rooms, high ceilings, and even a timber floor. Race knocked and then entered, without waiting for a response. In the living room we found Amelia, sitting in a canvas chair reading a book. This she hastily, and with some apparent embarrassment, thrust into a bag at her side as we entered.

"Sorry to disturb you, Miss Fell," said the colonel briskly, "but your father did say that we could use this room for our interviews."

"Interviews?"

"I believe I am 'helping the police with their inquiries,'" I explained with a nervous laugh. Amelia gave me an odd look, gathered up her bag, and left the room.

"Take a seat, Flinders," commanded Race. "This shouldn't take long."

Race and I both chose canvas chairs, while Chesterton carefully lowered his bulk into the largest chair in the room—a darkly varnished, solid timber affair that creaked as he sat down.

"Where would you like to begin?"

"With the movements of people in the tomb shaft yesterday afternoon," Race said, flipping open a small notebook. "With your permission, Mr. Chesterton, I will ask questions—you simply intervene when something occurs to you."

Chesterton nodded his agreement, but the expression on his face suggested a child-like bafflement at the colonel's brisk efficiency.

"When the work resumed yesterday, who entered the tomb?"

"Fell, of course, Wilding and I, as his assistants, and Narracourt, Poole, and Burton."

"No other members of the expedition?"

"Fell was careful to exclude just about everyone—except essential personnel."

"Why was that?"

"Well, it's very important that nothing be disturbed when a burial chamber is opened. It's a job for professionals."

"On that basis he excluded non-archeologists such as Dr. Lamb?"

"Precisely. And Dr. Lamb wasn't too happy about it, I can tell you."

"So, why did Professor Fell allow Narracourt, Poole, and Burton to be present?"

"Sir Edward Narracourt and Canon Poole, like Professor Fell himself, are archeologists. I guess he was happy to have them present as expert witnesses—as long as they stood back from the actual work and didn't interfere."

"And Burton?"

"Dr. Burton represents the American money that pays for much of this expedition, so Fell tries to be nice to him. Besides which, although Burton has no qualifications as an archaeologist, my impression is that he is a fairly well-informed and sensible amateur."

"And that's the complete list of those present in the tomb shaft?"

"Yes. Apart from the Egyptians, that is."

"Very well. Tell me about the Egyptians—who were they?"

"That's much harder to say."

"Why?"

"Well, I know it's a foolish thing to say, but they do all look very much alike to me. I mean, they all dress alike to begin with. They all wear that full-length, shirt-like garment."

"The *galabiyah*."

"Eh?"

"That's what it's called—a *galabiyah*."

"I see. And, of course, there's that sort of cloth wound around their head. That probably has a name as well."

"It's called a *keffiyeh*."

"I see. Anyway, partly because they all dress the same, I do find it hard to tell them apart. So I'm not sure I can answer your question."

"Do your best—tell us who was there."

"Farouk, of course, came and went quite a bit—supervising the men. There were various shovel men and basket boys who removed the rubble from the plastered mud brick wall, once Wilding and I had pulled it down. And each of the specialists on our team—Hoffman, Farnsleigh, and Burrows—has his own Egyptian assistant."

"Do you know the names of any of the workmen who were in the tomb?"

"I saw Hamoudi at one stage. Perhaps Abdullah was there. Hassan might have been . . . no, he wasn't. I can usually pick him because of his large build."

"So there were the six members of the expedition you have named, plus a small group of Egyptian workmen who came and went, is that right?"

I nodded.

"Was there any stage during which Dr. Lamb could have slipped past you, into the burial chamber?"

"Totally impossible," I insisted. "You've seen for yourself how narrow that shaft is. And for much of the time there were two groups of three of us—Fell, Wilding, and me at the workface, and Poole, Narracourt, and Burton farther back. When the workmen were clearing the last of the rubble and Burrows was taking his photographs, all six of us were together—virtually blocking that narrow shaft. A stray dog couldn't have got past, Colonel Race. I swear."

"You're not making this easy for us, Mr. Flinders," said the colonel, rubbing his chin thoughtfully. "Do you have any questions, Mr. Chesterton?"

"Hmm . . . Let me see now," rumbled Chesterton. "Mr. Flinders, are you an imaginative man?"

"Imaginative? No, not really. I think I have a rather dull imagination really. I don't see, or imagine I see, strange things—if that's what you're getting at."

"The function of the imagination," said Chesterton, staring at the ceiling as if he was staring at the stars, "is, not to make strange things common, but to make common things strange. The question is, Mr. Flinders, whether you have the eyes to see the difference between the two."

"Between the two what?" I asked, feeling puzzled.

"Between the strange and the common, the usual and the unusual."

"In the light of what Mr. Flinders has told us," said Colonel Race, interrupting this exchange, "I think I should talk to Farouk and some of his workmen next. Since I will conduct those interviews in Arabic, I wonder, Mr. Chesterton, if you would carry out another task for me?"

"If it is within my powers to do so, I certainly shall."

"Will you search Dr. Lamb's hut? I doubt there's anything to be found there, but the job has to be done."

"Search his hut? Very well, if you wish. And, unless you have any objection, Colonel, I shall ask Mr. Flinders here to assist me."

Race thought for a moment and then replied, "I can't see why not. He's not really a suspect. If you want him as your assistant, you may have him."

"Oh, I want him all right," chuckled Chesterton gleefully. "An unimaginative man is exactly what I want."

I didn't know whether to be flattered or insulted by that remark. But the result was that several minutes later Chesterton and I were standing in Dr. Lamb's hut, looking around and wondering where to begin our search.

Lamb's hut was the same size as mine and had the same basic furnishings. Chesterton stood in the doorway, looming black against the sunlight, like a giant in a fairy tale.

"Now, young Flinders," he boomed, "start rummaging, and tell me what you find."

"Well, let me see now. This is obviously his doctor's bag," I said, picking up a black leather Gladstone bag from the sandy floor of the hut and unfastening its clasps. "Contents—appear to be the good doctor's surgical instruments," I murmured as I rummaged through a set of stainless steel instruments, nicking my finger on a scalpel in the process.

"Nothing concealed underneath?"

"Nothing."

"Proceed, Mr. Flinders."

"Next item—a polished wooden box with metal clasps which, upon unfastening reveals . . . a first-aid kit. A very complete and well-equipped first-aid kit, by the look of it—bandages, splints, ointments, and the like."

"Nothing out of place? Nothing that shouldn't be there?"

"Not that I can see."

"Very well, move on, young sir."

I moved on to the rough wooden plank shelves. "Top shelf contains a row of brown glass bottles with Latin labels—which I take to be Lamb's supply of medicines. The only bottle I recognize is the anti-malaria tablets—the rest of the labels mean nothing to me."

"Next shelf?"

"Second shelf contains a dozen or so books. One copy of the *British Pharmacopoeia,* one copy of *Gray's Anatomy,* and the rest appear to be yellow-jacketed thrillers."

"Clearly a man of discerning taste."

"Against the back wall of the hut," I said, continuing my running commentary, "between the shelves and the bed is a sea chest, such as most of us have. This contains," I continued, opening the lid, "the doctor's clothing."

"Rummage deeper, young sir, rummage deeper," urged Chesterton.

I pulled the clothing out of the chest and laid it in piles on the palm-stick bed.

"Ah ha!" I exclaimed when I reached the bottom, "a brown manila envelope, which upon opening turns out to contain—letters."

"Reading a dead man's mail is distasteful," said Chesterton, "but necessary if his death is not to be in vain. Bring the letters over here to the sunlight."

I did so, handing half of them to Chesterton and retaining the other half myself. We both began reading. Within two minutes we had both made the same discovery.

"It seems to consist entirely of correspondence with the Medical Registration Board of New South Wales," I said.

"Hmm. . . Clearly he had been struck off the list of registered medical practitioners. These letters are all arguing for his re-admittance."

"Fell won't like this," I remarked, "his expedition doctor turning out to be a deregistered practitioner."

"The thought is hardly a pleasant one, I grant," Chesterton said, "but in practical terms, did it make any difference?"

"Well, no, not really. He set a few broken bones for injured workmen and treated the occasional infection."

"His work was always satisfactory?"

"As far as I could tell."

"I wonder why the good doctor was regarded by the authorities of New South Wales as not good enough?" speculated Chesterton. "Well, is there anything else in the chest?"

"Nothing," I replied, after making a careful examination.

"Then repack the doctor's clothes, and we shall take these letters to Colonel Race."

When we went in search of the colonel, we were told that he had joined the others at Dr. Lamb's funeral service.

I showed Chesterton the way to the old Coptic cemetery beyond the camp. This meant walking toward Hatshepsut's temple and then veering to the right, around the base of the lowest terrace. There, on the northern side of the ruins of the Coptic monastery, was an area with just enough sandy soil covering the bedrock to make burial possible (without going to the Egyptian lengths of digging into solid rock). We arrived to find the service underway.

The Rev. Dr. Billy Burton was reading from the Bible, ". . . For we brought nothing into *this* world, *and it is* certain we can carry nothing out." On these words Burton closed his Bible and glanced at Canon Poole, who took over.

"Man that is born of woman hath but a short time to live," read Poole from the prayer book in his hand, "and is full of misery. He cometh up, and is cut down, like a flower."

I glanced around the group at the grave side and discovered that the entire expedition had gathered for the funeral.

"In the midst of life we are in death," continued the canon while my thoughts wandered back to the puzzle of who killed Dr. Lamb. And why he was killed. And, even more puzzling, how it was done.

"Thou knowest, Lord, the secrets of our hearts . . ." (*Yes*, I thought, *God surely knows the identity of the murderer, but, without divine guidance, how will Race and Chesterton ever find out?* Once again I surreptitiously surveyed the faces of those gathered around the grave. I couldn't imagine any one of them as a killer. But then, Chesterton had said I wasn't capable of imagining anything much. Still, most likely one of these people was a murderer—a devilishly cunning murderer.) ". . . most worthy Judge eternal, suffer us not at our last hour to fall from Thee."

As the leader of the expedition, Professor Fell then stepped forward, took up a handful of the dry, sandy soil, and sprinkled it on the lid of the coffin, where it lay in the grave. The others followed his example: Amelia and Elspeth, then Mrs. Poole and Madeleine Sutton, and then the men of the party. I was the last in the line, and there must have been some gravel in the handful I picked up, for it fell on the coffin lid with a horrible, echoing rattle.

"Forasmuch as it hath pleased Almighty God," continued the canon, "of His great mercy to take unto himself the soul of our dear brother here departed, we therefore commit his body to the ground; earth to earth, ashes to ashes, dust to dust; in sure and certain hope of the Resurrection to eternal life, through our Lord Jesus Christ; who shall change our vile body, that it may be like unto his glorious body, according to the mighty working, whereby he is able to subdue all things to himself."

Canon Poole then took a step backward, and Billy Burton gave the eulogy:

"I guess we have to admit," he said, "that none of us knew our departed brother, Dr. Brian Lamb, all that well. Heck, the truth is, we hardly knew him at all. He was small of stature and quiet of nature. We didn't really see him do enough medicine to even know for sure if he was a good doctor or not. But in what he did for the members of this expedition, he did it diligently and well, and we should be grateful for that.

"He enjoyed being here in Egypt and had the genuine passion of the amateur archeologist. And all of us who find the story of Ancient Egypt fascinating can understand that. Dr. Lamb was a pleasant and amiable little man, and we shall miss him.

"Now, not knowing the man well, I make no pretence of knowing the state of his heart. Whether or not he had a personal friendship with the Living God, I do not know. But this one thing I know: that his abrupt and violent death is a reminder to us all to keep our relationship with God in good repair, for none of us knows when we shall go.

"And that means choosing which way we shall live.

"There are only two ways to live—our way or God's way. The Bible says: 'He that believeth on the Son hath everlasting life: and he that believeth not the Son shall not see life; but the wrath of God abideth on him.'"

Burton concluded with these words, and a thoughtful silence descended, to be broken after a minute or so by Poole's voice.

"Shall we pray?" said Canon Poole. "O merciful God, the Father of our Lord Jesus Christ, who is the Resurrection and the Life." *(What about the murderer? I wondered. Is he now damned forever? Or is the possibility of repentance and forgiveness still open to him? Or her? Might the killer be a her and not a him?)* "We meekly beseech Thee, O Father, to raise us from the death of sin unto the life of righteousness . . . Grant this, we beseech Thee, O merciful Father, through Jesus Christ, our Mediator and Redeemer. Amen."

And with that, the funeral service was over.

Pushing my way through the group, I grabbed Colonel Race by the elbow and led him to where Chesterton was standing, staring down into the open grave.

"We made one discovery in Lamb's room," I said.

Chesterton handed over the brown manila envelope containing Lamb's correspondence. "Read these at your leisure, Colonel," he said. "You'll find them instructive."

Race glanced at the envelope with a puzzled expression, and then I asked him, "Did you find out from the Egyptian workmen who was, or wasn't, in the tomb shaft yesterday afternoon?"

"Ah, no. I'm afraid not. It would certainly be possible to compile a partial list from those workmen who say they were there. But, since none of them is prepared to say who else was there, I could never make it a complete list."

"Flinders!" thundered a voice behind my left shoulder. I turned around. It was Professor Fell.

"You are an archeologist, not a blasted detective. Leave the murder to the experts. I want you back at work with me."

Murder. Murder most mysterious. That's what filled my mind that afternoon. The funeral service had finally brought home to me the chilling fact that here, in the Valley of *Deir el-Bahri*, was someone who was prepared to kill—and might kill again.

As Fell led the way back to the shaft entrance, I saw that the others were already at work. Lined up at long trestle tables, cleaning and sorting, were Sir Edward Narracourt, Canon Poole, Lawrence Wilding, Madeleine Sutton, Mrs. Poole, and Amelia. I must have stopped to stare when I caught sight of her, because Fell's voice interrupted my thoughts, urging me on.

"Flinders! Menes has already waited three and a half thousand years—don't make him wait any longer."

I hurried to catch up. On one of the lower levels of the terraces we had already passed Elspeth Fell taking Frances Chesterton on a guided tour of the site. As I gathered up my notebook and pencils from one of the trestle tables, I noticed that John Farnsleigh and Nat Burrows were also working—sketching and photographing the objects from the tomb. Billy Burton was bustling around from table to table. Only the taciturn Ambrose Hoffman was missing. Off surveying a remote corner of the site, I assumed.

Then the murder once again sprang, uninvited, into my mind. At that very moment Mr. Chesterton and Colonel Race were, I knew, discussing the case and planning their strategy. I wished I could be with them.

"Are you ill, Flinders?" asked Professor Fell.

"Ah, no, sorry, just a bit distracted, that's all. I'm with you now."

As we re-entered the shaft, all the distractions fell away, and I was once again captured by the thrill of exploring an ancient and vanished civilization.

All that afternoon Fell and I again worked side by side in the burial chamber. Working with an experienced archeologist like Fell was teaching me much about the practical side of our work that I never learned at the university.

He began the afternoon shift by removing the items of furniture—several wooden chairs and a low table—from the chamber. This gave us clear access to more small items that had been stacked underneath them. As he worked, Fell dictated notes, which I scribbled down in a small book.

Halfway through the afternoon, we stopped for the tea break.

"I've poured your tea for you," said Amelia as we emerged from the mouth of the tunnel. At first I thought she was talking to her father, but then I realized she was looking at me.

"Milk and two sugars. That's how you like it, isn't it?" she said as she handed me the mug of hot tea.

"Yes, it is. How did you know?"

"Oh, I notice these things."

We walked some distance from the others and sat, side by side, on a large boulder.

"How is it that you're looking after the tea this afternoon?"

Amelia was wearing a lemon dress and had changed the ribbon on her hat so that it matched the color of the dress. I noticed how careful she was to keep herself screened from the sun, and, as a result, how pale and soft and lovely her skin was. I had looked closely at her hands as she poured the tea, and they were so soft that I longed to reach out and stroke them.

"Well, something has upset Rami, and she's fallen into a tearful mess, so Farouk's family is all at sixes and sevens fussing around her. Miss Sutton is busy typing up Papa's notes, and it's below my step-mother's dignity. So it was left to me."

I noticed how delicate her gestures were as she drank her tea.

"It couldn't be left to anyone better."

"So that's your estimate of what I'm good for, is it? Maid service?" she said, with a mischievous twinkle in her eye.

"All I meant, Amelia, is that you are reliable."

"Well, if that's all you meant, then you are forgiven for the insult."

"Are you reading any interesting books at the moment?" I asked, looking for something else to talk about.

"What to you mean by that?" shot back Amelia, suddenly defensive.

"Nothing special," I protested innocently. "I was just looking for something we could chat about."

"Oh, I see. Well, as it happens I have just started to read a most interesting book."

"Tell me more."

"It's the autobiography of our friend and colleague the Rev. Dr. Billy Burton."

"Really? I had no idea he'd written his autobiography. How did you lay your hands on it?"

"Dr. Burton lent it to Mrs. Poole. She read it and passed it on to me. Rebecca—Mrs. Poole—described it as 'a very colorful story.' It's called *Saved from the Darkness.*"

"Certainly sounds colorful. If the book's as much fun as the title, you must lend it to me when you've finished."

"I'd be delighted to."

At that moment a gust of wind whistled around the cliff face and whipped Amelia's broad-brimmed straw hat off her head. I put down my mug of tea and ran after it. The hat bowled along, across the top terrace of Queen Hatshepsut's Temple, like a cartwheel. I was gaining on it when it disappeared from sight over the edge of the terrace.

By the time I came to a red-faced, puffing halt at the terrace edge, the hat had landed on the sloping ramp that ran through the middle of the temple—where it was picked up by Wilding. He recognized it at once and strode briskly toward where Amelia was waiting for the hat's return.

By the time I caught up with them, Wilding was turning on his best Oxbridge accent. "I believe this is your property, Miss Fell."

"Why thank you, Mr. Wilding. How kind of you to return it to me." Amelia held out her hand to him, that soft, pale, delicate hand that I longed to touch.

Wilding held her hand much longer than necessary, or so it seemed to me, then bowed his head politely, and walked off in the direction of the shaft tomb.

"He may have . . . ," I began as he walked away. But I could not continue and had to stop to catch my breath. "He may have returned it to you . . . ," I finally managed to gasp, ". . . but I chased it!"

With that, I turned around and followed in Wilding's footsteps, mopping my sweating brow with my handkerchief as I walked.

"Mr. Flinders!" Amelia called out behind me. "Philip!"

But I didn't turn around. Why didn't I? Because, I think, at that moment, I was feeling extremely foolish.

That was the moment at which I resolved that if I was rejected by Amelia, it would be face to face. I was not going to allow Wilding to go on playing his little games. I would speak to her directly, I decided. Yes, and that meant it was time to summon up my courage and ask her . . .

"Come on, back to work," said Fell, slapping me on the back good-humoredly, "back to good old Menes's tomb."

In the next two hours we completed the task of removing the last of the small objects, and Fell turned his attention to the paintings on the walls of the burial chamber. Some of these showed Menes, his wife and children, while others depicted gods and goddesses. Before long, I was once again enveloped by the world of Ancient Egypt.

"Professor, these three scenes here on the back wall," I asked. "The first depicts Anubis, I take it?" As I spoke I was pointing at a stylized picture of the jackal-headed god of the dead, seated on a shrine.

"Quite right," muttered Fell.

"But what's this next one? A kneeling goddess?"

"Yes. Notice her gesture. She is protecting the *shen*-sign, which means to 'encircle' or to 'enclose,' referring, I would think, to protection of the mummy. And in the third one . . ."

"That's Menes again?"

"Precisely, kneeling below a sycamore tree receiving libations from the goddess within. Now I would guess that . . ."

"Professor, can you hear that?" I interrupted.

"Hear what?"

"Listen carefully."

Fell listened for a moment, his head to one side.

"Wind, by the sound of it," he said, "echoing down the tunnel."

I was about to respond, when a second sound could be heard—the sound of running feet. A moment later Farouk was at our side, out of breath, and gasping out the word, *"Samma! Samma!"*

"Sandstorm," Fell translated. "We'll have to get back to the camp quickly."

"Is it that dangerous?"

"You haven't see a *khamsin*—I have. Hurry!"

Farouk and Fell set off down the shaft, and I hurried after them. As we approached the mouth of the tunnel, the sight that met our eyes was ghastly. It was as if a blood-red curtain had been dropped over the sun. A sinister crimson light filled the valley, and the scream of the wind filled our ears.

Suddenly a gust of wind swept into the shaft. Fell shouted, "Hold on!" but before I could, I was thrown back against the tunnel wall. The air was full of fine dust that blocked the nostrils, choked the mouth, and threatened suffocation.

"Cover your mouth with your handkerchief!" shouted Fell. "Like this!" I followed his example and tied my large white bandanna around my face so that it covered my nose and mouth. Farouk covered his face with the end of his *keffiyeh*.

At the next hot, furious gust of wind, I braced myself against the rock, but I could still feel it buffeting my body, as if trying to tear me out of the tunnel and fling me bodily across the valley. Already several inches of sand had built up in the tunnel mouth, and it was growing deeper by the minute.

"We can't stay here," yelled the professor, over the wail of the wind. "We have to make it back to the camp. We should be safe inside the common room—it's a sturdy enough building—if we lock all the windows and doors. I'm worried about the others—must see how they are."

With that, he launched himself into the swirling torrent of air, with Farouk close behind him. I took off my battered old felt hat—there was no point in losing it outside—and threw it on the tunnel floor. Then I followed in the footsteps of Fell and Farouk.

Once outside the mouth of the shaft, I felt as though I had been gripped by a giant hand that shook me like a doll. Both the trestle tables were gone. Picked up, as the storm started? Or blown away?

I staggered across the top terrace of the temple. Visibility was terrible. Through the clouds of dust I could just make out the white of Farouk's *galabiyah*. It acted as a beacon, guiding me across the terrace and toward the ramps that led to the valley, and to relative safety.

Already the ramps were covered with deep drifts of sand that caught my feet and caused me to stumble.

"Flinders! Are you there?" shouted Fell over his shoulder.

"I'm here, Professor! Keep moving!" I shouted back.

"Keep up with us, Flinders, or you're a dead man!"

The hot wind from the desert had launched itself with fury into the heart of the prevailing wind that swept up the Nile Valley. It seemed like a mortal combat between the two forces of the air. They pushed and wrestled and buffeted each other; they advanced, paused, fell to grips, and clutched in deadly embrace; rolled around and around, this way, that way, in a delirium of rage. They moaned, and it was like the sound of a great crowd; they gasped, fell silent, then gave forth a mighty scream of sudden pain; and around and around they rolled again, flinging out wild banners of burning sand.

As we struggled down the valley toward the camp, it was as if we were pushing back waves of swirling water, instead of wind. How long it took to make that journey I will never know; my mind was concentrated on the effort of drawing each moment's breath.

Eventually a dark shadow loomed out of the crimson twilight. From its size I knew that it had to be the common room. Farouk's sure instincts had guided us to safety! Just as we turned toward the building, I heard a woman's scream, faintly, in a slight lull in the wind. It came from somewhere to my right. As I turned in the direction of the scream, I knew—don't ask me how I knew, but I did—that it was Amelia.

I called her name. My voice was lost in the wail of the wind, then the torrent of air around me had one of its momentary lapses, so I shouted louder, "Amelia! Amelia!"

"Philip! Over here!"

I rushed in the direction of her voice. And there she was—on the ground, holding her leg, with sand already beginning to sweep over her.

"What happened?" I asked as I knelt down and placed an arm around her shoulders.

"I was trying to get from our house to the common room," she gasped, coughing and choking on the sand, "when something struck me. A piece of corrugated iron, I think, from one of the store huts."

I tore a piece of cloth off the sleeve of my shirt and gave it to her to hold over her mouth.

I glanced at her leg: even through the layer of blown sand I could see that it was bleeding freely. I lifted her up. "Put your weight on me.

It's not far to the common room. You were almost there when you were hit."

I tried to retrace my steps through that swirling, whirling, confusing wind. Eddies of sand swept by, revolving in living funnels, swaying, dancing, and for a moment I lost all sense of direction, and then, mercifully, the clouds of wind-born sand parted, and the common room emerged ahead of us.

With Amelia's arm around my neck, and my arm around her shoulders taking most of her weight, we staggered up to the building and pounded on the door. For a moment I thought we hadn't been heard, then came the sound of bolts being slid back, the door was opened a crack, and we were pulled inside, wind and sand swirling inside with us.

The door was pushed closed behind us, and abruptly the volume of the howling dropped, and the air was still.

"Flinders! Where did you get to? I told you to stay . . . ," began Fell, and then he saw his daughter. "Amelia, my dear, you're bleeding! What happened?"

"Something hit me. A piece of iron, I think . . ."

"Never mind that now. Mrs. Poole! Here, quickly—with your first-aid kit, if you please."

Amelia's wound, I could now see clearly, was a long but shallow cut.

"Oh, you poor dear," clucked Mrs. Poole as she knelt beside Amelia. "You gentlemen can leave her to me now."

Fell and I walked away from the place where the patient was lying on the floor, while Mrs. Poole pulled up Amelia's skirts and began cleaning the wound.

"What happened?" asked Fell anxiously.

"I heard a scream," I explained. "Just as we were approaching this building. Didn't you hear it?"

"I didn't hear a blasted thing. Except for this foul wind, of course."

"Anyway, I heard a woman's scream, so I turned back to investigate."

"Damned brave of you, Flinders." Fell grasped my hand firmly.

"What happened?" asked Billy Burton as he, Chesterton, Race, and several of the others walked up to us. Fell repeated the story, and there were numerous comments about how fortunate Amelia and I were to be alive. The words were a background buzz in my head. My mind was flooded with a sense of relief and that awful sinking feeling that comes after an escape from danger. It was the sudden realization of how close we had been to death that made my stomach feel as though it had been vacuum pumped. I looked around with something like affection at the familiar faces of our party and with real gratitude at the solid, mud-brick walls that now surrounded me.

"The wound has been cleaned and dressed, and you may speak to the patient now, gentlemen," announced Mrs. Poole. "The wound is only superficial. There is no serious damage."

We turned around and found Amelia, seated at the trestle table and nursing a cup of cold water in her hands.

Fell moved over and took a seat beside her. "Tell me what happened, dear," he said solicitously.

"When the sandstorm started," she said, "I thought it would be safest to stay in our house. So I locked and bolted the doors and windows and waited for it to die down. Then the wind started to lift the roof, and sand began to pour in, so I thought I should try to make it across here. After all, it's not such a long way across the compound. And I would have made it, too, if I hadn't been struck by . . . well, whatever it was."

"Once the roof went," agreed Colonel Race, "you had no choice. You did the right thing in trying to make it to this building."

"But then that . . . thing . . . came bowling out of the dust. It knocked me over. That's when I screamed. When I tried to get up, I could feel the pain in my leg. Once I was on the ground, the sand started covering me immediately. If Philip hadn't . . ." And at that, she started to cry.

"Delayed shock," said Mrs. Poole briskly.

But Amelia was stronger than Mrs. Poole took her for. She wiped her eyes on a small, lace handkerchief that she extracted from her sleeve. Then she turned to me, took my hand in hers, and looked directly into my eyes.

"You saved my life, Philip."

I think I blushed. I certainly coughed and cleared my throat and stammered something about "my pleasure, Miss Fell."

I knew there would not be a better time to talk to Amelia. I would tell her my feelings for her, feelings that had been growing over the last two months. Not here, of course, in front of the others, but at the very first opportunity. And I would ask her . . .

Yes, I would do it!

Satisfied that his daughter was safe, and not seriously harmed, Fell turned to his wife.

"Elspeth, how could you leave Amelia alone in the house when the storm blew up?"

"I was not in the house when the wind began," she replied icily, her attractive face screwed into a frown. "I was out. Walking. Naturally I hurried to this building for safety as soon as I saw the danger. I thought you'd be pleased that I'm safe."

"I am, my dear, of course I am," he said apologetically. Fears for the safety of his own family settled, Professor Fell turned his concerns to the rest of the expedition and began a head count.

John Farnsleigh, Nat Burrows, Sir Edward Narracourt, Canon Poole, Billy Burton, Miss Sutton, Lawrence Wilding, Colonel Race, Frances Chesterton as well as her famous husband, Elliot Jones, Farouk, Rami, their two sons—they were all there.

"Where's Hoffman?" he asked.

He was right. Ambrose Hoffman was missing. No one could remember seeing him since the *khamhsin* began.

"We'll have to send out a search party," said Fell grimly. "Danger- ous, I know, but it's got to be done."

"Leave it me," Colonel Race volunteered. "I think this sort of thing is more in my line than anyone else's. Farouk—will you come with me?"

Our headman nodded. The two took wide strips of linen, soaked them in water, and wrapped them around their faces. Then the common room door was opened a crack, and sand started to pour in as they slid out into the hot, howling gale. Struggling against a wind like a giant fist, Wilding and I pushed the door closed behind them.

For perhaps half an hour there was little conversation in that room. Some of us paced back and forth, others sat in silence, others held whispered conversations. I took a seat beside Amelia, but we didn't speak. The tension was electric.

Then came the sound that we were waiting for—a pounding at the door. Quickly we opened it, and in staggered—two figures.

"No sign of Hoffman?" asked Fell anxiously as Race and Farouk dusted the sand off their clothing.

"Not a sign anywhere," puffed out Race. Even the tough little soldier was knocked about by his battle with the wind. "We checked all the huts and storerooms. He is in none of the buildings."

"In that case," muttered Narracourt, "he's a dead man."

It was a melodramatic statement, but the nodding heads around the room suggested it was true.

"Tell me, Farouk," I asked our head man, some little time later, "how do your men survive this sort of thing?"

"At the first sign of *khamhsin*—they head for cliffs. They know what to do. They know where it will be safe for them. They come back in morning. You see."

In subdued tones Fell asked Farouk if Rami could prepare a cold supper for everyone, and, with the wind still rattling, roaring, and howling around the building, the company gathered for the strangest meal of our time in Egypt.

What a strange time that was. Outside, the killer wind howled for blood, while inside a killer sat with us at the table, a killer whose ingenuity concealed his, or her, identity.

During the supper of cold chicken, bread, and goat cheese, Chesterton appeared to decide that our spirits needed lifting and that it was his job to do it. He talked on a wide range of subjects. In the course of half an hour, he touched on the origins of the Christmas cracker, merry-go-rounds (on which he particularly enjoyed riding), Beowulf, Buddhism, Thomas Henry Huxley, the films of Charles Chaplin, and Mr. George Bernard Shaw, whom he had once described as a coming peril but whom he now regarded as a disappearing pleasure.

With his enormous bulk, numerous chins, and words that fizzed like firecrackers above the scream of the wind, he was like Father Christmas and Old King Cole rolled up into one.

Having disposed of Bernard Shaw, he moved on to the current fad for occultism—the reading of tarot cards, the holding of seances, and the rest of it. Enthusiasts for this sort of thing Chesterton labeled "unselfish egoists," which got a rise out of Narracourt.

"A nonsense expression!" challenged Sir Edward. "Unless, of course, you can define what you mean."

"An unselfish egoist," responded Chesterton, "is a man who has pride without the excuse of passion. Of all conceivable forms of enlightenment the worst is what these people call the Inner Light—the worship of the god within. Imagine a man—I'll call him 'Smith.' That Smith shall worship the god within turns out ultimately to mean that Smith shall worship Smith. The Ancient Egyptians with their idolatrous worship of cats and crocodiles were bad enough—Smith and his worship of the god within is far worse. Christianity came into the world to assert that a man is not to look inward, but outward—to behold with astonishment and enthusiasm a divine Commander-in-Chief. The fun of being a Christian is that a man is not left alone with the Inner Light, but definitely recognizes an outer light, fair as the sun, clear as the moon, terrible as an army with banners."

And so he rolled on, teasing Narracourt, irritating Wilding, and entertaining all of us enormously.

At last the company left the trestle table and began to move about the room, forming little conversation groups. Amelia and I gravitated toward each other.

"How is the leg feeling now?"

"Much better, thank you. The question is, how can I ever repay you for saving my life?"

"Do I have to answer immediately?" I said with a smile, "or may I think about it?"

"Now you're teasing me," responded Amelia playfully.

Before we could say any more, we became aware of a row at the other end of the room. Farouk and Rami were shouting at each other in Arabic. He grabbed her by the arms and tried to hold her. She broke away, ran to the door, and began sliding back the bolts.

"Stop! You can't go outside!" called out Fell, who had been watching the drama.

Before she could wrench open the door, Colonel Race was at her side, restraining her. When she saw she was defeated, she collapsed on the floor and wept.

"Poor Rami," said Amelia. "I wonder what's wrong?"

"Probably just the sandstorm," I suggested.

"Men! You're so insensitive. Can't you see it's more than that?"

So saying, Amelia hurried to Rami's side, with me trailing in her wake. She knelt beside the weeping woman, put an arm around her shoulders, and comforted her. For a short while I crouched beside Amelia, then stood up, to find myself part of a small group gathered around the two women: Race, Farouk, and Fell.

"What's all this about, Farouk?" demanded the professor.

"I can't say. She must tell you," he replied, nodding at his weeping wife.

Race began to ask Rami questions in Arabic. Slowly the sobbing stopped, and she began to answer, haltingly at first, and then more fluently. After several minutes of this cross-examination, Race turned to Fell and said, "Well, that's clear enough."

"Not to me it's not," growled Fell. "I followed bits of the conversation but not all of it. Please explain."

"She told me that the escaped prisoner I came here to hunt—Mamur Zapt—is her brother. She has been hiding him in the camp for almost a week now. The food you've been missing, Professor, went to feed him."

"Is he the chap I saw trying to climb into the kitchen window the other day?" I asked, "the one we chased and lost?"

"That was him all right. Rami kept warning him to stay away from this building, to remain in hiding, where she could safely bring him food. But he cared nothing for risks, and he came to the kitchen several times. He broke in the night before we saw him, Flinders. Rami says she saw evidence of his raid, a broken water bottle, the next morning."

"Of course!" I exclaimed, "the glass on the bench top that Farnsleigh cut his hand on."

"No doubt. Well, even though he's a wrong 'un, she loves her brother dearly and fears for his life in this windstorm. She foolishly imagined she could make it through the storm to his hiding place."

"And where is that hiding place?" Fell inquired.

"One of the caves in the cliff face," replied Race, lighting his pipe. "I don't know which one, as yet—but I shall."

A much calmer Rami scrambled to her feet and was led by Farouk back to the kitchen. I helped Amelia to her feet, and, having done so, I was most reluctant to let go of her hand—so I didn't, and Amelia didn't withdraw it from my grasp.

"Why didn't Farouk tell me this?" fulminated Professor Fell. "He must have known!"

"Of course he knew," said Race calmly, "but loyalty to his wife closed his mouth."

"Well . . . I suppose one can't complain about loyalty," Fell muttered. "Good thing on the whole."

"If Mamur Zapt survives this storm—he shall not escape me," said Race as Chesterton joined us. "Ah, Mr. Chesterton, why don't we put our enforced incarceration to good use? I propose that we claim one corner of this large room and resume our interviews with witnesses. Will you assist once more?"

"I will," replied Chesterton, "as long as you allow me to have my own assistant by my side."

"Who did you have in mind?"

"Young Mr. Flinders here," he rumbled, thumping me heartily on the shoulder as he did so. "His complete lack of imagination makes him extremely useful."

"If you say so," Race commented doubtfully. "I have no objections."

Thus it was that, a few minutes later, we were sequestered in the quietest corner of the room, with Lawrence Wilding before us as the next witness.

"The question, of course, is," began Colonel Race, "just how Dr. Lamb managed to get past you and the other folk in the tunnel in order to get himself murdered in the burial chamber."

Wilding tilted his head back and, looking at us down the aristocratic bridge of his nose, replied, "You're asking the wrong person entirely."

"Really? Then who should I be asking?"

"The Spirits of Ancient Egypt. Oh, I heard our distinguished guest here taking cheap shots at occult belief. But I have been present at seances at which Great Spirits have appeared and spoken words of power far beyond the understanding of mere mortals."

"Is that all?" asked Chesterton. "I have seen far more astonishing things than that. I have seen a man walk through the solid steel wall of a bank vault. Unfortunately, the man's name was Houdini, and he was performing a magic trick on the stage of the Palladium."

"For the time being," Race said, "let's stick to the material realm. Personally, I find that quite puzzling enough. Mr. Wilding, can you give me the names of the people who were with you in the shaft yesterday afternoon?"

Wilding did so, and his list tallied exactly with mine. Race then took him over the sequence of events, and, again, he added nothing to the account I had already provided. After tracking backward and forward over this handful of facts for some time, Race finally thanked Wilding for his help and dismissed him.

Nat Burrows, the photographer, was next.

"When were you summoned into the shaft tomb, Mr. Burrows?" Race began.

"I wasn't looking at my watch. About the middle of the afternoon, I would guess."

"And you were ready as soon as you were called?"

"Alawi and I had been waiting all day; we had the equipment ready."

"Alawi?"

"My Arab assistant. Not that he's very much use. I tried to teach him how to develop plates, but I might as well have tried to teach him to fly to the moon. All I got for my trouble was several ruined plates. So, all I use him for now is lugging equipment about."

"So, when the two of you entered the shaft, Alawi was—where?—ahead of you or behind you?"

"Behind me. He was carrying the tripod; I had the camera."

Race glanced at me, and I nodded in agreement.

"When you reached the burial chamber, what did you see?"

"Several Arab shovel men and basket boys removing the rubble from the plastered mud-brick wall. Oh, and the burial chamber itself, of course. Quite remarkable."

"And what did you do?"

"Took about a dozen photographs. I covered the chamber from every angle I could get at without disturbing any of the antiquities. I can show you the results tomorrow. So far, I've developed the plates, but I haven't made any prints yet."

"Yes, I'd like to see those photographs—they may reveal something useful. Unlikely, but they may. How long did this process take?"

"Well, let me see. Alawi moved the tripod after each shot. And I had to reload the flash plate with powder after each shot. Say, two minutes per shot, so, altogether, perhaps twenty-five minutes I would say. But I'm guessing—I didn't look at my watch."

"Listen!" said Chesterton, suddenly leaning forward in his chair. Seeing Chesterton move quickly was always slightly alarming—a bit like seeing Mount Everest suddenly move two feet to the left.

"Listen for what?" I asked.

"Just listen!"

I did. "I can't hear anything."

"Exactly!" Chesterton said, leaning back triumphantly. It took a moment for the penny to drop, and then I understood—the moaning, howling sound that had been a constant backdrop to our evening meal was gone.

"The wind has died down."

"It actually fell away completely several minutes ago," said Race calmly, refilling his pipe. "By the way, Mr. Burrows, thank you for your help, and we're finished with you now."

As Burrows left, I stood up. Conversation in the room was dying away as others realized that the sandstorm was over, and the threat had passed. I walked across the floor toward Amelia. For the first time, in the newly fallen silence, I could hear the gritty scraping noise that my boots made at every step. I looked down and realized, perhaps fully for the first time, that the floor of the common room was covered with sand. There was a thin, gritty layer everywhere and in front of the door, mounds and streams of sand several inches thick.

"No wind!" I said, somewhat idiotically, when I reached Amelia.

"Isn't it wonderful!" she cried and threw her arms around me and hugged me. It certainly was wonderful.

Sometime later I became aware that someone was tapping me on the shoulder. It was Colonel Race. "Now that it's safe to venture out, there is a job to be done, and I would prefer it were done at once, tonight. Will you come and help?"

"If you wish. Will you excuse me, Amelia?"

"Certainly, Philip. But I'll see you again, later, won't I?"

"Of course you will."

It turned out that Race's "job" was searching Hoffman's hut. While Race pushed the common room door open—with some difficulty, there being a buildup of sand behind it—I lit a hurricane lamp.

"Why the urgency?" I asked, once we were walking down the row of huts.

"Hoffman's disappearance may have nothing to do with the murder. But it would be unwise for me to make that assumption at this stage. So I want to search his hut before there is any chance of it being interfered with."

As we walked to the hut, Colonel Race explained that he had instructed Farouk, together with any men he might be able to round up, to make a complete search of the campsite in the morning.

"For Hoffman's body," explained Race. "No point in attempting a search in the dark. And even in the morning I doubt they'll find it under all these deep sand drifts."

Hoffman's room was identical to mine—and to that of every other single male on the expedition team: a square, ten feet by ten feet, mud-brick hut with a floor of desert sand and gravel and a palm-thatched roof.

Race and I began with Hoffman's sea chest, since this had proved fruitful in Lamb's hut. This time it wasn't—it turned out to contain nothing except neatly folded and stacked clothing.

The one item of furniture that was peculiar to Hoffman's hut was his drawing board. Upon examination, we found this to hold several large sheets of cartridge paper, layered one on top of another and each holding a detailed drawing of one aspect of Queen Hatshepsut's temple. The top drawing appeared to be incomplete.

The other noticeable items in the hut were pencils. They were everywhere. There were pencils on the drawing board, on the rough plank shelves, scattered on the palm-stick bed, even lying on the floor. Among the pencils on the shelves were a chipped china mug, a half-empty brandy bottle, and a pile of papers.

"Ah, these might be useful," said Race, seizing the papers. Together we thumbed through them. There were several letters from his wife in Battersea, a report torn out of a magazine of an architectural conference at Brighton, an advertisement for a patent medicine that supposedly cured rheumatism, a letter from a publisher interested in an illustrated book on the ruined temples of Ancient Egypt, a letter from a London bank making threatening noises about a mortgage, Fell's original letter offering Hoffman a place on the expedition team, and a page torn out of the *Illustrated London News* showing photographs of various Egyptian antiquities.

"Shouldn't you wait until he's properly dead before you do that?" boomed a voice from the doorway. It was Chesterton, his bandit moustache looking particularly threatening in the flickering lamplight and his several chins quivering.

"Hoffman is dead," pronounced Race with calm certainty. "Lacking the knowledge of the local Arabs, no European could survive that sandstorm."

"In that case," said Chesterton, "why did he die?"

"Why? I don't understand?" I said.

"It's simple enough. Why did he not join us in the safety of the common room?"

"There are two possibilities," Race replied quietly, as he relit his pipe. "Either he tried to and failed. Or else, being guilty of the murder of Dr. Lamb, he didn't try—but attempted to flee under cover of the sandstorm instead."

"Flight being evidence of guilt?"

"Quite frequently. Whether that is so in this case is for you and me to discover, Mr. Chesterton."

"And what about you, young Flinders? Can you imagine Hoffman murdering Lamb?"

I thought for a moment before replying. "No—I don't think I can."

"That's useful to know," rumbled the writer of detective stories. "What the unimaginative mind cannot see may not be there."

"And anyway—why would he? I mean, why would Hoffman murder Lamb?" I asked, having entirely failed to comprehend Chesterton's last remark.

It was Race who replied, "Aye, that's the question. So far we have uncovered no motive in this case, not a glimmer of a motive."

"Have you, in fact, uncovered anything useful at all in Mr. Hoffman's room?"

"I'm very much afraid not," admitted Race, gazing wistfully around the hut as though he rather hoped a clue would leap out and bite him on the ankle.

"Then there is nothing to detain us here," said Chesterton as he turned around and, leaning heavily on a crutch-handled walking stick, led us back to the common room.

We found Miss Sutton making a fresh pot of tea and everyone strangely reluctant to return to their own rooms, despite the late hour and the end of the sandstorm. Or, perhaps, it wasn't so strange after all. The threat we had faced together had somehow brought us closer. There was a lingering feeling that together we were safe.

Over tea, Race arranged the next interview—with John Farnsleigh, the expedition artist—and the four of us gathered in a group of chairs in a far corner of the room.

"Well, Mr. Farnsleigh," began Colonel Race, "when was the last time you saw Dr. Lamb alive?"

"I thought you might ask me that," the artist replied, "and I've been trying to remember. I worked all through the lunch hour, you see. And when the others arrived for the afternoon shift, I was just finishing my work."

"Which was . . . ?"

"Well, the plastered wall that sealed off the burial chamber was decorated. And since the wall had to be destroyed to get at the tomb inside, those decorations had to be recorded. Burrows took some photographs, but, of course, that only gives us black and white images. So I had to paint exact, to-scale, colored copies of the decorations as well. It was rather a slow job."

"When you were working—through the lunch hour, that is—were you alone in the tomb shaft?"

"Yes. Apart from Ahmed, my Arab assistant, of course."

"When you finished, and the others arrived, what did you do?"

"Well, I had actually completed the last of my drawings just before they all turned up. The watercolors were still damp, and Ahmed and I were spreading them out in the sun to dry."

"And that's when the others arrived to begin work for the afternoon?"

"That's right."

"Who was there—in that group?"

"Just about all the men of the expedition party. None of the ladies was there. Neither were you, Mr. Chesterton."

Chesterton nodded his agreement.

"Oh, and I don't think Hoffman was there either," continued Farnsleigh.

"Was that unusual?"

"No. Hoffman had his own work to get on with—elsewhere on the temple site. His job was to draw up detailed architectural plans of the whole site."

"So, apart from Hoffman, Chesterton, and the ladies, all the other team members were present?"

"Yes."

"Including Dr. Lamb?"

"Yes. I remember him bouncing around like an enthusiastic schoolboy, wanting to see the burial chamber and Fell telling him he would have to wait. I'm certain that was the last time I saw him."

"How well did you know Lamb?"

"Hardly at all," insisted Farnsleigh, rather too earnestly I thought. "I mean to say, he was just the expedition doctor. My only dealings with him were to get my weekly anti-malaria tablets and to have the occasional wound cleaned and bandaged. On the morning he died, he fixed up a cut in my hand. But apart from that, well, he was such a quiet little man, one hardly got to know him at all."

"Do you know of any enemies the doctor may have had? Or any reason why anyone may have wanted to kill him?"

"I was thinking about that tonight—when the wind was howling around outside. And it has me completely puzzled. Not only do I not understand how Dr. Lamb was killed, I can't begin to fathom why—it makes no sense to me."

There was nothing more the artist could add, so Race dismissed Farnsleigh and summoned Canon Poole in his place.

"Dreadful business, this murder," said the canon, shaking his head sadly and making clucking noises with his tongue.

"Quite so," responded Race dryly. "Murder is never pleasant. Now, you only arrived on the morning of the murder, is that correct?"

"Quite correct."

"In the brief time you were here, did you see or hear anything that might hint at a reason for this murder?"

"Oh, the reason is clear enough."

"It is? Then please share your insight with us, dear Canon."

"I put it all down to Genesis 3."

"I beg your pardon?"

"I am referring to the third chapter of the first book of the Bible. It describes the rejection by the human race of our Maker and Ruler. This rejection, of course, has the effect of damaging human nature, and human relationships. Resulting in murder. The very first crime committed was the murder of Abel by Cain. That is what lies behind the murder of poor Dr. Lamb—Genesis 3."

"Most helpful, I'm sure. However, I was looking for a rather more immediate motive."

"Ah, yes, I see what you mean. No, I'm afraid I can't help you there."

"Now, Mr. Poole, you were in the tunnel during the opening of the burial chamber—is that correct?"

"Quite so."

"Who was with you?"

In reply, Canon Poole recited the list of names already provided by me and Wilding. He corroborated the details we already knew. All the evidence continued to point in the same direction: the sheer physical impossibility of Dr. Lamb's murder.

Sir Edward Narracourt was the next witness summoned by Race.

"I have to tell you that I don't entirely approve of this," he said stiffly as he took a seat. He brushed an imaginary fleck of sand from the sleeve of his khaki shirt and sniffed loudly.

"Approve of what?" asked Race.

"Of my being cross-examined in a criminal case. It's never happened to me before. It's . . . it's . . . undignified."

"I assure you that you are a witness, not a suspect, Sir Edward," Race said calmingly. Unfortunately, his well-intentioned remark only inflamed the situation.

"A suspect? I should certainly hope not! If there is the slightest hint . . ." His remarks died away in a kind of outraged splutter.

"Sir Edward," intervened Chesterton, "you are a scientist—a trained observer. Your observations may be useful in bringing a murderer to justice."

Somewhat mollified, Narracourt leaned back in his chair and asked, "What do you want to know?"

"When was the last time you saw Dr. Lamb?"

"Lying in the sarcophagus with a knife in his chest."

"What was the last time," said Race, with a weary sigh, "that you saw the doctor alive?"

"I can't recall. He was an unimportant little man. I paid no attention to him."

"During the opening of the burial chamber, you were in the tomb shaft?"

"I was."

"Who else was there?"

Narracourt gave the same short list as everyone else.

"Sir Edward," Race persisted, "you're an intelligent man. How did Dr. Lamb get past your group in that narrow tunnel? How could he slip past unseen in order to be murdered in the burial chamber?"

To my surprise Narracourt actually looked uncomfortable when asked this question.

"I wish I knew," he said, scratching his head. "I was there. I saw everything that happened. All the information I need is in my memory of that afternoon. My mind should be able to reason this puzzle out. But I have to reluctantly confess myself to be stumped."

"Then, ah, my good sir," rumbled Chesterton, who I thought had fallen asleep, "you give no credence to the notion of an Ancient Egyptian curse doing its devilish work here?"

"Stuff and nonsense! Utter poppycock! There must be a perfectly logical explanation for what happened to Lamb. It's just that, at the moment, I cannot see what it is."

"By the way, Sir Edward—when was the last time you saw Hoffman?"

"Hoffman? Let me think. I believe he joined us to help move the antiquities to safety when we saw the storm blowing up. There were a number of us carrying the antiquities down to the storeroom before the storm struck. I'm sure Hoffman was with us then. There was a lot of bustling backward and forward, so I could be mistaken. But I'm fairly certain he was with us then. Of course, I haven't seen him since, poor devil."

After Narracourt left us, our mugs of tea were topped off, and Fell planted himself in the spare chair facing Race, Chesterton, and me.

"Any clues yet?" he asked.

"It's early days yet, Professor Fell," Race replied cautiously.

"Which I take to be a no. Hardly surprising, of course—it's a baffling business."

"I take it you did not know that Lamb had been deregistered from medical practice in New South Wales?"

"Of course not! What do you take me for? I would never have employed him if I had known."

"Could anyone else have known?"

"I can't see how. Anyway, if someone else on the expedition knew, why didn't they tell me?"

"Why indeed?" muttered Race.

"What about Hoffman?" Fell asked. "Does his disappearance have anything to do with Lamb's death?"

"We simply don't know at this stage, Professor," replied Race with a shrug.

"It must have, surely," Fell continued. "I mean to say . . . too much of a coincidence . . . and all that sort of thing. There must be a connection, mustn't there?"

"That's one of the things we're hoping to find out. Could you ask your secretary to step over here for a few moments, to answer some questions?"

"Yes, certainly, of course."

Madeleine Sutton sat in front of us looking very prim and proper and rather stiff. She wore a plain, white blouse and a long, plain skirt in some dark-brown material. Her hair was pulled severely back into a bun, and there was a look on her face that said she was giving us her full attention. She was the very picture of brisk, impersonal efficiency.

I recalled the diary entry I had read: "Guilty! Guilty! Guilty!" What on earth, I asked myself, did this woman have to be guilty about? Was it something to do with the murder? Should I tell Race and Chesterton? To do that, I would have to admit that I had invaded Miss Sutton's privacy by reading her diary. I would think about it for a little longer, I decided, before I told anyone.

"How long had you known Dr. Lamb?" Race asked.

"Since the start of the expedition," replied Miss Sutton with a sniff. "I certainly didn't know him before then."

"So that means you met . . .when exactly?"

"All the members of the party gathered for the first time in Cairo. That was just over three months ago."

"Did you like him?"

The question seemed to surprise Miss Sutton. "Like him?" she replied, with a lift of her eyebrows. "I never thought about him. I neither liked him nor disliked him."

"What about the other members of the expedition? Was there any tension between Dr Lamb and anyone else?"

"Not as far as I could observe. What are you implying, Colonel? That a member of this party murdered Dr. Lamb? Preposterous. That sort of thing couldn't happen on one of Professor Fell's expeditions. It just couldn't."

"Then who do you suggest killed the doctor?"

"One of the natives, of course! Surely that's obvious."

"And why would they want to do that?"

"I don't know! Don't ask me! Really! No one understands how a native's mind works. One of them took a dislike to him and killed him. That's all."

"Did you ever see Dr. Lamb having a disagreement with one of the Arab workmen?"

"See? No, I didn't see anything. It's just obvious; that's all there is to it."

"And how did this . . . er, native . . . actually manage the murder?"

"How? I can't imagine how! I can't answer that. But I can tell you one thing—they are a devious and deceptive lot, these natives. Take my word for it—one of them killed poor Dr. Lamb."

"What are we to make of that?" asked Race, smothering a yawn, after Miss Sutton had left us.

"I suppose it's possible one of the Egyptian workmen was involved in the murder. Do you think it's possible, sir?" I asked Chesterton.

"What matters is not what happened, but what you think happened; not what you saw, but what you thought you saw."

"I don't understand," I said helplessly.

"My dear young Flinders, I am beginning to see a faint glimmer of light in this dark business."

"Then please share it with us," pleaded the colonel.

"Not yet! This small idea of mine is too frail a thing to be brought out and handed around in company just yet. I think I shall retire for the night," he added, lumbering to his feet. "Frances!" he bellowed to his wife, across the room, "it is time we were in bed."

"He's probably right—it's bedtime," Race admitted. "I'll see you in the morning, my boy."

Other members of the party were also, if somewhat reluctantly, leaving the comfort of the common room and returning to their huts for the night. Had I missed Amelia? Had she gone? No, there she was, on the other side of the table, still waiting for me. I pulled up a chair and sat down beside her.

"Tired?" I asked.

"Yes, I am rather," she admitted with a smile.

"Hardly surprising. Let me walk you back to the expedition house. Ah, the thought just struck me—you said the roof of the house began to collapse. I wonder: is it habitable tonight?"

"Papa thought of that some time ago. Farouk and his sons, under Papa's direction, have effected some temporary repairs and swept out the worst of the sand. Apparently our rooms are habitable."

"Then, may I walk you home, Amelia?"

"Thank you, Philip. I would be delighted if you would do so."

As we stepped out into the mild evening air, Amelia laid her hand gently on my arm, and in companionable silence we walked across the camp grounds to the expedition house. There was lamplight shining from several windows when we arrived.

"Papa and my stepmother are already there, I see," Amelia said. "Well, goodnight, Philip."

She turned to face me. I took a step closer. *Would she mind if I kissed her?* I wondered. I bent my head toward hers, but just at that moment, the front door of the house crashed open, and Fell emerged carrying a blanket, which he shook vigorously.

"Papa! That sand is going all over us!" protested Amelia.

"Sorry, my dear. I didn't see you there. Who's that with you? Ah, Flinders. See you in the morning, Flinders. Bright and early, mind. We'll start the morning shift at the regular time. Come on in, Amelia— Farouk's sons have cleaned out your room for you."

I watched Amelia until she had disappeared into the house then walked down to my own hut.

There was a foot of sand piled up against the walls on two sides. Within, I found that all my lighter possessions had been blown around. Fortunately, the space was so small they couldn't be blown far. Half of my palm-thatched roof was missing, and my blankets needed a vigorous shaking before the bed was fit for sleeping in.

But I was tired, and no discomfort could have stopped me from sleeping that night.

When the alarm went off, I felt as though I had slept for half an hour, not half a night. Forcing myself out of bed, I staggered to the canvas bath behind my hut to find the bath filled, not with water, but with sand. Then I remembered the *khamsin* and all the events of the previous night.

I walked up to the common room, where I found a basin of fresh water set up on a re-erected trestle table by the side wall of the building. Here I stripped to the waist and washed as thoroughly as I could. Then I returned to my hut, dug into the bottom of my trunk for some clean clothes, and changed out of the crumpled, dusty clothes I had fallen asleep in. I found a clean, white shirt and a pair of khaki shorts which, together with a change of underwear and socks, made me feel more human and look more respectable.

Taking my shaving kit with me, I returned to the basin of water at the common room to complete my transformation from disheveled wreck to an approximation of a human being. Then I was ready for breakfast and was surprised by my own appetite.

I found an exhausted company of archeologists seated around the common room table in sleepy silence, but the bread was hot and fresh and accompanied by that special smell that only freshly baked bread has. I devoured the bread and the hot, sweet tea and even enjoyed the bowl of *ful,* which, as usual, we were served for breakfast.

The common room door flew open, and in staggered a disheveled-looking Elliot Jones.

"What are you doing up at this time of the morning?" I asked, surprised by his appearance.

"I couldn't sleep," he mumbled, then fell into a chair at the table.

As he slouched there, head between his hands, I asked, "What kept you awake?"

"Are you kidding?" he responded, raising his head to stare at me with red-rimmed eyes. "There's something happening in this camp. First, harmless Doc Lamb is killed by a murderer who can walk through solid rock. Or who can carry his victim through solid rock to die in an Ancient Egyptian tomb. I don't like that sort of thing. It's unnerving. And then Hoffman disappears. Why? How? No one has a clue. It makes me nervous. Who'll be next?"

"What makes you think there'll be a next?"

"There's an old saying that these things come in threes. There'll be another—you mark my words."

"And you're worried that it might be you?"

"It might be any of us! Why not me? If this wasn't such a good story . . . If I hadn't promised my editor . . ."

His voice trailed away as he closed his eyes and slowly shook his head. No one else in the room said anything, so, trying to be reassuring, I said, "Colonel Race is investigating. And Mr. Chesterton is helping him. Between them, they'll solve the mystery."

Jones's eyes shot open, and he stared at me with a wild-eyed look that was quite alarming. "You may not believe in that 'curse of the pharaohs' stuff . . ."

"As it happens, I don't . . . ," I began, but Jones wasn't listening.

"Let me tell you something. We journalists get around a lot. We see a lot of strange things. There are forces at work here that frighten me, Flinders. And if you're not frightened, too, then you're a fool."

For a while no sounds emerged from Jones except for a low kind of moaning, then he asked, "Can a man get a cup of coffee around here? Or is there only miserable English tea?"

"Rami has some excellent Turkish coffee," I replied. "Go and ask her."

Jones managed to push himself to his feet and staggered off in the general direction of the kitchen.

"If you ask me," commented Wilding, from farther down the table, "that man's been hitting the bottle."

I hadn't asked Wilding, and didn't particularly want the man's opinion, but I felt compelled to make polite conversation with him.

"Well," I said, "journalists do have something of a professional reputation as hard drinkers."

"Mostly faked," said Billy Burton, who had risen early to help with the task of sorting, cleaning, and cataloguing all those antiquities from Menes's tomb that had been rushed into the storeroom as the storm approached.

"When I lived in New York, my boy," he continued, "I knew a reporter on the *New York World-Telegram*—knew him well, I say, I knew him like a brother. I tell you that man should have died from alcohol poisoning. His kidneys should have been pickled and his liver should have turned purple. At every social event in the city he was there with a glass of Kentucky rye whiskey in his hand. Turned out he never drank the stuff! Not a drop! Just nursed a glass all night long, I say, just held it in his hand, getting gossip for his paper as those around him got drunker and drunker. That's the truth about journalists, my boy, I say, that's the absolute truth, and you'd better believe it."

"I wasn't talking about journalists," persisted Wilding, "just our friend Mr. Elliot Jones. And to be in the state he's in this morning, he must have hit the bottle when he went back to his hut last night."

"Who's been hitting the bottle?" demanded Jones belligerently, as he staggered back from the kitchen nursing a mug of coffee carefully with both hands.

"No one. That's the whole point," I said quickly. "Dr. Burton here has just been defending the reputation of the entire journalistic profession."

"That's all right then," Jones muttered, as he lowered himself cautiously into a seat. He nodded toward Burton as he added, "Most gracious of you, sir."

"Not at all, son, I say, not at all," beamed Burton expansively. "To tell you the truth, when I was a wild, young lad, I was in the clutches of the demon drink myself. I was a slave, a slave I tell you, to alcohol. Of course, that was in years past. I took the pledge long ago, and today I am one of the leading lights in the Temperance Union of Chicago. I tell the whole fascinating story in my book *Saved from Darkness*—you ought to read it one day; you'd find it mighty instructive, son, I say mighty instructive."

There was a hiatus while Jones sipped his coffee noisily and the rest of us ate quietly. Then Wilding resumed, in his slightly mocking voice, "You seemed to be getting on very well with the lovely Amelia last night, Flinders, old chap."

"Miss Fell," I said with careful emphasis, "suffered a dangerous blow last night. It could have cost her life."

"But it didn't," Wilding went on with an impish grin. "Instead, it turned you into quite the little lifesaver. Should we cast a medal for him, do you think, Dr. Burton? Or possibly present him with a citation?"

"Save it, Wilding," I snapped. "It's time we were getting to work anyway."

I rose from the table looking around, automatically, for my battered old felt hat. Then I remembered that I'd left it in the tomb shaft at the height of the storm. At that moment Fell flung open the common room door, calling "Come on, you lot. There's work to be done and lost time to be made up for."

A gradual stirring around the breakfast table resulted in Wilding, Farnsleigh, Burrows, Burton, and me straggling out of the door to follow Fell up to the worksite. I had gone no more than five paces when a heavy hand was clapped on my shoulder.

"Hold on there, young Flinders—I want your assistance this morning."

It was Colonel Race, dressed in a clean uniform, looking fresh and chipper, like a man who'd never seen a sandstorm in his life.

"I'd help if I could, but Professor Fell . . . ," I protested.

"Never mind the professor; I've explained it to him. This is urgent."

"What is?"

"I've identified the place were Mamur Zapt is hiding, and I want your assistance to take him."

"How did you find out . . . ," I began.

"Very early, before the rest of you were up, I followed Rami Bahri. She led me to the place."

"Well, I don't see what I can do."

"Mamur Zapt is a dangerous man. To my certain knowledge he's killed four people. Two of them with his bare hands. I need a young man like yourself, preferably armed, to watch my back. Don't worry—I'll do the hard part."

Obviously, I was looking worried.

"You have a revolver?" Race continued.

I nodded. "In my hut."

"Run and fetch it. And some ammunition. I'll wait for you here."

"Are you sure the professor . . . ," I stuttered, looking for some way out of a dangerous assignment.

"Leave Professor Fell to me. You fetch your revolver."

It seemed I had little choice. I found the old service revolver my father had given me the day I left for Egypt. I kept it wrapped in a piece of linen on one of the rough plank shelves in my room. The linen had a fine layer of sand over it, but inside, the revolver was still clean and well oiled—no sand had got through into the mechanism.

Putting the revolver into one pocket and a box of cartridges into the other, I rejoined Race, who was waiting impatiently.

"This way," he said as he strode off in the direction of the cliffs that gleamed like old gold in the early light. "Zapt is a wily bird, and we'll need to be quick. No telling when he'll leave his present hiding place."

The gravel road we were walking on rose slowly, and as we drew closer to the temple area, I paused and turned to look back in the direction from which we had come. The sun was rising over the vast temple complex of Karnak, on the other side of the Nile. On the near side, and in a direct line between where we stood and Karnak, were the ruins of the Qurna temple of Amenhotep III. All that remained of the temple were the Memnon Colossi, huge seated statues, the northern-most of which, according to local superstition, was said to utter a cry at sunrise each morning.

"Come on," said Race impatiently.

With some reluctance I resumed the trek toward the western cliff face. As we approached Queen Hatshepsut's mortuary temple, we veered left, toward the ruins of the temple of Amun and Hathor, built by Tuthmosis III. This whole valley of *Deir el-Bahri*, I knew, was traditionally connected with the local cult of the cow goddess Hathor.

Climbing up the increasingly steep and rocky surface, Race led us still farther to the left, toward the mortuary temple of Mentuhotep. We walked up the broad ramp, or causeway, that led to the open, flat forecourt of Mentuhotep's temple.

In the eastern part of the forecourt, where we were standing, was the opening known as *Bab el-Hosan*. This was connected by a long underground passage to an unfinished royal tomb. To our right was the crumbling remains of the kiosk of Tuthmosis III, and directly ahead of us the colonnaded portico. Beyond that, at the western end of the forecourt, was another terrace with reliefs showing boat processions and hunting scenes. And beyond that again was the dominant feature of the temple, the mastaba—the above-ground superstructure that some archeologists believe later evolved into the pyramid. It was surrounded by a pillared walkway on all sides, featuring, in its west wall, the ruins of six statue shrines.

Standing in the temple forecourt so soon after sunrise, I was struck by the power of Ancient Egypt. These constructions were vast; the sheer willpower behind their building must have been monstrous. At that moment I understood how superstitious minds could believe this force of will able to reach down through the centuries and take revenge upon the violators of its tombs.

Despite the warmth of the early morning sun, I shivered. I have always thought of myself as an unimaginative chap, but just then I could picture the great power wielded by those temple-building pharaohs and the iron wills with which they commanded that their tombs be guarded for all eternity.

"Get a move on, Flinders," complained Race. "We're nearly there."

We climbed up to the western terrace and found ourselves facing the inner part of the temple, cut directly into the cliff. There were two small courts here, with the ruins of the columns that once surrounded them. In between the courts was the entrance to an underground passage. I was familiar with this edifice, having visited it shortly after arriving at *Deir el-Bahri* two months earlier. It was a typical royal tomb in construction and completely empty—having been looted many centuries earlier.

"You recognize this place?" asked Race in a whisper.

"Yes," I said, automatically dropping my voice into a whisper in response to his.

"You've been inside?"

"Some weeks ago—yes, I have."

"Good. I thought you probably had. This place of much interest to archeologists?"

"Not really. Completely empty. Was mapped by Naville in the 1890s. Look—what's going on?"

"He's a clever boy, is old Mamur Zapt."

"Meaning what, exactly?"

"That's where he is. In there." So saying, Race gestured toward the entrance to the underground passage. "He knew the safest place to hide around an archeological camp was an old tomb that had long since ceased to interest the archeologists."

I peered into the dark rocky entrance. This task was looking more unappealing every moment.

"Take off your boots," ordered Race.

I said nothing but gave him a quizzical look.

"From here on, our footsteps must be completely silent," he explained. Having removed his boots and set them to one side, he drew his revolver from its holster and spun the cylinder.

"Got your weapon?" he asked.

I nodded. Squatting down on the rock I pulled off my boots, then I pulled out the revolver and the box of ammunition and carefully loaded each of the six chambers.

"Single action or double action?" asked Race, nodding at the weapon I was loading.

"Single."

"Then cock the hammer before we enter the underground passage."

"I don't fancy firing a shot down there. I'll kill myself with a ricochet!"

"Zapt is dangerous! Have your revolver cocked and ready!"

I did as I was told, but once Race took the lead and stepped into the entrance to the underground passage, I quietly released the hammer. That made me feel much safer.

"We need a light," I whispered.

"Ssshh! He'd see a light. We'll move slowly and let our eyes adjust."

The narrow rock tunnel, I remembered, ran straight into the cliff for some 150 yards and then opened out into the tomb proper. The farther we advanced, the more the light behind us faded, while ahead was nothing but pitch darkness. And that darkness, I kept reminding myself, hid a man who had already killed four people—two of them with his bare hands.

Race crept forward very slowly. This had the dual benefit of reducing any sound we might make in that echoing shaft almost to zero and of giving our eyes time to adjust to the loss of light. As my eyes slowly adapted, I found that I could make out the walls of the shaft for a yard or two ahead.

Every few yards Race would come to a complete halt and listen intently for a minute or so and then resume his forward movement. Progress was painfully slow, and nerve wracking.

Most of my forward view was blocked by Race's back. The floor of the shaft under my socks was hard, cold, and damp. My mind started playing tricks on me—imagining I heard a sound, thinking of places I would rather be, out in the sunshine, anywhere but here.

The next time Race stopped, he crouched down, and I glanced over his shoulder at the passage ahead. For a moment I thought I saw a dim movement, but I wasn't certain. Race crept forward, slowly and silently, another yard, and then another. Then, suddenly, he was gone! An arm reached out of the darkness, seized his uniform, and with a loud grunt of effort pulled him into the blackness.

I was alone. Straining my eyes, I looked desperately for some movement, some indication of what was ahead. Straining my ears, I struggled to hear what was happening.

"Colonel?" I called. My voice echoed through the hollow chambers of the mountain.

"I have him," said a heavily accented, guttural voice. Two figures shuffled forward into my dim line of vision. The colonel was struggling to breathe, with an arm around his throat and a hand holding a revolver to his temple.

"Shoot, Flinders! Damn you, shoot!" gasped Race.

"You shoot, your friend dies," said the voice. My single-action revolver was not cocked; I could not have got a shot off quickly enough. I knew I was beaten.

"Throw down your gun!" commanded the voice.

With a clatter my revolver landed on the stone floor of the shaft. A leg shot out from behind the colonel and kicked the revolver out of reach. I still couldn't see the face of our adversary, the mysterious and murderous Mamur Zapt.

"Turn around," was the next guttural command, "and place your hands against the wall."

I did as I was told. *Am I about to be killed?* I wondered. The question entered my head in a surprisingly calm way. I seemed to be looking at the possibility of my own death with the dispassionate detachment of an outsider.

"You English—I despise you." I wanted to tell him I was Australian, not English, but I thought it prudent not to interrupt. Besides which, nationality seems to diminish in importance as one faces the possibility of imminent death.

"You cannot deny us our Egypt for much longer," he growled. "We have been ruled by too many foreigners. Yesterday, the French; today, the English—tomorrow, the Egyptians! We shall rule ourselves! Egypt shall return to its ancient glory, and you feeble English shall not stop us!"

This impassioned speech was the last thing I heard for some time. It felt as though the back of my head had exploded; there was sharp pain, a shower of fireworks in my brain, a ringing sound, and then—nothing.

When I came to, my head was throbbing. It felt as though there was a mule inside my skull, kicking impatiently to be released. And each kick was a sharp stab of pain. I tried to feel my head and discovered that my hands were tied behind my back. The mule kicked again, and I groaned out loud, but no sound emerged. Then I realized that I was also gagged.

I tried to move into a more comfortable position but discovered, as I now expected I would, that my ankles were firmly lashed together. I managed to squirm into a more comfortable, and slightly more upright, position. I blinked and looked around me. In the dim light I could make out Colonel Race, propped against the shaft wall opposite, similarly bound and gagged. His eyes were open, staring at me. I tried blinking to indicate that I was all right, but any form of communication was impossible.

My first reaction was to feel angry, and my second to feel stupid. The brawl between the Egyptian nationalists and the British protectorate government was none of my business—why did I have to be dragged into it? And I was especially angry with the crafty, powerfully built man who had attacked, bound, and gagged us. At that moment I felt like administering some swift and painful punishment to him. Leaving us here, trussed up like Christmas turkeys. It was so . . . so . . . uncivilized!

Then a sense of my own foolishness overwhelmed the anger. It was my own stupid fault for allowing the colonel to talk me into this in the first place. And in the second place, if I had had my revolver cocked and ready to fire, as instructed, then perhaps the attack would not have succeeded. I looked into Colonel's Race eyes. Was that a look of reproof I could see? Was he blaming me for our predicament? I supposed he must be. After all, he had brought me along to "watch his back"—which I had singularly failed to do.

Then I started to worry about when we would be found. This old tomb shaft was never visited by the archeologists in our party. Was it ever visited by anyone? Surely not, that's why Mamur Zapt chose it as his hiding place. That being so, it could be days, or weeks, before we were found. Might we starve to death before they found us?

No, of course not, I reassured myself. We would be missed. Search parties would be sent out. Someone would think of looking in this old tomb. And we would be found. There was nothing for it but to be patient.

How long we lay there, I do not know. But it was not for days and not even for hours. The first sign of our rescue was the disappearance of the light. The dim light around us vanished, as if the entrance to the underground passage had been blocked. Then there were noises: the stamp of boots and a wheezy breathing, as if an asthmatic elephant were stumping toward us.

The wheezing and stumping grew louder and finally revealed itself as—Chesterton! He loomed over us, filling the shaft to the bursting point.

"Hmmph! I thought I'd find you two here," he wheezed. "At least, I hoped I would."

How on earth could he have expected that? I wondered.

"Turn around," he ordered, producing from his pocket as he said this, a Scout knife. A moment later I could feel my hands being cut free and then my gag released.

"Ah, thanks for that," I gasped, my head pounding again with the effort of speech. "I thought we'd be here for days before anyone found us."

"If you thought that, you must take us all for nincompoops!" growled Chesterton as he released Colonel Race. "If you wish your location to be a secret, you should not leave your boots lying at the entrance."

"Thank you, sir," said the colonel as his gag came out. "What time is it? Does that man have much of a lead on us?"

"You can forget about chasing your convict now, my dear Race. I should imagine he is well clear by this time. It is almost the middle of the morning, and, unless I am much mistaken, your encounter took place an hour or two ago, at the very least."

So, I had been unconscious a good while. I felt the back of my head. It was very tender, and sticky with dried blood.

Chesterton reached out a large hand and helped me to my feet.

"Why did you come looking?" asked Race.

"My original intention was to watch Fell and his team at work. But when you two were noticeable by your absence, I inquired after you. Fell gave me to understand that you had both set out on an adventure of your own—and not returned. I thought it advisable to take up my stout walking stick and go for a stroll. By sheer good fortune—or possibly the hand of God—I came upon the subtle clue of two pairs of boots, pointing me as clearly as a street sign in the direction of their owners. Come along—back to the camp, where the tender ministrations of Mrs. Poole shall be applied to your wounds."

With muscles still cramped and aching, Race and I moved slowly as we followed Chesterton's massive bulk down the passage toward fresh air and sunlight. I had never seen a man who looked so entirely out of place. In that narrow stone passage Chesterton looked like a model ship that had, somehow, been jammed tightly into a glass bottle.

Outside, we both sat down on the rock and pulled our boots on.

"My revolver!" I said, suddenly remembering it.

"Gone, I'm afraid," said Race. "The rebels keep any weapons that fall into their hands."

"My father will give me curry about that when I get back to Sydney," I said. "It was his old Army revolver."

"I apologize, young Flinders," muttered Race. "I shouldn't have dragged you into this. It was never your affair, and I shouldn't have exposed you to that risk. I'm just glad that we're both still alive. But," he continued as he rubbed his chin, "this won't look good in my report."

"It's I who should apologize," I insisted. "I was supposed to watch your back, and I let you down entirely. If only I had taken your advice and had my revolver cocked and ready to fire, the outcome might have been different. Sorry about that."

"If you two have quite finished apologizing and groveling to each other—a perfectly sickening display for an outsider, I do assure you—then Mrs. Poole and her first-aid kit await. Let us be off."

"These blasted rebels," said Colonel Race as we walked, "are getting entirely out of control. We need to deal with them with a much firmer hand; squash the movement once and for all."

"You may succeed in squashing it once," responded Chesterton, wheezing as he walked, "but you'll never squash it for all."

"What do you mean?"

"I mean that democracy is part of the human spirit and is likely to break out like measles—just when least expected."

"Can you imagine the sort of government Mamur Zapt, and men of his ilk, would provide for their people? It would not be good government. What we provide is far better for them. That's what matters. Not who elects the government, but how well the government is run."

"Nonsense!" exploded Chesterton with a loud laugh. "Utter nonsense! Government, my dear Colonel, is like blowing one's nose or choosing one's wife. What matters is not how well it is done, but that one does it for oneself."

To avoid an argument between those two, I changed the subject: "Colonel, could Mamur Zapt have anything to do with Dr. Lamb's murder?"

"Possible, I suppose. What are you suggesting?"

"Well, if Dr. Lamb had stumbled across his presence—could he have killed him to silence him?"

"Zapt and his kind are cutthroats. His history of violence suggests that he would be more than ready to kill for his own security."

"Meaning that Mamur Zapt has what nobody else appears to have in the Lamb murder case—a motive."

"A possible motive," corrected Race, "on the assumption that the doctor had discovered Zapt's whereabouts."

"However," wheezed Chesterton heavily, "as much as I hate being the fly in your ointment, young sir, if the political zealot was the murderer, why did he kill Lamb where and how he was killed? Why kill him at exactly that place where the entire expedition was concentrating its work? Would it not have made more sense to commit the murder and hide the body as far away from the rest of the party as possible?"

Of course it would have, so I was unable to reply to Chesterton's question. Another good theory up in smoke.

Our rescuer lodged Race and me in the common room then went in search of Mrs. Poole. She couldn't have been far away, for, within a few minutes, she was at our side, examining our wounds and clucking sympathetically.

"This may hurt a little," she said, "but I have to try to find out how much damage has been done."

"Ow! It hurts like blue blazes when you press on my skull like that!" I complained.

"Hmm . . . It's a nasty blow. But neither of you seems to have a broken skull. Of course, you really should have an X-ray. Colonel, would a doctor in Luxor be able to arrange for an X-ray?"

"Only by sending us to Cairo."

"That's the nearest?"

"None closer, I'm afraid."

"At least I can clean the wounds."

"And please give me something for the headache," I said. "It feels like it's splitting my head open."

Ten minutes later our wounds were cleaned and treated with antiseptic, and I had washed down several aspirins.

"And now you two should both lie down and rest until lunchtime."

"Too much to do, Mrs. P., much too much," said Race, snatching up his pith helmet. "I'm off to talk to some of the Egyptian workmen. I may be able to get a line on where Zapt is likely to have gone from here." These last words were spoken as he was stepping out through the door.

"You'll be more sensible, I hope," said the canon's wife, fixing me with a gimlet eye.

"I'd really rather do something than just sit around," I protested. "I'll walk up to the work site—just a slow stroll, I promise you—and see if there's some light work I can do."

"If you refuse to see sense, I can't make you," she responded, packing away her first-aid kit.

I stepped out into the blazing, scorching sun of the late morning. The heat made me remember my missing hat. At a steady pace, I walked toward Queen Hatshepsut's temple and up the broad ramps to the top terrace. There I found most of the expedition members at work at several trestle tables, on which antiquities from the tomb were spread out.

Fell, Narracourt, Burton, and Poole were taking items out of the boxes into which they had been hastily packed as the sandstorm approached. These were being properly cleaned and catalogued and repacked carefully for transportation. Amelia and Frances Chesterton were helping with the cleaning, and even our artist and our photographer, Farnsleigh and Burrows, had been roped into the work.

"At last," Fell grunted with satisfaction, "you've given up gallivanting around with the colonel. Did you catch your man, by the way?"

"He caught us, I'm afraid."

"What on earth do you mean?"

"He knocked us out, tied us up, and escaped."

"Oh!" cried Amelia, "Are you all right? You haven't been hurt, have you?"

"I'm fine," I replied, delighted by her concern and determined to ignore the renewed pounding in my head brought on by the sun. "I'll just rescue my old hat from the tomb shaft and give you a hand."

Inside the entrance to Menes's shaft tomb I found a drift of sand two feet deep. Beyond it, covered by only a few inches of sand, was my battered old felt hat. I shook it clean, clapped it on my head, and stepped back out into the sunlight.

Thus protected from the heat and glare, I walked back to Fell and reported for work.

"Why don't you work with Amelia on the pottery table?" he suggested.

So for the next hour or so Amelia and I worked happily side by side. For some time we talked about nothing but Ancient Egyptian pottery, but, somehow, running through the conversation was the feeling of a link, the sense that we belonged side by side, together, just as we were at that moment. At times, as we passed the pottery pieces across the table, our hands brushed, and there was an electricity between us. I was certain Amelia could feel it too.

"Philip," she said, quietly and hesitantly, after a lull in the conversation.

"Yes?"

"I have decided there should be no secrets between us."

"I agree. And I assure you that I have no secrets from you, Amelia."

"But I have been keeping a secret from you."

I didn't say anything, but my face must have looked astonished. What deep secret could Amelia possibly have?

"Several times when you have come upon me I have had to quickly hide a book I was reading or a notebook I was writing in to keep my secret."

"Ah, yes. I have noticed that. So, what is the secret?"

"Well. It's a little embarrassing to admit it, but the truth is . . . that I am extremely fond of romantic novels."

"Romantic novels?"

"Yes. Rosie M. Banks and Leila J. Pinckney are my favorite writers."

"Is that it? Is that all? Why keep that a secret?"

"Well, you are a university graduate, Philip, and I was afraid you would think less of me if you discovered me reading a novel such as *The Love Which Prevails.*"

"Foolish girl," I said with an affectionate chuckle, "of course I wouldn't think less of you."

"I discovered that Mrs. Poole shares my enthusiasm for romantic literature."

"Ah, those are the private conversations that I interrupted."

"Precisely."

"So, that's your secret, is it? Well, if that's all?"

"That's not quite all, Philip."

"What else is there?"

"I have begun to write a romantic novel. I have ambitions—they probably seem to you to be foolish, childish ambitions—to one day see my name in print as a romantic writer."

"Amelia, my dear. Anything you are ambitious to do, I encourage you to do. I support you in your plans. I think it is a fine and noble ambition and not something to be embarrassed about at all."

"Oh, Philip. You are so understanding."

I would have happily stayed there working by Amelia's side and talking to her all day, but we had to stop when Fell called the lunch break.

As we worked, an intention slowly formed itself in my mind. Then, as we strolled back down to the campsite for lunch, the intention firmed into a resolve. I would do it, I decided; I would definitely do it. And I would do it now. No point in waiting for some romantic, moonlight moment—I would simply lose my nerve. No, I was determined that the moment had come.

Back at my hut, I stripped off my shirt and washed; then I put on a clean shirt and combed my hair. Three times I dropped the comb. I was very nervous; I had never done this before, and, if Amelia said no, I was sure I would never have the nerve to do it again. In my sea chest I had a bottle of medicinal brandy. Should I take a sip to steady my nerves? No, she might smell it on my breath. I stood in front of the mirror and combed my hair again, then took a deep breath and said to myself, "Now or never."

Thus prepared, I slowly walked in the direction of the expedition house. If Amelia emerged with her father, or with anyone else for that matter, my plans would have to be put on hold. However, if she emerged on her own, then . . .

I waited no more than three minutes, and then the door opened, and Amelia emerged. She was alone.

"May I walk you to lunch, Amelia?" I asked.

"I should be delighted if you would, Philip," she replied.

So saying, she placed her arm through mine.

Thus encouraged, I seized the moment and said what I most wanted to say.

"Amelia. There is something I want to ask you."

She stopped and turned toward me. "Yes?" she said.

"The fact is . . . look, I've been bottling this up . . . and I can't bear to wait any longer . . . what I want to ask is . . . Will you marry me?"

"Will I . . . ?" Amelia was startled by my proposal.

"I love you, Amelia. More than anything else in the world I want to marry you." Nerves made my voice hesitant and husky. I reached out and clasped her hand and found it to be trembling. "I want us to be together for the rest of our lives," I said urgently. "Will you marry me, Amelia?"

For a few moments several competing emotions crossed her face. After the initial surprise her eyes became warm and her lips began to smile, then a change came, like a cloud passing across the face of the sun. Her expression hardened, and she replied, "No. No, I'm sorry Philip, for I don't wish to hurt you. But no—I shall not marry you."

"Why?" I blurted out before I could stop myself. "Perhaps this is the wrong time. This is not a very romantic moment, I realize that. Or? You're not in love with Wilding are you?"

"Wilding? That swine? Of course not!"

"Then . . . ? Then . . . ?"

Amelia took my hand and speaking softly said, "If I were ever to marry anyone, it would be you, dear Philip. But I shall never marry."

"Never?"

"Marriage is a farce and a fraud, and I shall live and die a spinster. I shall never marry!"

With that, she turned on her heel and marched off toward the common room. I stayed where I was, lost, bewildered. I stood in that scorching sun, unmoving, trying to make sense of what I had just heard.

"Don't just stand there, old chap," Nat Burrows said, slapping me heartily on the shoulder as he walked past, "Lunch awaits." I fell into step beside him, and we walked to the common room together.

"Now, Flinders, you've been hanging around with Race and Chesterton rather a lot,' chatted Burrows, "so you must have some idea of how their investigation is going. Are they getting anywhere? I mean to say, this is a dashed mysterious business. How did Lamb get inside the sarcophagus of Menes, inside a burial chamber, hundreds of feet underground? Dashed mysterious. 'Curse of the pharaohs' and all that sort of stuff. So, do they have any clues?"

"Clues?" I replied in a daze, "No. Well, honestly I don't really know. But they don't seem any closer to explaining the inexplicable."

Neither was I. How could I explain the inexplicable behavior of Amelia?

Once the expedition party was gathered around the long trestle table in the common room, Fell asked Canon Poole to give thanks for the meal, which he did. Then I discovered what was troubling Amelia.

"Ahem!" Fell cleared his throat to attract our attention. "I have an announcement to make. I shall now explain to all of you what has happened so that there is no need for gossip or innuendo. And after I have explained, I would appreciate it if there was no more discussion of this matter, for the sake of myself and my daughter. In other words, I would ask you to consider our feelings and say nothing about this, either to us, or to each other."

About what? What on earth was he babbling about?

"The fact is," Fell continued, "that my wife, Elspeth—Amelia's stepmother—has left. That is to say, she has left me. Left us. When I arrived back from the dig, I found a note waiting for me at the house. And, upon inquiry, I discovered that she had been seen to depart an hour or so ago, in a pony cart, with Mr. Wilding. So that's it then. Elspeth has, ah, run off, with, ah, Wilding. This is, of course, sad news. Divorce and all that. End of a marriage. Bound to be some scandal. But what can't be cured must be endured. So, that's the end of the matter. And I ask that there be no further discussion. Thank you. Enjoy your lunch."

Fell's face was bright red as he spoke, whether with anger or embar-rassment I couldn't tell. After he finished, there was a stunned silence. Farouk and his sons served the food in silence.

Elspeth and Wilding? I'd never guessed! Then all those times I thought he was interested in Amelia, it was really . . . I felt extremely foolish and dull and blockheaded. And how awful for Amelia. I had proposed to her just after she had heard of her father's second marriage breaking up. No wonder she said the things she did about the institu-tion of marriage. Perhaps, after she calmed down . . . ? Perhaps, there would be a time when I could ask her again?

"By the way," said Fell again, after several minutes of heavy silence, "I've decided that I'm fed up with having a journalist hanging around the dig. Jones, you are to pack your things and clear out straight after lunch."

Jones glared daggers at Fell, but nothing more was said. It didn't need to be. The tension at that table was now thick enough to cut with a knife. Rami may have prepared a nice meal for that lunch, I will never know, for I didn't taste a mouthful of it. We all ate like machines, unaware of what we were eating, not sure where we could look without feeling uncomfortable. We needed some conversation, something to divert our attention from the scandal of Fell's marriage. But no one seemed to want to start.

"Are you satisfied with the way the cataloguing is proceeding, Pro-fessor?" said the Rev. Dr. Billy Burton finally.

"Cataloguing? Ah, yes. Yes, quite satisfied. It's all going very well."

"Excellent! Excellent!" enthused Burton. "How long until it's complete?"

"Complete? Well, perhaps, a week or so."

"Excellent! Excellent! That is particularly good timing. For I shall have to leave in a week's time."

"Leave?" I asked, "Where are you going, Dr. Burton?"

"First to London, my boy, to the thriving metropolis, I say, of London. There I shall deliver my famous and popular lecture entitled 'The Bible as History.' Upon completion of which, I shall sail for the United States where I have a lecture tour, a nationwide lecture tour, due to commence in a little over eight weeks."

"Tell me about the lecture," I prompted, not really caring what Burton spouted to the waiting masses but concerned that lunch not lapse back into frigid silence.

"You'd like to know what I lecture on, my boy? Then you shall, you shall indeed. In my talk, illustrated with hand-colored lantern slides, I demonstrate that archeology proves the Bible to be historically accurate—I say accurate down to the smallest detail."

"But can you? I mean is it?"

"Of course I can! And yes, yes my boy, it is—absolutely."

No one else seemed inclined to take up the conversational cudgels, so I soldiered on.

"What sort of evidence do you produce?" I asked.

"Evidence? Why I produce more evidence than you could carry in a bag, that's what."

"Such as . . . ?"

"Such as the Hittites—to give you a 'for instance.'"

"The Hittites?"

"That's what I said, I said the Hittites."

"Who are the Hittites?"

"Not 'who are,' but 'who were'—ah, the ignorance of the younger generation. Beggin' your pardon, my boy, no offense intended. The Hittites are a group of people mentioned in the Bible, in the Old Testament to be precise. But until a few years ago no one had found any trace or sign of the Hittites—except in the Bible, of course. Now, you can imagine what that led the enemies of the Bible to say, can't you? You can imagine, can't you, my boy?"

"I imagine they said the Bible wasn't true, because there was no evidence of the Hittites. If they really existed, someone else would have written about them, or archeologists would have dug up their remains."

"Exactly! Exactly! That's just exactly what those folk said. And now they've got egg on their faces. Because just thirteen years ago—in 1906 to be precise—a German named Hugo Winckler was digging in Turkey, and he found the ruins of the city that was the Hittite capital. There it was, about a hundred miles east of Ankara, the buried ruins of the Hittite city of Hattusa. What do you think of them chickens, eh?"

"Very impressive."

"You said it, my boy, you said it. And that's not all, not by a long shot. Right here in Egypt, clay tablets have been found recording a battle between Ramses II and the Hittites in 1287 B.C. Ramses was even captured by them for a while. He was rescued when the Egyptians won the final battle. You can find the victory inscription across the river at Karnak. The archeological evidence proves the Bible is right, and has been right all along, and the doubters are completely wrong."

At this point Billy Burton leaned back in his chair and hooked his thumbs in his braces. It was clear that he now had up a head of steam.

"Are you familiar with Genesis chapter 40, I say chapter 40, my boy?"

"Genesis chapter 40? No, I can't say that I am."

"There you will find the story of pharaoh's chief steward and the grapevine."

"So?"

"So, the doubters said the story wasn't true because grapes never grew in Egypt. But . . . ," he said, wagging an admonitory finger at me, "but—just across the river from here at Luxor, in the ruins of ancient Thebes, archeologists found a temple painting depicting Egyptians picking grapes and making wine! So much for the doubters, eh boy?"

"Indeed, Dr. Burton."

"Well may you say 'indeed,' my boy. For the evidence is there, indeed—evidence that the people, places, and events described in the Bible are real people, real places, and real events."

"I"m sure it's a very entertaining lecture," I muttered.

"Don't sound so patronizing, my boy. It's your profession that is the star of my lectures."

"My profession?"

"Archeology, young sir, don't be dense! I'll give you another 'for instance.' Take the case of that great and distinguished archeologist, Sir William Ramsay. I take it you've heard of him?"

"Sir William Ramsay," I replied, closing my eyes to concentrate, "born Glasgow 1851, contributed much original work in the field of classical archeology. His book *The Historical Geography of Asia Minor* was a set text in my university course."

"And so it should be. A great book. Well, back when he was plain William Ramsay—probably just 'Bill' to his friends—he set out to prove the Bible was wrong. In particular he set his sights on the book of Acts, in the New Testament. He reckoned it was not written by

Luke, the Greek doctor, as an accurate historical record—but by someone else a hundred years later."

"So what did he do about it?"

"Do about it? He had the sense, my boy, the good sense not to push his prejudices, but to go and investigate. Back in 1880 he made his first journey to the places described in Acts. He spent years traveling and digging and studying ancient writings. He felt sure he could prove Acts to be full of errors."

"And?"

"And he was wrong. The more he investigated, the more he found Acts was not full of mistakes, after all. He was most impressed with how the writer got those small, seemingly unimportant details exactly right. That, he claimed, was the mark of a writer who knows what he is talking about and is careful to be correct and accurate in his account. Have you read his other great book?"

"Which book?"

"Which book! The book he called *St. Paul the Traveller and the Roman Citizen.* Just one of many excellent books Sir William Ramsay has written on how accurate and reliable the New Testament is. In one of those books he announced that he had become a Christian."

Burton looked at me for a moment and then added his punch line, "One of your own, my boy—an archeologist. And the story of Sir William Ramsay is one more reason we can have confidence that the Bible is true."

By the time Burton finally started running out of steam we were finished with lunch and down to the tea and coffee.

People began to leave the table and mill around, carrying their mugs with them. Amelia drifted in my direction, and then, when no one else was close, she said quietly, "Thank you for that."

"For what?"

"I could see what you were doing at lunch. Getting Dr. Burton talking to cover up father's embarrassment. I appreciate it."

"Well," I muttered, "it just seemed . . . well, you know . . ."

"Yes, I do know. And thank you."

For a moment we sipped our tea in silence.

"About this afternoon," I began, "before lunch. Perhaps I asked at a bad time. Perhaps if we talked about it again, at some other time . . ."

"No! I'm sorry, Philip, truly I am. But my mind is made up."

There was a tense and awkward silence between us for a moment, and then she said, "I think I should go now."

And before I could respond, she turned and slipped quickly out the door. Through the common room window I could see her walking briskly across the compound toward the expedition house, head held high. If she had been downcast that would have made me feel better. But seeing her face lifted up, her lips grim, her chin resolute, my spirits sank.

I felt hopeless, and yet, something inside told me I must not give up on Amelia. I could make her happy, I knew that, if only she would give me a chance. My confused and whirling thoughts were interrupted by the sound of banging.

I looked around and saw Elliot Jones thumping an enamel mug on the trestle table. In his other hand he clutched an almost empty brandy bottle.

"Attention! I want everyone's attention!" he slurred loudly. "I have an important announcement to make. In fact, a couple of announcements."

He was speaking loudly and slowly, enunciating each word with the deliberate care of a man who knows he is drunk. Every face in the room turned in his direction.

"You all listening to me now? Good. Since I am being kicked out of this miserable sand trap, I have a few home truths I want to share with everyone. Everyone. The whole lot of you."

He swung the hand carrying the brandy bottle in a wide arc as he spoke. For a moment I feared the bottle would go flying out of his hand and cause someone an injury. But the gesture threw Jones off balance, and he collapsed into a chair.

"You all paying attention?" he asked again, "Good. Because you lot are so pretentious."

He had to try saying the word "pretentious" several times before he got it out.

"So very pretentious. But I know a secret or two about you lot. Or about some of you, anyway."

"Mr. Jones, you are drunk," snapped Madeleine Sutton.

"I know I am drunk. I know that. But that doesn't make any difference. I am going to announce to everyone—to the whole world—what I know about some of you people."

"Won't someone do something about this . . . this . . . wretch!" cried the exasperated Miss Sutton.

John Farnsleigh and Nat Burrows started toward Jones.

"Burrows," slurred the journalist, "you're one of the people I want to talk about. I know what you've been up to."

"You don't know what you're talking about," muttered Burrows sternly, as he and Farnsleigh grabbed Jones by the arms and began propelling him toward the door. Jones resisted, digging in his heels and grabbing the furniture.

"You all think," shouted the drunk, addressing the whole room, "you all think that Burrows here is a fine fellow and a fine photographer. But let me tell you—he has broken his contract with the expedition. Yes, he has. He has been selling photographs of the dig. Against dear old Fell's explicit" (he had difficulty with this word) "explicit instructions. I know. 'Cause he sold some of them to me."

Jones became a dead weight in the hands of Burrows and Farnsleigh, and the two were finding him difficult to move.

"Pay no attention to him," grunted Burrows as he tried to get a better grip on the journalist's limp arms.

"That's right," slurred Jones, "just ignore me. It's the truth all the same. This pretentious Burrows has been taking photographs for you lot and then selling them to my lot. To me and Page and any other journalist who'd slip him a few quid. Copyright photographs. Pictures that belong to the expedition. And I tell you this for free—he's made a bit out of it too. He'll leave this dig a lot richer than when he arrived here."

"Don't believe him," said Burrows again, heaving Jones to his feet.

"If you don't believe me," shouted Jones as he was frog-marched to the door by Burrows and Farnsleigh, "just look at the next edition of *The Illustrated London News*. At least I think it's the next one. Maybe the one after. When it arrives from London, you'll see the pictures in print. Then you'll believe me."

By now the trio had reached the doorway, and there Jones grabbed the door frame and held on.

"I'm telling you the truth," he shouted pathetically, "and I could tell you more too. About dear old Fell, for instance . . ."

At that point Burrows gave him a mighty shove and sent him sprawling on the sand and gravel of the compound.

"Clear off," said Farnsleigh firmly. "No one wants to hear your drunken ramblings. Get your belongings and get right out of the camp."

Jones staggered to his feet, opened his mouth as if to say something, then apparently decided not to bother. He shrugged his shoulders and staggered off in the direction of his hut.

An embarrassed-looking Burrows looked back toward the assembled group.

"It's all lies, you know," he stuttered, as he wiped his forehead with a large red handkerchief, "all lies. All I care about is the quality of my work. I'm only here because it's a good place to take interesting photographs."

I, and probably the others as well, just wished he would stop protesting. But Burrows seemed unable to stop himself—the words just kept rattling out.

"That's all I care about—taking quality photographs in interesting places. My photographs have been exhibited, you know, in leading galleries. I have taken pictures of the most interesting places in the world—the Eiffel Tower on a foggy day, the Taj Mahal in brilliant sunlight, a thunderstorm swirling around the peak of the Matterhorn, Sydney harbor at sunset as the lantern-lit ferries come in to Circular Quay, giant waves breaking on the coast of Iceland, Moscow under a blanket of snow—I've photographed them all. And that's all I care about."

His voice faded away as the babble trickled into silence. Then he seemed to realize that he had protested too much. Looking flustered and embarrassed, he walked into the kitchen, where we could hear him asking, too loudly, for a fresh pot of tea.

For a moment there was an embarrassed silence, then the group in the common room resumed their seats and their quiet conversations. I found myself facing Billy Burton and Sir Edward Narracourt.

"Could that be true?" I asked in a semi-whisper. "What Jones said about Burrows selling photographs to the press, could it be true?"

"Well," replied Narracourt, scratching his chin, "it has happened before, at other digs. The photographs are supposed to be the property of the expedition, but if the photographer is on salary rather than being one of the archeological team, well, he can succumb to the offer of money."

"Yes, I've known it to happen," agreed Burton. "I say, and I say it sadly, my boy, that I've known it to happen in the past. Human nature, you know, my boy—a weak and corrupt thing is human nature."

Narracourt and Burton then started reminiscing about other digs they had been on and nefarious activities that had occurred at various sites. As they spoke, my mind drifted back to arguments I had seen, or partly overheard, between Burrows and the two journalists, and I had a strong feeling that Jones had told the truth. That being so, what was he about to tell us about Professor Fell? What secret could Fell possibly be hiding?

Thinking about the professor led me quickly to thinking once again about his lovely daughter. Before Jones's outburst I was steadying my nerves to try again to talk to Amelia, but now I just felt defeated. She didn't want me; that was the truth. It was a horrible truth. The worst truth in the world. But I had to face it: she just didn't want me.

Narracourt and Burton drifted away, leaving me in my silent, solitary gloom.

For some minutes I sat on a wooden bench, staring at my boots, wallowing in self-pity. I was awakened from my depressing thoughts by the bellowing voice of Chesterton.

"Archons of Athens! What's this I see? A fit young man, in the prime of life, sitting idle, with sorrow written upon every feature?"

I opened my mouth to respond, but before I could speak, Chesterton leaned over me and hissed in a conspiratorial whisper, "The game's afoot, Flinders! Will you join me, as my able, unimaginative assistant?"

"Yes, of course, but where . . . ?"

"Follow me."

As Chesterton turned to stride off, I leaped to my feet to follow him. To my astonishment he led me in the direction of the kitchen. Halting at the kitchen door, he turned and said (in what he probably imagined was a whisper), "I've heard of the little fracas that you witnessed between Hoffman and Farouk. I believe it should be inquired into. It's time the little matter of the disappearing artifacts was cleared up."

So saying, he pushed open the kitchen door and made that small room appear to shrink by inserting his enormous bulk into it. Farouk and Rami were standing at a bench: she was chopping vegetables, and he was watching her and keeping up a rapid flow of conversation in Arabic. This stopped abruptly when we entered the room.

"Farouk," I said, "Mr. Chesterton here would like to ask you a few questions about that incident the other day."

"Beg pardon?" responded our head man, a puzzled look on his face.

"I mean Mr. Hoffman's accusation that you had been stealing artifacts."

"That is all over. Finish," said Farouk, with a dramatic sweep of his hand. "I not talk about it anymore."

"But we need to talk about it, my dear fella," boomed Chesterton, grinning hideously in an attempt to look friendly.

"No. Not talk. Over. Finish."

"But since you didn't take the artifacts . . . ," I began.

"I not take," interrupted Farouk. "Professor say I not take."

"Precisely," I continued, "but if you didn't, then who did?"

"Eh?" responded Farouk, his eyebrows shooting up.

"We need your help, you see," said Chesterton. "We need to get these side issues out of the way, so that we can know whether they had anything to do with the murder or not. And you can help us. Young Flinders and I both believe you when you protest your innocence of the thefts. But who then is the thief?"

"Ah, well," Farouk shrugged his shoulders, "Allah knows, but Farouk does not."

"But you do know something that would help," insisted Chesterton, stabbing the air with his stubby finger.

"No. I know nothing!"

"Now hang on. Just go back a step," Chesterton said. "When Flinders here found you and Hoffman fighting, you said that you had found that small statuette and that you were returning it."

"That true. I find it."

"Then show us where," Chesterton snapped, leaning forward and towering like a mountain over our head man. "Show us where."

"Easy. Come with me. I show you."

Farouk then led the way back through the common room and out into the blazing, white light and oven-like heat of the compound. He turned left at the end of the common room building and led us down the flat area of gravelly sand behind the row of identical huts occupied by the single men.

"Here," said Farouk, coming to a halt behind one of the huts. "I found small, black statue in sand here."

"How did you find it?" demanded Chesterton. "Were you looking for it?"

"No. No. Not looking. One of the camp dogs was digging here in sand. I chase away dog. Then I notice what had been dug up."

"And then you tried to return it because you feared that your wife's brother—that Mamur Zapt fella—had stolen it. Am I right?"

Farouk just grinned and shrugged. Clearly Chesterton was right.

"Very good," muttered Chesterton. Then he turned to me and asked, "Whose hut is this?"

But before I could reply he held up his hand and said, "No, don't tell me. Let me tell you. This is—or, rather, was—Hoffman's hut."

"Yes, quite right. But what does it mean?"

"It means, Mr. Flinders, that Hoffman was the thief."

"Ambrose Hoffman?"

"Indeed. It was he who was stealing the smaller artifacts and selling them to the market dealers."

"But why?"

"He needed the money. Remember when you and Race went through his papers you found a letter from his banker demanding money owed on a mortgage. Poor Hoffman was desperate to make the payments, and he had a key to the storage hut where the artifacts were kept. He knew there was always some 'wastage,' and he thought the natives would be blamed for any disappearances. So he stole some of the smaller, more valuable items and traded them for cash, which, I presume, he sent back to his wife to make the mortgage payments."

"But, how did you know . . . ," I began, and then I ran out of words.

"His behavior, of course. Awful suspicious, attacking Farouk like that. Accusing a trusted head man of theft. Particularly when the piece Farouk was returning had been missing for a week. Hoffman was too intelligent to make that sort of mistake. So it wasn't a mistake. He was deliberately trying to throw suspicion away from himself. I think the murder had spooked him, and he was worried that everything would be carefully investigated and his thefts discovered."

"Why did he run away?" I asked.

"Same fear," muttered Chesterton, his head bowed as he scratched in the sand with his walking stick, all three of his chins wobbling as he spoke. "Fear kills logic. Hoffman would have had a small hoard of stolen treasures buried, or hidden, somewhere near this hut. Fearing discovery, he decided to take his hoard and flee under the cover of the *khamsin*. Foolish, suicidal thing to do."

"Farouk," I said, turning to our head man, "would he have gotten far?"

"Who do you mean, *effendi*?"

"Hoffman. If he decided to run away during the *khamsin*—would he have got far? Which way would he have gone?"

"Ah. Up ridge, toward Nile. He would have gone that way."

"And would he have got far?"

"Not far, *effendi*."

"Let's take a look, shall we?" proposed Chesterton.

Farouk led the way up the rocky slope behind the huts. Chesterton followed, leaning heavily on his crutch-headed walking stick. I followed behind.

We made slow progress. Farouk had to keep stopping and waiting for Chesterton to catch up.

Finally, we reached the top of the ridge looking down toward a small, palm-fringed oasis. Here, too, the *khamsin* had left signs of its progress. Heaped against the base of each tree was a deep drift of sand, while the pool of water itself, which seemed to have shrunk in size, was surrounded by low, long sand drifts.

Chesterton stopped and wiped his flushed red face with a spotted handkerchief, then waved Farouk on.

It was easier walking on the other side of the ridge, and it was downhill.

As soon as we reached the oasis, Chesterton collapsed, wheezing loudly, onto a rock in the shade of a palm tree. He handed me his spotted kerchief and asked me to wet it for him in the water of the oasis. I did so, and he proceeded to wipe his face, his forehead, and the back of his neck.

At last the wheezing subsided, and Chesterton barked, "Well, let's get on with it." He lumbered to his feet, like a solemn and determined elephant, and led us in a slow circuit around the oasis.

Chesterton poked his walking stick deep into each sand drift he came to. When I realized what he was doing, I found a fallen branch and imitated his example. Farouk sat in the shade and watched us.

I was the one who made the discovery, on the far side of the oasis, away from the camp. Pushing my branch in the drift of sand I struck an object—not a hard object, like a rock, but something soft and yielding.

"Farouk," I called out, "come and give me a hand."

Farouk and I shoveled away the sand with our hands while Chesterton towered over us, casting a welcome shadow. Within a minute we had exposed the khaki jacket that Hoffman always wore. Three minutes later we had exposed the whole body of the late Ambrose Hoffman. He had died a horrible death.

For a moment the three of us stood back and looked in silence at our grisly find. Then I noticed a sack of unbleached cotton, half hidden underneath the corpse. I eased it out and looked inside.

"Look at this," I said, holding it open to show Chesterton. The bag contained a whole collection of small, precious, Ancient Egyptian artifacts.

With some effort Chesterton knelt down and rummaged through the bag. His efforts produced a slip of paper, on which was written a name, Nabil Tannous, and an address in Luxor.

Without a word, Chesterton showed the name to Farouk.

"I know of this man. A market dealer. He is not a good man."

"Farouk," I said, "tell the others. Colonel Race and Professor Fell must know. And come back with two of your boys and a stretcher."

As Farouk disappeared toward the camp, Chesterton lumbered back to his rock and resumed his seat in the shade of the palm tree.

"What a waste of a life," I muttered.

"Every life lived without God is wasted" was the murmured response. "It's just that some are wasted in more foolish and tragic ways than others."

Hoffman's body was photographed by Burrows where it lay and then carried back to one of the storage huts. A messenger was sent into Luxor with the news. After the initial shock had worn off, Colonel Race settled down to writing an official report on Hoffman, and the rest of us returned to our duties.

Fell insisted that we work that afternoon. Despite Hoffman's awful death, there was much that needed to be done, and done quickly.

John Farnsleigh and I were put to work together in the tomb recording the wall paintings. Farnsleigh was to copy them, while I was to write a precise, and technical, description of their contents.

We worked in silence for much of the time, too shaken by recent events for small talk.

At length Farnsleigh asked the question that was on both our minds, "Do you think Hoffman could have done it?"

"Done what?" I asked, continuing to write.

"Murdered Lamb, of course. If Lamb had discovered Hoffman's thefts, would that have been enough motive for Hoffman to commit the murder?"

I finished the sentence I was writing and then looked up from my notebook.

"I'm not sure of anything anymore. I had always imagined that only the most powerful motive would ever push someone into murder, but now I'm not sure."

"I know what you mean."

"And there still remains the problem of how it was done. I mean, here we are, in the burial chamber—look around you, Farnsleigh. This is all solid rock, deep underground. How could Lamb have been spirited in here, either dead or alive? And if alive, how was he killed in here? I confess that I understand none of it."

"Just for the moment, leaving the impossibility of the crime to one side—who are the other suspects? Other than Hoffman, that is."

"Well, perhaps we all are."

"In a formal sense, I suppose Colonel Race has to suspect everyone. But realistically, who is likely to be high on the list?"

"Well, there's Mamur Zapt, of course. He's known to be a murderer, and he was here at the dig site. Perhaps if Lamb had stumbled across his presence he might have been murdered. But, again, why in the burial chamber?"

"Who else?"

"I don't know. Perhaps Wilding?"

"Come now," said Farnsleigh, "that's your personal dislike showing."

"Perhaps," I admitted, "but if Lamb had learned of the affair between Wilding and Mrs. Fell, would that have given Wilding a motive for murder?"

"Well . . . ," Farnsleigh muttered doubtfully, "I can see your point. But since Wilding was planning to run off with Mrs. Fell anyway—why not just do that? Why kill Lamb?"

"Perhaps they were not originally planning to run off together. Perhaps they only decided to do that after Wilding murdered the little doctor."

"It's a thought."

"And what about one of those journalists? They are a strange pair."

"Especially Elliot Jones. Mind you, I can imagine Jones killing someone in a drunken temper—but that hardly describes Lamb's murder, which was clearly very cunning, and very well planned."

"Yes, true. Which brings us back to Hoffman and his secret. Or, any of the rest of us, for reasons as yet unknown."

Farnsleigh grunted in reply and returned to his painting.

We worked a little longer in silence and then heard, in the tunnel behind us, a strange noise. As the sound came closer, I recognized the distinctive puffing and wheezing of Mr. Chesterton, and soon his shadowy bulk loomed around the corner of the tunnel, heralded by a flickering lantern.

"Ah, here you are," he grunted. "I've come for my first look at the burial chamber."

"Perhaps we could move out to give you a good look, sir," suggested Farnsleigh politely. However, it was immediately apparent that this was not practical, since maneuvering past Chesterton's bulk in the narrow tunnel would be an impossibility.

"Stay where you are, Mr. Farnsleigh—you too, Mr. Flinders," commanded Chesterton, "I can see quite well from where I am."

Given his height, Chesterton had to keep his head down and, hence, his various chins pressed against his chest.

"Fascinatin'—simply fascinatin'. Although I do wish the Egyptians were a larger race of people."

"Perhaps built more along your lines, sir," Farnsleigh suggested with a smile.

"I am not a small man, Mr. Farnsleigh, I grant you that. When I walk down the main street of my home town of Beaconsfield, I am either mistaken for the village idiot or for a Harrods delivery van."

For a while Chesterton stood there, taking in the details of the chamber and the wall paintings.

"I shall be delighted when we return to England to be able to say that I have seen an Egyptian tomb," he said at length.

"Do you return soon?" I asked.

"Frances and I are almost at the end of our holiday, and work awaits me in London."

"Do you look forward to going home?"

"I can hardly wait. With all its idiocies, England is still my home, my place in this world. I miss its quiet inner humor and insular geniality."

"And what about its idiocy?" asked Farnsleigh. "Do you miss that as well?"

"Of course! Of course! Only in England could ten thousand women march through the streets saying: 'We will not be dictated to,' and then go off and become stenographers."

"About the murder of Dr. Lamb," I prodded. "Are you any closer to a solution?"

"There is a gleam of light. It is a gleam that is becoming brighter by the minute. It shall not be long before that gleam is as brilliant as sunlight, and all is revealed."

Chesterton removed his pince-nez and began to polish the lenses. As he did so, he remarked, "It is, of course, a theological problem."

"Really?" Farnsleigh remarked. "I would have thought that only cold rational thinking could solve such a puzzling murder."

"Your mistake, young sir, is to assume that theology is irrational. It is not. It is the rational mind at its finest. A man is never thinking more logically than when he is thinking theologically."

Having made this remark, Chesterton snorted, wheezed once or twice, and then performed the difficult maneuver of turning around and making his way back up the tunnel toward the surface.

Farnsleigh and I resumed our work.

I scribbled in silence, working hard at identifying each of the people in the wall paintings, and precisely describing their postures and pictorial relationships. There was an illustration of a nobleman, possibly Menes himself, with his wife, dressed in the fine linen for which Ancient Egypt was famous. Below it were pictures of a woman kneading bread, a girl using a top-like device to spin thread, men at work in brickfields, and a scribe at work, possibly recording one of Menes's famous battles. We were perhaps an odd sight: two earnest young men in khaki recording the daily life of a vanished civilization.

Farnsleigh silently mixed his watercolors and copied the paintings with careful precision. Both of us were too preoccupied with our own thoughts to talk.

Perhaps another hour passed in this way, with only occasional, grunted comments between us. Then we stopped simultaneously at a sound. The tunnel echoed with the slap of leather shoes on stone, moving rapidly.

A moment later Amelia appeared, carrying a lantern, flushed and out of breath.

"Amelia! What's wrong?" I cried in alarm.

"Philip," she gasped, still out of breath, "I need to talk to you."

I laid down my notebook on the stone floor and hurried to her side.

"What is it? What's wrong?" I asked anxiously.

"Not here. Outside," she said.

"Is there anything I can do to help?" called out Farnsleigh.

"No. Thank you, Mr. Farnsleigh," Amelia replied, recovering her breath and her dignity. "I just need to speak to Mr. Flinders for a moment."

"Oh. Right-oh then," said the artist, looking puzzled as he returned, reluctantly, to his work.

I fell into step behind Amelia as she turned back toward the tunnel entrance.

"What has happened?" I asked again.

"Not here," she whispered. "Voices echo in this tunnel. Wait until we're outside."

I held my peace, burning with curiosity, as we made our way back to the cliff face. Once we had stepped outside and found ourselves blinking in powerful sunlight, I said, "Now what is it?"

"Let's move away a little," whispered Amelia, nodding toward the group of archeologists working at a trestle table. Fell, Poole, Narracourt, and Burton were grouped around a number of pottery fragments.

As we walked toward the far end of the terrace, Amelia explained. "I don't want anyone else to overhear. Just in case I'm wrong. There has been enough gossip at this camp. I don't want to start anymore."

At last we were out of earshot of the group.

"Now, tell me about it," I insisted. "My curiosity can't stand anymore of this."

"It's about him," she said, nodding at the group.

"Him? Who?"

"Dr. Billy Burton."

"What about Dr. Burton?"

"I've been reading his book. His autobiography."

"Ah, yes. *Saved from Darkness*—or something like that."

"Yes."

"Well, what about it?"

"He's a murderer."

"What?" I almost shrieked.

"Philip! Keep your voice down!" hissed Amelia.

"He's a what?" I whispered.

"A murderer."

"Dr. Burton is a murderer? How do you know?"

"Because he admits to it in his book."

"He actually admits to being a murderer?"

"Yes."

"You'd better tell me about it."

"It happened when he was quite young. I gather from the book that he was a very wild youth. The son of a drunken father, who became, to use his words, 'a slave to alcohol and Satan' when still a youth."

"Where was this?"

"In South Carolina—I forget the name of the city."

"And this led to murder?"

"It did. While he was still in his teens he killed another youth in a drunken brawl in a bar. But partly because of his youth, and partly because there was some element of self-defense in what he did, instead of being hanged, he only served ten years in prison."

"'Only' makes it sound easy."

"Oh, it wasn't easy. In the book it sounds just horrible. But while he was in prison he found a Bible and started reading it, and it changed his life. When he was released he became a preacher and temperance campaigner. Then a wealthy patron, a Christian businessman, put him through college."

"And the result is the Rev. Dr. Billy Burton we know today?"

"Exactly. But don't you see?"

"No, I don't. Not really. It's a colorful story. And, I must say, it's always inspiring to hear of someone who has overcome adversity."

"No. No. You're missing the point."

"Well, what is the point?"

"Dr. Burton has killed a man. He admits it."

"So?"

"And he was convicted of murder."

"Well?"

"Well, if he could murder once, he could murder again."

"You mean Dr. Lamb?"

"Yes! We have a convicted murderer in our midst, and we didn't know it. I mean to say, couldn't someone who has killed once, kill again?"

"I suppose so," I said doubtfully. "But to be honest—I find it very hard to imagine Dr. Burton as the murderer of Dr. Lamb."

"I know it's hard to imagine," insisted Amelia breathlessly, "but perhaps that's just because it's a new thought. Dr. Burton's history is a new piece of evidence we hadn't considered before."

"Perhaps." I was still doubtful.

"Who else on this expedition is a convicted murderer?"

"No one, of course. But that doesn't prove . . ."

"It's not proof. But it is a startling revelation, isn't it?"

"It's certainly that," I remarked, my eyes wandering as I did so to the group of archeologists around the trestle table. I could see Dr. Burton quite clearly: his round, florid face; his shock of white hair; his tall, solid frame; his endlessly cheerful manner.

"But I find it very hard to imagine . . . ," I protested.

"So do I," agreed Amelia, "but we have to face the fact, Philip, that this murder is completely baffling. That suggests to me that when the identity of the murderer is finally revealed, it will turn out to be someone completely surprising."

"Most likely. But . . . Dr. Billy Burton?"

"It may even turn out to be someone we find quite likeable," insisted Amelia, "and he does turn out to have aspects to his character we knew nothing about."

"Only because we hadn't read the book before."

"What do you mean?"

"I mean, my dear girl, that far from hiding his past, Dr .Burton advertises it by putting it in his book."

"Don't be patronizing," snapped Amelia, stamping her foot. "I am not your 'dear girl'!"

"I know. I know," I said quickly, holding my hands up in protest, "and I apologize. I understand now that you can't abide me."

"It's not . . . It's just . . . Oh! It's so hard to explain."

"Have you talked to Mrs. Poole about this yet?"

"Mrs. Poole?"

"Well, it was Mrs. Poole who lent you the book, wasn't it?"

"Yes, it was."

"And had she read it herself?"

"I'm sure she had."

"Did she make any remarks about Dr. Burton's self-confessed wild and wicked youth?"

"No. No, she didn't."

"Perhaps that's because she didn't see the confessions in the book as being all that significant. Not all these years later. Why don't you talk to her about it?"

"Perhaps I will," responded Amelia, apparently irritated because I had not enthusiastically endorsed her theory.

At that moment our debate was interrupted by a distant cry and the sound of feet running on gravel.

"Effendi! Effendi!"

It was Farouk shouting as he ran toward us up the sloping ramps of the temple ruins.

Amelia and I walked quickly toward the top of the final ramp, as did the group of archeologists. We were standing there together when Farouk arrived, puffing and out of breath.

"Dead," he gasped. "Dead."

"Who's dead?" demanded Fell. "Pull yourself together, man, and explain what you mean."

Farouk stopped trying to talk and took deep breaths. His eyes were wide and staring, and on his face was an expression I had seen there only twice before—naked fear. He swallowed hard, and then he said, "Alawi dead."

"Who's Alawi?" asked Poole.

"One of the native servants," Fell explained. "And you say he's dead, Farouk?"

"Yes. Dead. Hassan find body. Just now. Behind photo hut."

Fell said nothing but immediately led the way down the sloping ramps to the floor of the valley and then across to the photography hut. The door of the hut was closed.

"Behind hut," Farouk said, grabbing Fell's sleeve and pulling in that direction. We all followed.

There, in the shade of the hut, lay the small, dark-skinned body, the back of the head a bloody mess. Narracourt knelt beside him and picked up a limp wrist.

"He's dead all right," said Sir Edward, allowing the wrist to fall back into the dust.

"Could it have been an accident?" asked Poole hopefully. "Could something have fallen on him?"

"Perhaps," said Fell doubtfully, and as we looked at Alawi's wound, we knew that Poole was clutching at straws. None of us wanted to face the fact of another murder. We didn't want to know that there was a killer still at large in the camp. Amelia was clutching at my arm, and despite the heat, I could feel her shivering.

"Farouk, fetch Colonel Race at once," Fell commanded.

"Yes, *effendi*," said Farouk as he ran off.

"It wasn't an accident, was it, Papa?" said Amelia in a quiet voice.

"No, my pet, I'm afraid it wasn't."

"Struck down from behind," muttered Dr. Burton, "with a rock, or something. That would be my guess."

"Hmm . . . yes, a blow with a blunt instrument," Fell agreed.

"Oh, Philip," whispered Amelia. I looked down to see tears welling in the corners of her eyes.

"I can't take anymore of this," she said softly, her bottom lip trembling, then she buried her head in my shoulder. Horrified as I was by the latest murder, I could not help but enjoy Amelia's closeness. Gently I placed an arm around her shoulders. At that moment I glanced up to see Fell looking at us strangely.

"I think this might be it," called out Narracourt from a few yards away. At his feet was a small, round rock with a dark-brown stain that was rapidly blackening in the heat of the sun. Narracourt nudged the rock with his toe. "Better not touch it, I suppose, before Race gets here."

"Probably wisest," Fell agreed.

"Dashed horrible business," muttered Poole.

"Where's Mr. Burrows?" asked Billy Burton. "I say, if this guy Alawi was working with Nat Burrows, then perhaps, I say, perhaps, Burrows can tell us when he saw him last, and things of that sort."

"Good idea," snapped Fell, obviously pleased to have something to do.

As a group we marched around to the front of the photography hut.

"Burrows! You in there?" shouted Fell, pounding on the hut door.

"What's the problem?" called a muffled voice from within.

"We need to talk to you," explained the professor.

"Almost finished. Be with you in half a tick."

We waited in somber silence until the hut door opened a minute later.

"What's the problem?" asked Burrows again as he stepped, blinking rapidly, from the darkness of the hut into the blazing sunlight.

"It's your boy, Alawi," explained Fell. "There's no easy way to say this. He's dead. Murdered."

"Murdered?"

"Blow to the head," said Poole.

"Struck from behind," added Narracourt.

"Involved in some quarrel with the other natives, was he?" Burrows asked.

"We don't know yet," Fell said grimly. "Race will look into all that. Of course, there could be some connection between this murder and the death of Dr. Lamb."

"Surely not," said Burrows. "I mean, these *fellahin* are always rowing with one another. They'd as soon stick a knife in each other as look at each other."

"Be that as it may, it has to be investigated."

"Yes. Yes, of course," agreed Burrows as he locked and bolted the hut door. "Where's the body?"

"Behind the hut. This way," said Fell.

We returned, as a group, to the scene of the crime to find Colonel Race and Farouk kneeling over the body conversing in rapid Arabic. Looking at the faces around me, I was sure that all of us would rather have been somewhere else, but, somehow, this second murder held us in its thrall: it had a grim and horrible fascination that made it impossible to tear ourselves away.

"I think I found the murder weapon," volunteered Narracourt upon seeing Colonel Race. "Here—this rock. Surely those are blood stains."

Race stood up and walked over to where Narracourt was standing.

"Yes. About the right size. You're probably correct, Sir Edward," said the colonel. "And it would fit comfortably into a man's hand. That's what we call a 'weapon of convenience.'" Seeing the blank stares on the faces around him, he explained. "It is a weapon found on the spot, so to speak. In other words, Alawi was killed with whatever came to hand at the time."

"Does that mean this murder was unplanned?" I asked.

"Quite probably," agreed Race.

"Well, there you are then," said Burrows triumphantly. "A quarrel that flared up between two of the natives. You know how hot-blooded they are."

"Mr. Burrows," said Race with cool efficiency, "would you be so kind as to fetch your equipment and photograph the body for me, please? And Farouk, please send a messenger into Luxor immediately, informing the authorities of what has happened."

Farouk and Burrows departed.

"Once the body has been photographed," continued Race, "I would like your permission, Professor, to move it into one of the storage huts until a doctor arrives from Luxor to write a death certificate."

"Yes, of course," muttered Fell.

"As for everyone else," said Race, "why don't you return to the common room for afternoon tea. I intend to do a little scouting around here on my own for a few minutes."

We all took the hint and headed for the common room. As we walked in grim silence, Amelia stayed close by my side.

Then followed the quietest and gloomiest afternoon tea I can recall during my whole time on the dig. As Madeleine Sutton, John Farnsleigh, Mrs. Poole, and the Chestertons joined us, the news had to be broken to each of them in turn. On each occasion the result was the same: shocked disbelief that murder could strike twice.

Nat Burrows repeated his assertion that this was just a quarrel among the *fellahin* and had nothing to do with the expedition party. We all said we agreed with him, but, privately, I suspect that everyone else feared what I feared: that, somehow, this death was connected to the murder of Dr. Lamb.

Amelia and I sat together on one of the uncomfortable wooden benches with our tea.

"Poor Papa," she whispered, leaning toward me. "This dig means so much to him. If the Egypt Exploration Society back in London, or Dr. Burton's trustees back in Chicago, are unhappy about all this, the whole expedition may be canceled."

"Surely not," I protested, "not after this great success of discovering Menes's tomb?"

"Perhaps you're right," she said. "I certainly hope you are." A little later she placed her now empty tea mug on the table and said, "I think I'll go and lie down for a while."

"That's probably a good idea," I said solicitously. I took her arm and led her through the baking heat of the compound to the door of the main expedition house. She paused with her hand on the door latch, so, boldly I leaned forward and kissed her on the cheek. She turned to me, looking a little surprised, and then said, "You're sweet, Philip. You're really very sweet."

A moment later she was gone, and I was looking at the closed door behind which she had vanished. Slowly I turned around and began to retrace my steps. I had not gone more than a few paces, when a voice called from behind me.

"Flinders!"

I turned around. It was Professor Fell.

"I'd like to have a private word with you, if I may."

"Yes. Of course. Certainly, sir."

"Let's walk down toward the Luxor Road, where we can't be overheard."

"Certainly," I agreed, feeling puzzled and a little apprehensive. Was he going to ask me to keep away from his daughter? Fell picked up his pith helmet and clapped it onto his head, then he fell into step beside me.

"Rotten expedition," he muttered, after walking for some time in silence, "worst I've ever been on."

"But—Menes's tomb?"

"Ah, yes . . . But so many other things cloud the triumph of Menes's tomb that I almost wish I had never come."

"Surely not!"

"Well . . . perhaps not. It is a wonderful find, isn't it, Flinders?"

"Yes, sir. A wonderful find."

We walked a little farther in silence. I began to wonder when Fell would raise whatever it was he wanted to talk to me about. Apparently he was finding it difficult to begin.

"Look here," he said at last, "you're fond of my daughter, aren't you?" Ah, so that was it.

"Yes, Professor. I'm very fond of her indeed."

"I thought as much," muttered Fell and then lapsed into silence again. What would come next? A warning that I wasn't good enough for her? But Fell's next words surprised me.

"I gather that she is also very fond of you."

"Is she? Are you sure? It's just that . . ."

"Oh, she's a bit rattled at the moment by the outrageous behavior of that blasted Elspeth. But she'll get over it."

"Then, in the future, it might be possible . . . ?"

"Oh, I should think so," said Fell with confidence. "I should certainly think so." At that, my heart seemed to fly above the valley, soaring somewhere among the clouds.

"But it's not Amelia I want to talk about," Fell said, bringing my thoughts down to earth again. "Well, not directly about Amelia."

What on earth does the man mean? I wondered.

"You see, young Flinders," he continued, "I feel a need to unburden myself. I thought of talking to Poole for a while. But he is a clergyman, and whatever I wanted to get off my chest he would end up treating as some sort of confession. I didn't want to tell Billy Burton. He's a nice enough chap but a very narrow-minded moralist. And he does control the purse strings of his trustees' money. Chesterton just plain intimidates me. And then I thought of you. You're a straightforward young fella, and we get on well, don't we?"

"Well, yes sir, we do. I think."

"I think so too. And so I thought I could unburden myself to you, get it all off my chest, as it were, so I could stop thinking about it and worrying about it. And I could be confident that it would go no further."

"Certainly, Professor. I can keep a confidence."

"Good lad. And anyway, if you and Amelia are as fond of each other as you appear to be, well, perhaps you have a right to know."

"A right?"

"So anyway . . . Well, the fact is . . . ," Fell began, but then his voice just petered out. By now we had almost reached the turnoff where the Luxor road began. But still Fell walked, looking down at the ground and kicking the toes of his boots in the dust.

"Of course, it may all come out anyway," he said at length, "since that blasted Jones knows about it."

"Knows about what, sir?"

"Well, the truth of the matter is that, ah, not to put too fine a point on it, ah, that, ah, Elspeth and I were not married, as it were."

"Not married?"

"Not legally. Not in a church, you understand. Or even in a registry office. So you can see why I would find it hard to talk to Poole about this. Or Burton."

"So, that means that Mrs. Fell, er, Elspeth was . . ."

"My 'common law wife'—that's the usual expression they use in the newspapers."

"Oh, ah, yes, I see. Well . . ." It was hard to know what to say. "Amelia's mother . . . ?"

"Oh, I was legally married to Amelia's mother. Still am, if it comes to that."

I decided it was wiser not to say anything in response but just to keep listening.

"Not well, poor woman," continued Fell, after a lengthy pause. "She's, ah, in a nursing home under, ah, constant care."

There was a long silence, but I couldn't leave it at that point so I asked, "What's wrong with her, exactly?"

"It began with drinking. Amelia was away at boarding school. She didn't see what was happening, and we have no other children. Judith always tried to hide it from people. Somehow she managed to pull herself together when Amelia was home for the holidays. But before long she was drinking again. And then it was more than drinking. She became, ah, confused and, ah, incapable."

"Insane?"

"Oh, ah, yes, well, that's what the doctors said in the end. They recommended she be institutionalized."

"And she is still alive?"

"Yes."

"And because she is alive and insane you can never get a divorce from her?"

"Quite correct."

"So when Elspeth came along . . . ?"

"When it became clear that we were attracted to each other, I was honest—told Elspeth the whole story. She was—I should say 'is,' I suppose—a strong-willed, determined woman. It's one of the things I admired about her. Elspeth just wrote her own rules. So we went through a ceremony. We regarded ourselves as properly married. I should have known that if she ever got tired of me, she would just rewrite the rules again."

Professor Fell stopped in his tracks and stared at the ground for a long time.

"It's an unhappy story," I commented at last.

"Indeed. That is exactly what it is."

"What have you told Amelia about her mother?"

"Amelia thinks her mother is dead. It seemed the kindest thing at the time. By the way, you mustn't think that Judith's insanity is hereditary: the doctors told me there is no sign of that."

"The thought hadn't crossed my mind."

"Good. Good. Now, if anything should happen to me . . ."

"Such as—what, exactly?"

"Anything. There have been three deaths, two of them murders, in the camp. Anything might happen. And I'm concerned about Amelia. I wanted to tell someone I could trust, someone I could talk to, about this. So that if anything should, ah, happen to me, then, ah, Amelia will be taken care of. Will you do that?"

"Yes, of course."

"I want a solemn promise, mind, that in the event of something happening to me, you will look after Amelia."

"You have my most solemn promise, Professor. I love your daughter, and I will look after her—if she'll let me."

"Thank you, Flinders. You've set my mind at rest."

"Professor, you said that Jones knew about this matter."

"Yes, he did. He still does, of course. That blasted man used to be an attendant at the, ah, nursing home where my wife—Amelia's mother—is under care." As the professor spoke, I remembered that twice Page had referred to Jones as "that keeper of lunatics." So, Page at least knew something of Jones's background.

"He used his knowledge to blackmail me," Fell confessed. "Made me throw out Page and allow him sole access to the dig. But when Elspeth left, there didn't seem to be any point any longer in giving in to the man's demands, so I threw him out. That means, of course, that this whole ugly story may appear in the public print. Scandal is always damaging, and the trustees may choose to remove me from supervision of this dig. But, of course, if anything serious happens, you'll keep an eye on Amelia for me, won't you?"

"I promise."

"Good."

With that, Fell clapped a cigar into his mouth, lit it, turned his back, and walked briskly back to camp. It appeared that our private and confidential conversation was at an end. And from the abrupt way it had ended I took the hint that I wasn't to raise the matter again. The interview had clearly been very painful for him—as painful for him as it was embarrassing for me.

Slowly I followed in Fell's footsteps. Exactly what did the professor mean with his reiterated concerns that "something might happen to me"? Did he expect to be the next murder victim? Or was it worse than that? Was he involved, in some way, in the murders? Was he anticipating his own arrest? Was Prof. Henry Fell the actual murderer? I couldn't believe it.

Could he be implicated if one of the other suspects was found guilty? Hoffman? Burton? Wilding? Or someone else in the expedition party? My head was buzzing with questions, and I was feeling more puzzled and confused than ever.

When I arrived back at the camp I found that, in the wake of the second murder, the afternoon's work had come to a halt. So I went back to my hut and freshened up. The alarm clock sitting on the rough wooden shelf beside my shaving mirror told me it was almost time for dinner, so I stepped out of my hut into the vivid, crimson and gold light of an Egyptian sunset and walked toward the common room.

The common room was almost empty when I entered—the expedition team did not seem to be in a hurry to assemble again. John Farnsleigh was sitting by himself in a corner reading a back number of the *Strand* magazine, while Professor Fell and Sir Edward Narracourt chatted idly in the middle of the room. Apart from them, the place was deserted.

I nodded my greetings and, feeling rather thirsty, pushed open the kitchen door in search of some cool water. The kitchen was empty—of Rami or Farouk there was no sign—but a chicken and vegetable mixture was simmering on a low heat in a large, black pot on the stove. I rinsed an enameled mug and filled it from the rainwater cask. This late in the day the water was not particularly cool, but in my parched throat it felt wonderful.

Returning the mug to the sink, I was about to step through the kitchen door when I heard lowered voices on the other side.

"A confidential word, if you don't mind, Fell," said a voice I instantly recognized as Narracourt's.

"If you wish," replied the professor.

"I want to apologize for the, um, heat in our recent academic dispute."

This seemed to take Fell somewhat by surprise because there was a long pause before he responded. "Not at all, old chap, not at all. Think nothing of it."

"You've had some rotten luck on this dig but made a magnificent discovery as well, and I've been impressed by the way you've handled both of those things."

"Very kind of you to say so, Edward, very generous."

"As for the unresolved questions about the eighteenth dynasty . . ."

"Yes?"

"Would you be interested in doing some joint work? Perhaps writing a joint paper on the subject?"

"This is extraordinarily decent of you, old chap. What you propose strikes me as an excellent solution. Perhaps we could put together some of my work here with your work in the Valley of the Kings?"

"Indeed, that possibility had crossed my mind."

I felt like an eavesdropper listening to this conversation, but there was nothing I could do about it. I couldn't push through the kitchen door into the common room without alerting Fell and Narracourt to the fact I had overheard their conversation, and there was no other way out of the tiny kitchen. Although their voices were low, I could clearly hear every word through the thin paneling of the door. Narracourt was continuing. "By the way, have you ever noticed how quickly I've been able to respond to your papers in the past?"

"Yes, I have," growled Fell quietly. "I found it dashed puzzling. I presumed you were a quick writer, and you had some research assistants."

"In a sense I did."

"What do you mean 'in a sense'?"

"What I'm trying to do, as tactfully as I can, old chap, is to warn you against your secretary, Miss Sutton."

"Madeleine? Why should I be warned against her?"

"Because she has been supplying me with advance copies of the papers you send to *The Archeological Quarterly* for publication."

"She's been what?"

"Keep your voice down. Sorry about it, old chap, but it was academic war, and I discovered she was the weakest link in your team."

"But why?" Fell sounded genuinely puzzled, and hurt. "Madeleine's been with me for years. I can't believe she'd do that sort of thing. I thought she was loyal to me."

"She found it very difficult to do, if that's any consolation. And I believe she felt badly about it."

"Then why did she do it?"

"Oh, the usual reason—money. She has an aged mother she needs to provide for, so she was vulnerable to a financial offer."

"Hmmph!" Fell started to clear his throat, and I felt a volcanic explosion was near. But at that moment, a group of people, including, judging from the voices, the Pooles and the Chestertons, entered the common room talking loudly. Fell choked off his anger and swallowed whatever remarks he was intending to make.

Narracourt and Fell moved away from the door to greet the others.

I stood there stunned by what I had heard. What infernal cheek for Narracourt to coolly announce that he had bribed Madeleine Sutton. And while he was prepared to warn Fell against Madeleine, he seemed to have no qualms about his own behavior of tempting her with money!

Mind you, his remarks did explain one mystery: namely those comments in Miss Sutton's diary. Now I knew what she felt so "Guilty! Guilty! Guilty!" about—selling Fell's secrets to his mortal enemy. If I were Fell, I think I would have immediately canceled the truce with Narracourt. I felt very sorry for Professor Fell. He was a great archeologist, a man I both liked and admired, and, as leader of the expedition, he had suffered greatly. Most of it was not his own fault, although some might possibly blame him for the Elspeth-Wilding episode. And now to be confronted with this disloyalty by one of his oldest associates. My heart went out to him.

I waited a few more minutes and then slipped through the kitchen door into the common room where I mingled with the gathering crowd.

That evening Fell provided sherry from his private supply, perhaps feeling that everyone needed a tonic after the day we had been through. I don't know about the others, but in my case he was quite correct.

I stood near the doorway, chatting aimlessly with Nat Burrows and John Farnsleigh, waiting for Amelia to appear. When she finally did, she was a vision of loveliness, in a fresh white dress with a light cotton shawl around her shoulders and her hair brushed back and tied in a blue satin ribbon.

"Good evening, Philip," she said warmly.

"Good evening, Amelia."

"Is dinner served yet?"

"Not yet."

"Good. That gives us time to talk. And there is something that we need to talk about."

"There is?"

"I've been doing some thinking. In fact, I've been doing a lot of thinking," she continued.

"And have you come to any conclusion?" I asked.

"Yes. I've decided that I have been foolish. Very foolish."

"I don't understand."

"This afternoon, Philip," she said softly as she lowered her eyes and blushed, "you asked me a question."

"And you gave me a very definite answer."

"A foolish answer. If you should ever care to ask me again, the answer would be very different."

"Do you mean . . . ?" I stuttered.

"Yes. That's exactly what I mean."

"Amelia, shall we step outside, into the moonlight, where we can be away from this crowd for a moment?"

By way of reply she placed her hand through my arm, and we turned and stepped outside. In silence we walked across the compound, leaving the yellow lamplight and the chatter of voices behind. Then we stopped and turned to face each other.

"Miss Fell," I said nervously, "ah, Amelia—will you marry me?"

"Yes!" she whispered passionately. "Oh, yes! yes! yes!" And then we kissed.

As I held her close, we began to make plans in a kind of excited, breathless babble.

"You must come back to England with us, Philip," said Amelia, "and do your post-graduate work at Oxford—under Papa. And then, when we come back here next season, you can be Papa's senior assistant."

"Dinner's ready, you two," called Farnsleigh's voice from the doorway of the common room. "Are you coming in?"

"Coming," I called out.

"Shall we break the news?" I began to ask as we walked, arm in arm back across the compound. "No, I'd better ask your father before we say anything. Actually the prospect of asking him for your hand makes me quite nervous."

"He's a lamb, not a lion," laughed Amelia. "Besides which—he likes you."

Our arrival back in the common room seemed to be the cue for Fell to summon everyone to the table. Poole gave thanks, and dinner was served.

"Mr. Chesterton," I asked as we began to eat, "earlier today you talked about a 'gleam of light' that might illuminate the case. Have you progressed any further?"

"Oh, ah, yes indeed," said Chesterton as he swallowed a huge mouthful of food, "a good deal further."

"How far?" asked Amelia, who was seated at my right elbow.

"Well, not to put too fine a point on it, young lady," muttered Chesterton as he loaded his fork, "I have in fact, ah, solved the case."

"Solved it!" spluttered Fell.

"Oh, yes, quite," Chesterton said innocently, blinking short-sightedly at the startled faces around the table.

"Mr. Chesterton is speaking the plain truth," said Race quietly. "He conveyed his account of the matter to me this afternoon, and I was unable to fault it."

"But who is the murderer?"

"And how was it done?"

"You must explain," insisted a chorus of voices from around the table.

"I think this is as good a time as any," proposed Race. "Go ahead and tell them, Mr. Chesterton."

"Well, let me see. Where should I begin?" muttered the great man as he shoveled in another load of food and wiped his chin.

"Begin at the beginning," said someone.

"In that case, I shall have to begin in the Garden of Eden. That is where all stories begin, and it is certainly where this one begins."

"I don't understand," said Amelia.

"But you soon shall, my child, you soon shall. You see, we must begin by confessing that anyone around this table is capable of murder."

"I say, that's a bit rich," complained Narracourt.

"Not at all, good sir, not at all. We are, as a race, out of touch with God, and, therefore, out of touch with what it means to really be fully human. We are none of us complete, and, therefore, we are, all of us, corrupt."

Chesterton took a large swallow of tea from his mug and then continued. "If you wanted to dissuade a man from drinking his tenth whisky, you would slap him on the back and say, 'Be a man.' But no one who wished to dissuade a crocodile from eating his tenth explorer would slap it on the back and say, 'Be a crocodile.' For we have no notion of a perfect crocodile; no allegory of a crocodile expelled from a crocodile Eden."

"But there are good people," pursued Narracourt.

"None who are good enough," persisted Chesterton. "All the good you may find among men is a remnant to be stored and held sacred out of our primordial ruin. Man has saved his good as Robinson Crusoe saved his goods; he has saved it from a wreck."

"But your philosophy—your Christianity—is old hat," protested Narracourt with an impatient gesture. "That is the thinking of yesterday."

"I should certainly hope it is the thinking of yesterday, which is what makes it true today. Otherwise, you might as well say that a philosophy can be believed on Mondays but not on Tuesdays. You might as well say of a view of the cosmos that it was suitable for half-past three, but not suitable for half-past four. What a person can believe depends upon what is true, not upon the clock or the century."

"But what is true for you," persisted Farnsleigh, "might not be true for me."

"Utter poppycock!" snorted Chesterton. "Can the world be round for me and flat for you? Only if you, sir, are a nincompoop. It is true that some things change. London may be the capital of the British Isles in this century but not in the next. However, some things can never change. Two plus two equaled four a thousand years ago, and it still does. If God is God, then God is always there whether we acknowledge the fact or not. If human beings, by their nature, ignore God and, hence, are all capable of murder, then that fact is true for Ancient Egyptians and for modern Britons."

"Where is this getting us?" urged Fell.

"If everyone is capable of murder, then everyone is a suspect. And if everyone is a suspect, then we can proceed by asking who, alone out of this company, had the opportunity to murder Dr. Lamb and leave the 'why' until later."

"A novel approach, I suppose," Narracourt sneered.

"One that has produced results," Race said sternly. "Carry on, Mr. Chesterton."

"Yes," I added, "answer your own question: who, alone out of this company, had the opportunity to murder Dr. Lamb?"

"Why, isn't it obvious?" bellowed Chesterton, blinking furiously, like a schoolmaster with a rather dimwitted class. "Why, Mr. Burrows, the photographer, of course. Therefore, he is the murderer."

"That's a slanderous lie!" snapped the accused man. Burrows was not tall, but he was broad-shouldered and solidly built. As he spoke, his body seemed smaller, as if shrunken by the sting of Chesterton's accusation.

"Wait!" commanded Fell. "I confess I understand none of this, but let's hear Mr. Chesterton out."

"How could he have done it?" echoed several voices at once.

"Well, it's obvious, really," Chesterton muttered, removing his pince-nez and beginning to wipe the lenses slowly. "It's rather like a magic trick, in fact. Since what you claimed to see was quite impossible, the question I had to ask was: did you see what you thought you saw? If not, how were you deceived?"

"Hold on," interjected Fell. "What we saw was everyone who went into or out of the burial chamber. And we didn't see Lamb."

"Of course not. Because you were not meant to see him."

"Hold on again. Whose plan was it that we not see Lamb?"

"Why, Dr. Lamb's own, of course."

"Dr. Lamb didn't want us to see him?" Fell asked, clearly puzzled.

"Now you understand," Chesterton agreed, as he reached for the sherry bottle and filled his now empty tea mug full of sherry.

"I don't understand anything," said Fell plaintively.

"Dr. Lamb did not want anyone—but especially you, Professor Fell—to see him, so he made himself invisible."

This drew a snort, but no comment, from Narracourt. I glanced at Nat Burrows. The shocked look of a few minutes before had vanished. He was now scrutinizing Chesterton closely. His manner was calm, cold, and calculating.

Chesterton continued. "Professor Fell had banned Dr. Lamb from seeing the burial chamber on the day it was opened. But Lamb, as a passionate amateur Egyptologist, was determined that he would not wait to see inside the tomb. So, he did the obvious thing: he made himself invisible and crept past Professor Fell and the rest of you. He was in plain sight of all those inside the tunnel, as you stood in a line around the corner from the burial chamber, and yet not one of you saw him."

Chesterton beamed at the company, like a conjurer who has baffled his audience. Then, after drinking a deep draft of his sherry, he continued. "How can you see and yet not see? Who can you look at and not notice? In my detective story 'The Invisible Man' I pointed out that nobody notices a postman on his rounds. Asked, 'Who went to the door?' we reply, 'No one,' and yet the postman went to the door. But we don't notice him because he is just part of the scenery, and, hence, invisible."

"Yes, I remember now," said Amelia. "I read that story."

"Good for you, young lady," beamed Chesterton. "So, now we ask, who is invisible on this dig? Who would be invisible inside that tunnel?"

"I know!" I gasped. "One of the Egyptian workmen!"

"Precisely. Well done, Mr. Flinders. Now you can see the value of having an unimaginative assistant. He sees only what he sees and not what he imagines he sees. Eventually. You should really have come to this conclusion rather earlier, Mr. Flinders."

"I've been a little . . . distracted," I said blushingly. At which moment Amelia reached over and squeezed my hand, and my blush became even hotter.

"I object!" shouted Burrows. "A serious accusation has been made. I have been most seriously defamed, and I insist that the offensive remark be withdrawn—with an apology—or else be proved." The photographer's face was a mask of anger. In fact, it was more like a mask than a face. His protest struck me as an act—and an unconvincing act at that.

"It's proof that you want, is it?" rumbled Chesterton. "Very well then, listen to this. Dr. Lamb was determined to visit the burial chamber against the explicit orders of Professor Fell. He was, you remember, a man of small stature. He realized that if he darkened his face with coffee grounds, and put on one of those long, shirt-like garments all the Arabs wear, over the top of his usual khaki shirt and shorts, he stood a good chance of sneaking past the official party and seeing the tomb. But he couldn't do it on his own, since only a limited number of workers were being allowed into the tunnel. So he went to his friend Burrows and asked if he could take the place of Alawi, Burrows's Arab assistant. Burrows agreed. Suitably disguised, and further hidden by the load of photographic equipment he was carrying, Dr. Lamb walked right past the archeologists grouped in the tunnel—and was seen by none of them."

Chesterton cleared his throat and plowed on. "No doubt he was delighted with the success of this deception. It worked, and little Dr. Lamb got to see the burial chamber up close. Unfortunately, it was the last thing he did see. While the official party was out of sight around the corner, and while the Arab diggers were busy, Burrows removed the sarcophagus lid, and encouraged Lamb to climb in—having first removed the mummy. Lamb wiped his face clean, stripped off his Arab garment, and did what Burrows suggested. What did you say to him, Mr. Burrows? Did you offer to take a photograph? Did you suggest it would be a grand joke to play on the pompous officials?"

"Who's pompous?" demanded Fell.

"It's all lies," hissed Burrows.

"Once he was helpless in that narrow coffin, you seized one of the weapons that decorated the burial chamber and thrust it into his heart—perhaps holding your hand over his mouth to prevent him crying out. Then you replaced the lid on the sarcophagus, hid Lamb's Arab garment among your equipment, and proceeded to take more photographs."

"Wait! Wait!" urged Burrows. "I can prove this is all lies. When I came back down the tunnel, my assistant was still with me, carrying my equipment."

"That's true," Poole volunteered. "How do you explain that, Mr. Chesterton?"

"That was easy to arrange, wasn't it, Mr. Burrows?" said Chesterton confidently. "There were several workmen clearing the rubble. You simply grabbed one of them and thrust the equipment into his arms saying something like, 'Here, carry this.' Then the two of you walked out of the tunnel. You went in with an Egyptian assistant, and you came out with one. No one noticed they were different because no one notices the local workmen."

When Chesterton paused, there was a deep silence around the table. The more we were persuaded, the more deeply we were shocked.

"But why?" spluttered Burrows. "Tell me that? Why should I?" There was now a hint of desperation in his protest, and that made me nervous. Desperation, I feared, might make him dangerous.

"Now I have a confession to make," said Chesterton, without the slightest note of humility in his voice. "You see, I really don't know why. Oh, I can guess. And I think it's a very good guess. But at the moment a guess is all it is. Mind you, earlier this afternoon Colonel Race dispatched a telegram to Sydney, Australia. The reply to that telegram will provide the details to fill out my guess."

"What is your guess?" I asked. "At least tell us that much."

"Lamb had been deregistered as a medical practitioner, you remember? The question is, why? Clearly for something that happened in Sydney where he practiced, since it was the Medical Board of New South Wales that had deregistered him. Now, we know that Burrows was once in Sydney . . ."

"Do we?" Mrs. Poole asked.

"You heard him yourself. This afternoon, when he was talking about the places he had photographed, he mentioned, 'Sydney harbor at sunset as the lantern-lit ferries come in to Circular Quay.' It is not too hard to guess that while he was there he had some contact with Dr. Lamb, most likely contact that had something to do with Lamb being deregistered. Would you like to tell us about it, Mr. Burrows? Or shall we wait until the telegram arrives?"

All eyes were now fixed on Burrows, whose head was sunk in his hands. Without looking up at us, he said, "I'll tell you. There's no need to wait for the telegram."

A long, painful hush followed, and then Burrows continued quietly. "It was my sister. She was traveling with me in those days. Since both our parents were dead, it seemed the best way for me to care for her. While we were in Sydney, she became ill. The operation should have been a simple appendectomy. She died on the operating table. The coroner found that Lamb, the surgeon, was drunk at the time. He was deregistered and served three years in prison for manslaughter. Only three years! The charge should have been murder, not manslaughter. He deserved the death penalty. With both our parents dead, I was responsible for my sister. I knew that if ever the opportunity presented itself, I would extract the revenge to which I was entitled for the life he took."

"Then he turned up here at the dig?" asked Race.

"Yes."

"He didn't recognize you?"

"No. I was young at the time of my sister's death. My appearance has changed somewhat over the years."

"But you recognized him?"

"Yes. He looked exactly the same. And I could feel that old, burning hatred flaring up inside me once again."

"But you pretended to befriend him?"

"To get his confidence."

"And you waited for your opportunity?"

"Yes."

"And when it came, you murdered him?"

Burrows raised his head from his hands and nodded.

"Just as Mr. Chesterton described?"

"With only one change. I was the one who suggested to Lamb that he come into the tunnel disguised as Alawi."

"But Alawi knew that he had not been in the tunnel that day. When he finally realized how important that was, did he threaten to blackmail you, unless you paid him *baksheesh*?"

"Yes."

"And so you killed him, too, to silence him?"

"I had to." Burrows rose slowly from the table, his hands shaking. "I had to!" he gasped. "Don't you understand?" And then he began to weep softly.

Race rose from his seat and walked to Burrows's side. Talking his arm, he said, "Nathaniel Burrows, I arrest you for the murders of . . ."

Burrows wrenched his arm free before Race could complete the sentence. "Oh, no, you don't!" he hissed. And reaching into his pocket, Burrows produced an Army revolver—a souvenir of the Great War, no doubt.

"It's loaded!" he threatened, cocking back the hammer as he spoke.

"This will do you no good, lad," Race said firmly. "Now give me the weapon."

"Get back! Get away from me! I'm not going to surrender. I can disappear in this country. I know my way around."

As he spoke, he began backing toward the door.

"You're being very foolish, Mr. Burrows," said Race in his quiet, calm voice. "Just stand where you are and lay down the revolver."

"Not a chance! I'm not a murderer—just an executioner. What I did to Lamb is what the justice system should have done years ago. I executed him for taking my sister's life. There's nothing wrong with that. I'm not going to the gallows for that."

"And what about Alawi?" Race said, advancing slowly, step by step, toward Burrows. "Did he deserve to die too?"

Bang! Burrows pulled the trigger. It sounded like a dynamite explosion in that confined space. The bullet ripped chunks of wood out of the floor just inches from Race's toes.

"Come no closer! I'm serious. I've killed two men. I have nothing left to lose. I'm leaving now, and no one is to follow me. Do you understand?"

Bang! He fired again. This time chips of wood flew out of the rafter over our heads. While we were recovering from the deafening roar of the shot, he spun on his heels, darted out the door, and was gone.

"I'm going after him," said Race through gritted teeth. "Flinders, Farnsleigh—are you game for the chase?"

"I'm with you," I said, leaping from my seat. I glanced at Farnsleigh, but he didn't move.

"Philip! No!" cried Amelia, grabbing my sleeve.

"I can't let Colonel Race go on his own," I said rapidly. "It's too dangerous."

"It's too dangerous for you," Amelia said, tears in her eyes. "I don't want to lose you."

"You won't," I replied, with more confidence than I felt.

"Where's your revolver, Flinders?" asked Race.

"Mamur Zapt stole it, sir," I reminded him.

"Take mine," offered Fell. "It's in my kit bag—just there in the corner."

I pulled my sleeve away from Amelia's grasp and hurried to the corner of the room indicated by Fell. A moment's rummaging through his kit bag produced his revolver. I clicked it open and spun the chamber: it was fully loaded.

"I'm ready," I said.

Colonel Race flicked off the lights in the common room and then flung open the door. It was a wise move. It meant that we could step out into the compound without being silhouetted against a rectangle of light.

It was a full moon, and the compound was flooded with cold, silvery light. Once outside the building, Race and I looked to left and right, searching for a glimpse of the fleeing murderer. At first the whole area appeared to be deserted, then a distant shower of gravel caused me to look up. And there he was—on the ridge above the camp, clearly outlined by the moonlight.

I tapped Race on the shoulder and pointed, but he had already spotted the fugitive. He indicated with a gesture that I should circle around the ridge from the left while he did the same from the right. We split up and started out.

Carefully, so as not to give away my presence by kicking loose gravel, I began to climb the ridge. Where we had seen Burrows was approximately the same spot where I had talked to Amelia just four nights ago. So much had happened since then.

This was a ridge I had often climbed during the cool of the Egyptian evenings, and I knew where the firm ground lay and where to avoid the loose shale chips. Treading carefully I made slow progress, and by the time I reached the top of the ridge, Burrows was nowhere in sight. I released the hammer of the revolver and slipped it into my belt, then climbed onto a boulder to take a better view.

"Don't move," growled a voice behind me. "Take the revolver out of your belt and throw it onto the ground."

I did as I was told. There was an edge of panic in Burrows's voice that made me fear that any wrong move would send a bullet crashing through my skull.

"Good. Now, down off that boulder and turn around slowly."

Again I obeyed Burrows's instructions.

"I don't want to kill you, Flinders, I really don't." This was encouraging to hear. "But you shouldn't have come after me, you really shouldn't have. All I want is a chance to get away."

What I could see but Burrows couldn't was the shadowy figure slowly rising from the ridge line behind him. Colonel Race! All I had to do was to hold Burrows's attention until Race was in a position to do something.

"Don't be foolish, Burrows," I said, keeping his attention focused on me. "Can't you see it's all over?"

"Shut up, Flinders. I've got to think," growled the murderer. Behind his back Race slipped the revolver out of his holster and slowly cocked the hammer. Then he barked out, in his commanding military voice, "Just lower the gun and turn around, Mr. Burrows. The game's up."

Startled, Burrows spun around. As soon as his gun was no longer pointing at me, I stepped back, so that I was shielded by a boulder, scooping up my gun from the ground as I moved. Burrows looked back and forth quickly between Race and me. He could see the situation was hopeless—he was now covered from both sides.

Then, to my horror he placed the barrel of his gun into his open mouth. I swear I could see the knuckle whiten as he began to pull the trigger. I couldn't watch this. I closed my eyes. After the sound of a shot rang out, to slowly die in rolling echoes of thunder in the rocky ridges around me, I opened my eyes again. Burrows was alive! His gun was lying on the ground, he was clutching his wounded hand, and a thin trickle of smoke was drifting from the barrel of Race's revolver.

I realized I had been holding my breath and released it in an audible sigh. I was shaking with relief. Then I hurried to Burrows's side to assist Race who had already pocketed the fallen gun and seized Burrows by his unwounded arm.

The walk back down the ridge was slow and awkward. All the spark had drained out of Burrows, and he had to be helped or manhandled over slopes of shale chips that kept slipping beneath our feet.

Finally we were back in the compound. Standing at the door of the common room was Amelia. As soon as she spied our group, she ran across the open ground toward us.

"Philip, are you all right?" she called as she ran.

"Fine," I replied.

"When we heard that gunshot, I was so worried." Amelia threw her arms around me and buried her head in my chest. I let Race and Burrows go on ahead, while I stood there and held her. I would have been quite happy to spend the night right where we were, with our arms around each other.

"There are things you and I need to talk about," I whispered.

"Yes, there are," sobbed Amelia quietly as she dabbed at her eyes with a small handkerchief, "just as soon as I pull myself together."

With my arm around her waist, I led her toward the distant, warm glow of the common room. The members of the expedition had spilled out into the compound and were hurrying toward us.

"You're quite the hero, young Flinders," boomed Fell as he rushed up and shook my hand.

"Not me, sir. It was Colonel Race."

"You held his attention at the crucial moment," said the colonel. "Well done."

Amelia clung on to my arm, and when I looked down at her face it was glowing with pride.

The next to step up, shake my hand, and slap me on the back was Mr. Chesterton, saying how pleased he was by his trusty, "unimaginative" assistant.

As the others drifted back into the common room, a sense of peace settled over us.

It was all over now: the deaths, the fear, the tension—all were behind us. The mysteries had been solved, the puzzles cleared up, and Amelia and I had found each other.

We would have been quite happy at that moment if Chesterton had joined the others in the common room. Amelia and I wanted to enjoy the warm evening, standing in the moonlight—just us two. But Chesterton showed no sign of moving. He seemed to be gazing into the distance, as if he could see for a million miles.

I spoke to him, hoping that if I woke him from his trance he might join the others and leave us alone.

"So," I said, "the deaths are all over now."

"All over? Hardly," he harrumphed in his usual manner. "A murderer has been caught, but death still strides triumphant around this spinning globe."

Amelia shivered and looked at the exotic and rugged landscape around us as she said, "The whole culture of the Ancient Egyptians seems to have been focused on death."

"We should all be focused on death," Chesterton rumbled from beneath his bandit moustache.

"But why?" I asked. "Isn't that a bit grim?"

He turned and looked in my eyes as he said, "A recent survey of doctors has shown that ten out of ten people die." Then he smiled and said, "Every train ends up at the same terminus, so we might at least aim for the target with some thought and care."

"But that's so far away," protested Amelia. "I mean . . . at least for us young people . . . so very far away. Unless you have inside information on how long we shall live?"

"You really want to know how long you shall live?" asked Chesterton with his smile broadening. "Then I shall tell you. You shall live forever. You are immortal. Oh, your bodies shall die, but you—the real you—your memories, your consciousness, your personality, shall never cease to exist. And that, you see, changes everything. As Canon Poole said at Dr. Lamb's funeral: 'In the midst of life we are in death.' But it's also true that in the midst of death we shall find ourselves to be in life."

He walked several paces away from us, and, for a moment, I hoped he was going to leave the two of us alone, but he turned and faced us again, and then addressed us, as if we were the audience at one of his famous lectures.

"There are many reasons to believe we face an eternity of existence. There is something in every human heart telling us so. The human heart hungers for more than this life offers. There is an inescapable longing for something this world cannot satisfy. There is an emptiness of soul that cannot be filled by work, alcohol, or laughter. It cannot be satisfied with philosophy, music, or self-indulgence. Only when we have confidence in an afterlife can we find something large enough to satisfy this longing for significance. Belief in immortality is a timeless, universal phenomenon. From the artifacts of the Ancient Egyptians around us to the silliest of modern spiritualists who think they have contacted those who have 'passed over,' people of all times and places in history have believed the human soul survives death."

Somehow the stillness of that warm night and the echoes of Ancient Egypt all around us made his words clear, and nothing more than simple truth—uncommon common sense.

"And," he continued, "immortality changes *everything*. Once we face the reality of immortality, suddenly we realize that this life is so small, and what lies beyond so large. This is the lobby, that is the building; this is the school, that is the career; this is the overture, that is the performance. We either live this life preparing for that other, larger, life, or we waste it."

There was a longish pause, and then he continued, speaking as much to himself as to us. "We shall all end up in court. Not just sad Mr. Burrows, but all of us. And we shall face, not an earthly court, but the High Court of the Cosmos—the Court of Last Resort. And we shall be charged, not with murder, but with treason. Yes. With waging civil war against heaven. With being rebels against our Maker and Ruler. We can't spend most of our time ignoring God in this life and expect His approval in the next."

"But when the evidence is considered," said Amelia, squeezing my hand gently, "I do hope that I shall be found good enough for heaven."

"Oh, my dear young lady," Chesterton replied with a wheezing laugh, "all the good people go to hell. Only bad people go to heaven."

"But . . . but . . . ," I spluttered.

"Anyone," explained Chesterton, looming up before us in the Egyptian night, like a vast colossus of wisdom, "anyone who thinks he or she is good enough for God will discover that God is unimpressed by self-approval and will end up in hell. Only those who realize they are too bad for heaven, and ask for forgiveness, will get there. There is only one door to heaven, and the word stamped upon it is 'forgiveness.'"

"And how do we find that door?"

"By coming to know the door-keeper. Follow the Man who is both the Door and the Door-Keeper."

"Man? What man?"

"The Man who said: 'I am the door: by me if any man enter in, he shall be saved.'"

"But . . . who? Where . . .?"

"Do you have a Bible on your shelf, my boy? Try looking in St. John's Gospel, chapter 10 and verse 9. Goodnight, you two. And I wish you well for your lives—your very long lives, both in this world and the next."

With those words, he turned and was gone.

Amelia and I turned toward each other, reached out for each other, and, at that moment, could think of nothing better than being together forever. And ever. And ever.

Kel Richards is one of Australia's leading radio and television journalists, currently working with the national NewsRadio network. He has written several best-sellers in Australia, both fiction and non-fiction. Richards is also a popular evangelist and speaker in his country. Richards is married with two children.

Additional copies of this book and other book titles by
RiverOak Publishing are available at your local bookstore.

If you have enjoyed this book, or if it has impacted your life,
we would like to hear from you.

Please contact us at:

RiverOak Publishing
Department E
P.O Box 700143
Tulsa, OK 74170-0143

Or by email at: info@riveroakpublishing.com

Visit our website at: *www.riveroakpublishing.com*